HARMION

BOOK ONE OF *THE HARMION SERIES*

RICHARD A. SWINGLE

LWP

Cataloguing in Publication Data is available from the British Library

ISBN 978-1-916117-00-6 (B-format)
ISBN 978-1-916117-01-3 (Kindle eBook)

Printed and bound in Great Britain by Clays Ltd, Elcograf S.p.A.

www.richardaswingle.com

BILL HIATT - A MAJOR HARMION CONTRIBUTOR

As far back as he can remember, Bill Hiatt had a love for reading so intense that he eventually ended up owning over eight thousand books--not counting e-books! He has also loved to write for almost that long. As an English teacher, he had little time to write, though he always felt there were stories within him that longed to get out, and he did manage to publish a few books near the end of his teaching career. Now that he is retired from teaching, the stories are even more anxious to get out into the world, and they will not be denied.

https://www.billhiatt.com/my-books-2/

https://www.amazon.com/Bill-Hiatt/e/B009CWEWD8

https://www.facebook.com/writerbillhiatt/

https://twitter.com/BillHiatt2

RICHARD PINCHES AND LIZ HOWARD - MAJOR HARMION CONTRIBUTORS

Richard Pinches was born in 1965 on his parents' farm in Henley-on-Thames. It is here that he still works in a converted barn as a videographer and photographer. Richard started his photography career after graduating from art college in 1985. Quickly progressing to setting up his own studio on his parents' farm in 1988, he converted some barns and began shooting commercial and advertising briefs for many global brands from 3M to Xerox.

Richard first started shooting commercial videos in the mid nineties but it is the digital era that has seen him expand considerably in the realm of the moving image. This has been helped by his extensive studio that includes his own in-house digital team, drive-in car infinity cove and sound proofed green screen stages. Richard collaborates with a wide range of creatives in his production company, which he owns with his producer/director partner, Liz Howard. Richard and Liz started working on short films in 2011. They have now worked up to feature films and continue to work in this creative field.

http://www.meadowsfarmstudios.co.uk/

KEY CONTRIBUTORS

Julian and Helen Pletts - Helen Riley Photography -
www.helenrileyphotography.com

Sharon Mansfield and Lisa Grima - Her Last Bow -
www.herlastbow.co.uk

Ilaria Ceccarello

Neil Wallace - 1st Assistant Director -
https://www.imdb.com/name/nm0908801/

Declan O'Dwyer - Film and TV Writer, Director -
https://www.imdb.com/name/nm1398781

Christopher Anderson - Fireglass Studios –
www.fireglassstudios.com

Anonymous - Great Ormond Street Hospital -
https://www.gosh.org/

For my Family,
for always believing in my dreams and helping me to follow them

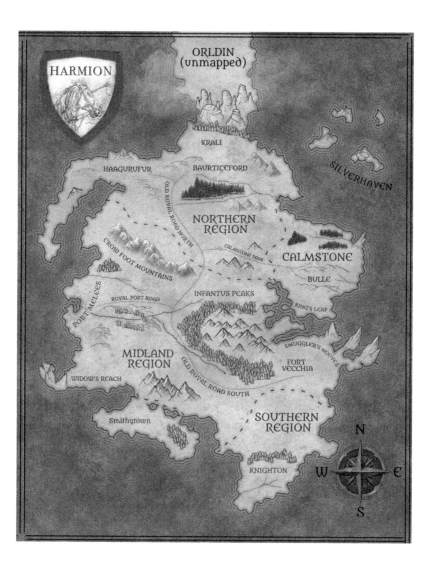

PROLOGUE

B ranches creaked and swayed in a cool evening breeze as the purple sun cast beams of light upon the ground. A light autumn mist cowered amidst an aged and scarred forest, recording ancient stories now lost in time.

Digging its claws into thick bark, a squirrel clambered to the top of the highest tree, jumping from branch to branch. Below it, footsteps drew closer until a partly-clothed man, painted in tribal markings, passed beneath.

The man was old, weathered like the forest, with a face riven with creases and folded skin like the hump of an exotic beast. He dressed in leather skins that matched the complexion of his own thick and twisted body. The old man invited the air in through deep breaths. Despite his appearance, this was no shaman. He was covered head to toe with tattoos and markings that had stretched or faded with age. The markings had been burnt into his skin with red-hot knives and spearheads, the pain afforded by each scar now reduced only by the conditioning of time. A series of black lines upon his brow produced an unchanging expression of fear and only served to age him more.

He held a simple spear to balance his stride, the blood-stained handle beautifully carved out of a robust wood; many sharp tools would have been ruined against its rind. The spear gave the old man an appearance of authority. He held his head with pride and the creatures of the forest parted in his presence. His eyes, dark and narrow, peeked at the clearing around him, full of movement from the animals scurrying around the bushes, fleeing from where he stood to rest. Breathing caused him to wheeze and he coughed. Tears filled his eyes though the tears were filled with sadness rather than pain. Dissatisfied he crouched closer to the ground, leaning on his spear, and listened to the distant echoes through the earth.

Standing to reconsider his direction, the tribe leader managed a step towards a series of rocks with green moss growing thickly through the cracks and earth. Tasting the bright green moisture and rubbing his fingers together, a colourful paste formed in his palms. He smeared it across his bare thigh to dry his hand and considered the path forwards.

The light began to dwindle in the forest as dusk set in. The squirrel continued to leap from tree to tree, following the man as he carried on through the old forest, curious and afraid. Thunder roared but neither lightning nor rain followed. Suddenly a herd of wild deer tore through the undergrowth escaping some hidden threat. The squirrel clinging onto the branch trembled as the tree shook from the roots upward.

The tribe leader took refuge behind a stump and watched as the herd ran past him. He scratched his nose, the bone piercing that protruded his nostrils causing him some discomfort as it rattled like a buzzing fly.

The freshness of the air lessened and the painted old man struggled to breathe. The humidity was now so fierce that he appeared to be suffering from a fever as sweat trickled down his face, stinging his eyes. He bent down to grab a weed by the side of a tree. Pinching up a handful, he rubbed the plant beneath his mouth, inhaling the vapour and sending a cascade of relief through his enclosed lungs. The next stride he took through the diminishing landscape brought on a suffering he could not have anticipated. His eyes flickered shut unwillingly and he barely breathed another breath as he stumbled forward, the ground beneath his feet a black and dusty charcoal. The air filled with a thick ash that stretched up into the skies where the great old trees now looked like a vision of lifeless ghost giants. A plague of mist spread through the forest like the shadow of a cloud sweeping across a field beneath a setting sun. The squirrel climbed higher, searching for air to breathe. It spluttered blindly and fell from its branch, disappearing into the foggy abyss.

No life could exist here, no animal could feed off the grass and weeds, no man could hunt for prey. The air would sustain no life as it filled the painted man's lungs with ash and death.

The last sight he saw before his eyes filled with the searing black dust, was an expanse of desolation. A cadaver of a great old tree stood reaching its limbs towards a dried-up lake where water had once flowed. It was as though the earth itself was a corpse, rotting and hopeless. Dread descended upon him.

1

As swirling dust parted over a febrile landscape, the rags of a makeshift infirmary billowed in the winds of a humid dawn. A hundred tents were crammed together, drapes hanging to separate the injured soldiers who stirred sullenly and in silence. The rising light woke them from far sweeter places than their current reality. The night before had been long and bloody, thousands had met to put an end to the ongoing battle and Augustus was sure to concede defeat. After all he had barely sent one good man for each of the ten against him that previous evening. Not by choice or tactics, but by necessity. Some might consider it a valiant effort that his 11th Legion had managed to sharpen the odds closer to their favour. A generous tactician might have calculated them now at eight to one. And why not? As perhaps in these, their final hours, they would clutch at any morsel of hope. The strategist had offered such comfort to Augustus and in return was rewarded with the rare luxury of a hot bath to replenish his strength for the final stand. But had last night not been that final stand? Surely those who were not killed would now be taken prisoners of war, captured, every last man and woman. In the respite afforded by the morning's peace, the 11th Legion expected final defeat. Only Augustus considered surrender to be an insult to his vain ambition.

"Blindness" was the word Augustus had been accused of. What insolence! The man who uttered it never spoke another word and any who felt troubled by the matter knew to keep their mouths shut for they needed every last soldier in this hopeless fight. But Augustus knew in his heart that fighting was the right course. He would strike again during this peaceful morning and take no further rest for he had no use for it and his sword was still sharp and ripe for the killing.

'Sire, we've found him. He was not alone.'

The voice came from a scrawny scout on horseback. Augustus spun to face the excited fellow.

'Go on, man.'

'There was a woman with the traitor, sire. And she is with child.'

His face reddened. His fists clenched. In that moment Augustus knew he'd lost his advantage and, for now, preparations for the morning's attack would have to wait.

'Take me to him.'

Augustus was led through the lines of the injured. Moans and cries were the only sounds, but he'd heard their song before. The badly wounded liked to remind him of their suffering and he cursed them for it. No matter. He would reward their cowardice with honour.

'Medic.' Augustus shouted his request as he rode on.

Three men approached him, all dressed in white, though you'd barely know it for the vermillion stains that their bloodied gowns exuded. The moment took Augustus by surprise as he admired the strange beauty of the perfect red.

'Many of the fighters have lost their limbs and those that

have not may yet still,' blurted out the boldest of the healers as they scurried along after their mounted leader.

'My concern is not with those that cannot fight, but those that can.'

The words fell like thunder as Augustus glared down at the trembling physician.

'You'll send any man or woman that can walk to the front lines to await my command. Including those who have only one arm. Ensure they are given short swords. If a man is bleeding internally and his death may be slow and cruel then send him too. Inject them with fire and give to them whatever numbing of pain they may need; you are permitted to exhaust the supplies. Order the alchemist to create as potent a brew as they see fit. Better for these soldiers to die fighting than pissing in their breeches.'

'But, my lord…'

'Speak another word and you'll lead the charge yourself!' Augustus bellowed as he halted and turned. In those raging eyes the healer could see he had been afforded mercy. This was not a man who offered second chances. The healer's skill to save lives was the only reason he still clung to his. He left to carry out his orders.

The scout barely acknowledged the interruption and led onwards to the forest outskirts where the traitor had been restrained.

The forest was old. The wood was musty and dank in the manner of a man in his final years. Beneath the sadness of one tree was where they had tied the traitor and beside him a battered and muddied woman, who was indeed with child and looked as though she might birth at any moment. She was of foreign blood, with tanned skin and black hair, and striking green eyes. Even in her captive condition he could see she was a beauty. In spite of her pregnant form, Augustus revelled in his carnal delectation and felt his blood warm as he strode towards the traitor whose eyes would not meet his own.

'I rather imagined I'd find you hanging from the gallows some place south of here,' he paused. 'Remove that gag at once!' Augustus ordered the soldier standing by the traitor's side and the man obeyed. 'I see they've been taking good care of you.' Augustus continued. 'Speak, wretch.'

The traitor opened his mouth. The sight of a gaping hole where a tongue once flexed sent a bolt of rage through Augustus.

'Who is responsible for this? Tell me at once!'

'He did it to himself, sire, the moment we captured him he bit it off himself.'

Augustus noted that the captor's hands were bloodied and bruised. He had clearly had his morning's entertainment.

'So why gag the man if he cannot speak?'

'Sire, he was a mess, drooling and slobbering all over us. It's a wonder he never passed out from the loss of blood.'

Augustus took a deep breath and prepared to address the hopeless mute before him.

'Well, I suppose I will have to do all the talking. I'd rather hoped to hear your story, quite an adventure you must have had for yourself. You see we've been condemned to lose this battle on account of your little escapades and apparent love affair. Had you obeyed your orders and brought me a band of even five hundred men we could have struck the enemy down and today we'd be feasting on their corpses. I'll not ask the reasons why as I'll assume the response will be less than adequate.'

The man managed a grunt and Augustus took that for agreement. He continued.

'So many years, wasted and thrown away like a fine spice caught in a breeze.' Augustus turned then to address the soldier with the bloodied hands. 'Did you at least find out where he had been staying all this time?'

'No, sire, we learnt nothing, even when we beat his woman. He was travelling with other villagers who fled at his command; they looked like a modest bunch, not a single fighter among them. We found no sign of the twenty men he left with.'

Augustus pondered the response for a while. Then he spoke again. 'Very well, today is not the day for answers.' Returning his attention to the traitor, Augustus stood over the man. 'I'm to ride out with the 11th for one final moment of glory. To die in battle will be the legacy of this legion you've betrayed, your former brothers and sisters. Your own fate will be to watch your woman and the child inside her taken from you, and you'll never be able to speak of the pain to another living soul so long as you live. And for that I must thank you myself.'

Augustus walked slowly to the foreign woman, an islander he presumed. He drew his sword, still crusted red from the previous night's mayhem that, to him, seemed as though it had taken place in another life. As he raised his sword a horn blew and the earth shook.

'Cavalry!' shouted the soldier on horseback.

'To your posts, men! Now!' roared Augustus. 'Not you.' He pointed to one of the captors. 'Your business is here with our guests. If I have not returned when the battle is done, kill the woman and child.'

'And what of the traitor, sire?'

'Lock him in the pit, with any luck they'll mistake him for one of us and take him to the torture camps.' Augustus looked down at the traitor one last time as he grappled the saddle of his horse. 'I will pray for you, traitor. Let your life be long lived so that the suffering you have brought upon yourself will fester and rot your spirit.'

Augustus mounted his steed and turned to ride towards the

front line where his pathetic army of cripples awaited their orders. Behind him he heard the faintest of moans from the traitor who grunted a hopeless whine through his rags.

Augustus was prepared for this moment, for it was the pinnacle of his existence and he was no longer fighting for the war, or his legion, but for revenge. He would fight as though he were more than just a man, as without victory his business with the defector would not be complete. And no other man deserved the satisfaction of causing pain to the traitor as he did. The traitor who in a past life had been his best friend, some might say his only friend. Augustus had not cracked a smile, enjoyed a song or laughed at a quip since the day the traitor had left on his orders to bring back a band of fighters to aid their cause. *Why had he betrayed them? What had caused him to turn his cloak and bed down with the island girl?* Three years had passed so quickly now it seemed, as his mind designed its own impression of the journey that his friend, no, that the deserter had embarked upon. He began to accept he might never know the answers to the questions he'd carried all these years, for the man had removed his own tongue.

He shook his head as if to shake off lingering thoughts. He needed to be focused as by now Augustus had reached the front lines, and the vista of the battlefield clouded as a thousand soldiers on horseback came thundering towards him with the dawn light rising in their faces. He smiled. For he knew then that the sun would be his ally.

With a cry to battle, Augustus threw aside his thoughts, for now was not the time for brooding. He had business to deal with and that business was death. And with his band of cripples, made up of no more than two hundred soldiers, Augustus rode to certain death.

2

H idden far to the south of the blood lands where the Forty Years War had commenced there existed a small settlement. A modest but idyllic village called Knighton where there lived no more than a dozen self-sustaining families. Among them were several widowed men and women, grown old and alone. The long war had taken everything from them, husbands, wives, sons and daughters. Even some of the older generations had joined the fighting when soldiers had become scarce. Those who stayed battled with the drying fields and adverse weather that had stolen the usual harvests. Resources were now short and it was no easy task to provide for those who remained.

Although the war had ended earlier that year, life continued unchanged for many, as they had known no time before the war. There was no victorious side just a rabble of men and women who had strength enough left to stagger home, confused by the events that had occupied their entire lives. Most of them had forgotten what they were fighting for or even who opposed them. Few were still alive to boast of a more prosperous time when trust between neighbours had existed. At least for this Knighton was rare, for the village had stood alone throughout the war. Too far to the south and too remote to be of interest to any of the armies, only once had a legion of brutal soldiers passed through. They were afforded the hospitality of stables, food and water and in return left the villagers to their lives before they went about their business. Perversely, it was the so called honourable soldiers, who all professed to have the worthiest cause of protecting the homelands of the poor, that had caused a greater disturbance by bringing injured fighters to the village for recuperation or burial. Caring for a dying soldier or one incapable of fending for themselves was a heftier burden than that of the indifference of the soldiers who wanted nothing more than a hot supper and a place to lay their head for the night.

One such injured soldier who had been brought to the village was Tritan Léon. Tritan's wounds had appeared fatal at first but a young healer from the village, treating the injured fighters far from home to the north, had found it necessary to bring Tritan back for the treatment he needed. Thomas was a skilled surgeon and believed that any man with even a fool's hope deserved his attention. It was by chance that he had come across Tritan, lying abandoned by his comrades under an old oak tree, with his guts hanging from his midriff. The healer had found him covered in snow, which had helped to slow the loss of blood.

Thomas had been on his way back home to Knighton for respite after a cruel winter of fighting. In the frozen northern climate he had lost several toes to frostbite and now walked with a limp. His one consolation was the gravitas it gave to his position amongst the villagers and he wore his affliction as a badge of honour, as was his way. It had meant that he was unfit to return immediately to the heart of the fighting and instead he set up a practice in the village. His father had been among those who had died in the third decade of the war and it was left to Thomas, as a teenager, to raise his two younger brothers. When he left for the war the boys had remained unsupervised and had grown now to disappoint.

Thomas had become an eligible bachelor, an accomplished and young surgeon, just into his early twenties. Few men of his age remained and it led to many fathers seeking his hand in marriage to their daughters. One local farmer, who had been ill and knew his time was short, had arranged for such a union to take place with his daughter, Marilia. The engagement was set to last until the war was over and so Thomas enlisted her as a healer's apprentice to aid him with his practice.

Returning Tritan to health was a full-time job. His body required regular turning and he drifted in and out of consciousness, afflicted by fever. Marilia would spend her days washing and feeding the soldier, massaging his body so that his blood could flow freely through his veins.

One morning she went to attend to Tritan but his bed was empty. He had been incapable of leaving his quarters for months. As she turned to leave there he stood, naked in the doorway. She had known it from nursing him whilst he slept, but she was still caught off guard by his muscular form. Often she had found herself imagining Tritan as she kissed her betrothed and her longing grew. She had fallen in love with him without ever speaking a word or knowing his mind. It was this moment that had led to their affair. Strength had returned to Tritan, months of repressed carnal instincts took hold of him, and Marilia could no longer ignore her own feelings. She broke her vows to Thomas who had waited patiently throughout the engagement. It was the end of her union to the healer.

Years later, the pain still twisted inside Thomas like an ironic knife to the heart. Thomas had blamed himself of course, although he carried a strange pride for having saved Tritan's life. It was the work of a miracle after all and he knew he was famous for it. At least those who knew him would remember the deed for a short while.

But Tritan resented Thomas for his gift of life. The pride of dying in battle had been denied him, for war was all that he had known. He was born in its clutches and the battlefield was his schoolyard, the sword his teacher and mother was a word he had never known. He had been told that in childbirth she had died and he had lived, a fact that his father had never allowed him to forget nor for which he had been forgiven. It had been almost a decade since Tritan had seen Augustus, the strange and brutal man who had raised him, or rather trained him in arms. Tritan's fear of Augustus had led to his belief that sons were an encumbrance to their fathers. Now a father in his own right, Tritan had come to resent his own son. There was no space in his heart for love at a time when he was a killer of men.

Now, Tritan spent his days drinking wine and hiding in the stable with the only one he truly trusted with his life, Diablo. The horse had been with him for many years, blinded by the arrows of war. Tritan's companions had offered to put the horse down on his behalf after the steed had been sedated for they knew the anguish it would cause him but he refused them and took to training the blind horse to ride under his command. And what great deeds they had achieved, they rode with such fearless strength that it was as though their minds were one. Tritan guided the horse from one battle to the next, though now these were just memories. Their purpose was spent, for the time of fighting was done and a dried up river needs no bridge.

Tritan's nine-year-old son, Pietrich, had inherited none of his father's traits and no two souls could have been less alike. At times the boy felt his mother Marilia might be the only parent he would know. Even so and in spite of their awkwardness he loved his father. The knowledge that Tritan too had once been a child made it easier to find empathy with him; such was the wisdom of this boy who was for certain insightful beyond his years.

THE CLANGING of a bell rudely awakened Tritan. His head pounded from a restless night's sleep; he could feel the pulse in his skull and cursed the skin of wine that lay to his side before uncorking it and draining the remainder of its contents. The continuous sound of the bell thumped inside his head and he slowly pulled himself up onto his feet. He brushed the hay from his body and staggered into the cracks of light that broke through the wooden slats in the barn. The beams reflected off the dust and blinded him. The sun was fierce and his photophobia was as hard as ever to shake. This almost daily occurrence, though well practiced, caused him ill feeling as though he were a creature emerging from some long hibernation. But the bell signalled one thing and one thing only. Approaching danger. It had been sounded only once throughout the war; he had heard it from the slumber of the bed where he had spent his recovery, a false alarm caused by approaching traders. *Why would it be sounding now?* With that thought Tritan forced his transition from sloth to lion and marched out into the village to face whatever may be waiting for him.

Many villagers had gathered at the edge of the crop fields by the forest perimeters. Pitchforks, hoes and even broomsticks had been gathered by the mob that stood disconcerted by a harangue about a threat to two children who had been seen running out into the woods. Jonah was the speaker, and a brute as the eye beheld, but on the inside he was as soft as a feather bed. Tritan knew this and the rage inside him erupted as he sought out his enemy. There was none.

'They were last seen running out into the forest an hour ago,' said Jonah to Tritan who had grabbed a pitchfork from a petrified old villager. Tritan, confused, turned his attention to Jonah and his simmering rage abated. It was as though he'd run headfirst into an inferno with a water bucket filled to the brim only to find the flames were already extinguished.

'Pietrich, your boy, he ran off with Eira into the woods.'

'And for that we raise the alarm? I thought the dark skies had descended upon us,' rebuked Tritan.

Eira's mother Kayla, pushed her way through the crowd to face Tritan.

'Consider your son's wellbeing trivial if you must but I won't have it said that my Eira is naught worth a worry. If any harm's come to my lass, you will pay in kind. She's only just turned eleven years of age. That son of yours better not have led her astray.'

'Eira is two years his senior.'

Kayla could not tell if Tritan intended to defend his son or if he merely needed an excuse for an argument. Thankfully, Jonah spoke to distil the brewing confrontation.

'We've more important things to do than argue amongst ourselves. Two children's lives are endangered and this bickering is an insult to them. If she's ensnared them they have as much hope of escaping as a fly caught in a web.'

She was an outcast, Isabelle, once rumoured to be a villager herself, but her own loss led her to unforgivable actions. Her child had supposedly died of some ailment that could not be determined. Grief had driven her mad and one night she had slipped into one of the village homes and stolen a newborn baby before fleeing into the forest and holing up in an outhouse of her own design. She'd been found the following morning, the babe clutched in her arms and a knife at its throat as though its life could be traded for that of the child she had lost. The *haggard old lady* was all she was known as now, her true identity lost to time. Tales had been born about her and Tritan suspected many of them were not true. She had used to work amongst the other villagers, not a skilled healer but more a student of experimentation and her concoctions had aided many of the people of Knighton, though this fact was certainly one lost to the present generation.

The villagers began to assemble but Tritan was already over the fence and into the depths of the forest. The rest followed his path.

'Spread out, ten foot abreast,' shouted Jonah.

The villagers scoured the forests; they were twenty strong and covered many acres in good time. Tritan had almost lost the crowd for he had moved so fast. The pain inside his head was fierce and his clothes were sodden with sweat but his instincts told him not to slow. His calves began to ache and his hands twitched as he bent down to massage his affliction. The base of his ageing back cracked and stiffened and he cursed the one enemy he would never defeat: time. He'd spent much of his life in difficult circumstances and this current plight was hardly one of those. He almost laughed at the thought of this absurd search party desperately hunting for the two children.

Eira fascinated Pietrich more than anything else in this life; her advanced age and intelligence had given rise to ambitions in Pietrich that no schooling had ever mustered. But at this time Tritan thought of how children were born to play and explore and mischief was their duty. He'd never had a childhood, as most would describe it, but perhaps the greatest gift he could afford his son was to differ from him in that matter. He knew from where the villagers fear had stemmed. The haggard old lady of late age, perhaps sixty, had been banished from the village when Tritan had not known it, so he knew not what to expect. Though Tritan believed that no harm would come to the children, for she had not killed the babe that day and had settled close to the village perimeter for want of her own child and nothing more. But Tritan had a part to play; there was nothing that offended him more than the appearance of weakness. Especially where these pathetic villagers were concerned. Not a single soldier among them. He respected Jonah for his strength but pitied him for his conscience. As for Kayla, they traded goods as required but no friendship existed between them. Throughout the brief time Tritan had spent attending village council meetings, Kayla had always voted against him; he suspected out of malice regardless of whether she agreed or not.

As Tritan took in his surroundings he realised he was alone. He had doubled his efforts and as his mind wandered he damned the drink that was his lifeblood, for he knew it weakened him. The forest had grown dark though the sun shone brightly above; thick branches cloaked with leaves flooded the ground with a shade that passed the world into night. Tritan looked ahead into a clearing and squinted as salty sweat caused his vision to blur.

Eira sat upon a stool and beside her was Pietrich, each of them held a small steaming wooden bowl and hovering over them was the haggard old lady, a proud cracked smile on her face as she watched the children supping her broth. She had the appearance one might expect of a character from an old tale. Folded skin and hard tired eyes, her back was rounded but she moved with no discomfort and as Tritan came into view her vision proved sharp as she spun around to meet his gaze. In the flutter of a robin's wing, Tritan had thrust the pitchfork towards the haggard old lady, who stood unmoved; she knew an empty threat when she saw one.

'Come join us, there's plenty to go around. You'll not go hungry at my table,' the haggard old lady said.

'Speak another word and I'll turn your little tea party into a wake.'

Tritan advanced his step.

'Tritan, these are my guests, as are you. I don't have any wine however, for that you'll accept my great apologies.'

'What have the children been telling you? Tell me all, and quickly.'

'Oh, nothing that concerns you, I know you and everyone who lives in the village. I make it my business to know and it grieves me that I have such a truthful picture but in return there is barely a drop of honesty in all the oceans of stories told about me. I was especially moved to hear of all the rituals I hold with the newborns. I believe they are eaten alive and their bones offered to some distinct god of my own branding. Tell me, where are the bones of these poor babes?'

'I'm not interested in what you have or have not done, it's the children I'm after, not you.'

Tritan gripped his pitchfork as a dog emerged barking furiously from the hut beyond the camp. It tackled Tritan, biting at his legs, trouser cloth embedded between rows of foul teeth. The haggard old lady took this moment to flee from the scene and Tritan swept the dog aside making to pursue her.

'Stop! Leave her alone, she's just lonely.'

It was Eira who blocked his path now. She was indeed a brave one.

'Out of the way, girl,' bellowed Tritan.

He tried to circle around Eira but she dared to obstruct him further and the old woman disappeared beyond view. The incessant barking continued, although now from a secure distance as though the animal knew it would not be shown such mercy twice.

Pietrich, unlocking himself from the immovable fear he had suffered, ran the other way out of the clearing and into the depths of the forest, more afraid of Tritan than anything that could be out there in these woods, for if he provoked some foul and hungry beast he fancied his chances of negotiation with it higher than he did with the man he called father.

As Tritan ran after Pietrich, Eira called out to him, afraid.

'Please leave him be, it's my fault.'

But Tritan had gone; the faintness of her cries fell to the dirt. The boy was quick, Tritan had to give him that, perhaps he had inherited something of value from him after all, even if in all other matters they could not be less alike.

It did not take long until Tritan had managed to stretch out his arm and force his son to halt. The two of them stood panting, facing each other but no words passed between them; they rarely did. Tritan had only known the child a short while; after he had fully healed Tritan had returned to the war and eight long years had gone by since that day. Tritan had never found his previous companions, those who had left him for dead. The 11th had purportedly disbanded, and so he had joined with the first battalion who would have his sword. In those final years, Tritan could not be sure what side he was fighting for but he was certain that he didn't care. He had become a sellsword, nothing more.

Pietrich was overwhelmed by an urge to run but he held fast. Now that Tritan had caught up to the boy, he found himself at a loss as to what to do. His usual actions were unsuitable. He would not strike the child, though he knew harsh words should pass from his lips. He coughed and his throat was so dry that it sent a sharp pain across the roof of his mouth. Normally in times like these he had tied the offender with a rough rope and dragged them back to the stronghold, the rope inevitably cutting severe grooves into their flesh and the floor scraping at their skin. But he feared such actions would cause a mutual suffering as though the pain of the child could be felt in Tritan's own soul. He drew his head back to the situation at hand. This was no prisoner but just a boy, a boy for whom he was responsible.

'I'm sorry, Father,' said Pietrich.

AS THE SEARCH party set about its return course to the village, Kayla scolded her daughter and Eira turned to look at Pietrich with hope that he might be forgiven with greater ease. Pietrich followed a few steps behind Tritan, occasionally looking up to stare at the bear of a man; the patterns of sweat that soaked through from his back to the shirt were a marvel. This austere beast who had taken countless lives now marched ahead of Pietrich, his protector. Though their estrangement could not be questioned, the fear that had sent a gelid shiver up the boy's spine, was now replaced by a strange feeling of comfort, a safeness that no other could afford him. He wondered in that moment if he would ever truly know his father.

3

She could feel the familiar emptiness inside her; she felt it every night as she wondered why her bed was always her solitary refuge. The longing for something lost in time. That was her restlessness; the hole to her side became a part of her as she felt the barrenness inside, aching in the cool autumn night. She moaned and rolled and turned. It was no good. Her hand stretched out across the ruffled night sheets to the void where her husband had not slept since his return from the war. She'd heard the excuse several times; that it was for her safety as his dreams brought out the worst of the past and his mind could not subdue the acres of pain and so his body would kick out in a furious remonstration.

Marilia believed she would have suffered any amount of physical hurt to feel complete again. She had harboured her love within their newborn when Tritan left. She prayed almost every night that he would return safely and see their son. Pietrich had grown knowing his father through his absence. Marilia wondered whether this was the cause of the boy's softness but she had never believed it to be a weakness, for compassion surely was a stronger pillar than hate.

As she stirred she guessed that the sun was not due to rise for several hours. She could tell by the intensity of her headaches most nights. The lack of sound sleep worsened her focus but then she recalled her son having gone missing the previous day and decided to rise to visit him. As she walked from the partition of the cottage where her bed lay, the old oak floorboards creaked and moaned against the backdrop of the silent village.

Marilia drained a jug of water that had been infused with fruits and spices into a cup and lit a candle. She pulled out a stool beside the rolled-up blanket that Pietrich lay asleep upon and placed the items slowly and carefully onto a panel shelf by the open window. The candle flickered in the subtle draught as she took a sip of water to assuage her dry throat. Without thought her hand went to stroke her son's head and although she regretted disturbing him she didn't retract for he brought her much comfort.

'It's not yet light, Mother.' Pietrich spoke softly.

'Yes, my sweet, don't rise. I'm afraid I was restless and you captivated your daft mother's attention as effortlessly as ever.'

Marilia held the cup of water to his mouth to share in her refreshment and the cool water ran down his throat like an elixir of life. He shuffled about and eventually sat up to address her.

'You've done it now. I'll be a zombie all day long.'

'The chickens will be glad for the rest without you there to chase them.' Marilia smiled at him.

'Eira can still cause them trouble.'

The cheeky grin he produced was so adorable Marilia hardly wanted the moment to end.

'Pietrich, you must listen to me now, for I must be serious

and you cannot question me as is your manner. I love you dearly and have told you many times before that we cannot wander alone into the woods; none of us are safe without the protection of the rest of the village. Disappearing is a villain's trick. I cannot know where you are at all times but I must know that you are safe or else it would drive me to madness.'

'But, Mother, I wasn't alone and I am nearly ten.'

'We are still in a period of convalescence, these are strange and possibly dangerous times that may never truly end so you must accept my word.'

She held his hand and shook it with a desire for acceptance. Pietrich could not look his mother in the eye at this moment but he opened his mouth hesitantly to speak.

'What's wrong with that old lady in the forest? She was kind to us and all we've ever heard are stories of her horrific deeds. It doesn't seem right is all I mean.' Marilia blessed him for his ability to forgive, but forgiveness was strung like a rope and it could be unwound until it bore no weight at all. 'If she lost her child, isn't she just lonely?' he added.

'She's suffered a great loss, and sometimes great suffering may drive a good person to evil. A killer is not a killer until the first life they take; a person may live a lifetime before such an act is committed. We should not denounce the life they lived before but it doesn't change who they are now.'

'Father killed the day he was born, does that mean he has always been a killer?'

Marilia was taken aback by the question and could not find the words to answer. Pietrich could see he had stepped onto a rickety bridge and so he spoke again. 'Why do we have to have war?'

'I don't know, sweetheart, I don't know.'

Suddenly there came a crashing sound from behind the drapes that separated them from the rest of the kitchen. Marilia held her hand to her son's mouth to keep him quiet. They waited for a few moments but no further sound came and so Marilia slowly crept from behind the drapes to check on the disturbance. A pot had fallen to the floor and smashed into pieces. She collected the fragments and noticed spilt wine across the wooden table where the food was usually prepared. Lettuces, carrots, potatoes and other vegetables had been stained by the fierce red wine and Marilia did her best to rescue them. As she moved to the doorway and looked out into the night she caught a glimmer of a shadow entering the barn across the field and she knew Tritan had been there listening to them. For how long she had no idea. Undoubtedly he had slunk over to find more wine, a quotidian ritual from which nothing could prevent him. This was perhaps the only predictable behaviour of Tritan's that Marilia had conceded to. For his other habits, she had less forgiveness. She imagined the palliasse on which he slept every night, like some dog, guarding the stables. It riled her that a straw bed could bring him more comfort than being by her side. When she had nursed him back to strength he had lived inside her and Pietrich had come as no surprise. Now she could barely recall the roughness of his skin. How heavy would he feel when lying on top of her? How much of her breasts would fill the grasp of his hands?

The breeze shook her and a shiver ran down her spine, though Marilia could not tell if it was just the cold she had felt. She closed the door and returned to Pietrich who was still concerned about the intrusion into their home. Marilia comforted him and felt the need of a white lie for she wanted to enjoy the night with her son and think no more of his broken father.

'It was nothing, just one of your chickens playing havoc and trying to even the score.'

'In that case, Mother, I'd better get my rest and come the

morning I'll tip the scales back in our favour.' Pietrich spoke the words through that same cheeky smile that she always loved so dearly and Marilia lay down beside him and blew out the candle and neither of them felt need to speak another word.

TRITAN FELT BETTER RESTED than most nights; perhaps the knowledge that his family thought of him in his absence was a strange comfort. Did Marilia know how he longed to lay at her side? Tritan guessed not. Surely, she was relieved to have her own space away from him whilst his shame kept him away. At any rate, he had been able to ready the cart earlier than usual and this was just as well for although he had no interest in the autumn-winter festival he was aware of its importance amongst the rest of the villagers and it was due to start the following evening. All of the villagers would meet in the market square to divide up their share of provisions. One proportion would be put aside for the forthcoming feast, a foolish endeavour for those whose supplies were growing scarce. Part of Tritan despised this sort of collectivism and he thanked the skies that the population of the village was not greater.

He sauntered down the dawn-lit path with Diablo in tow, pulling the cages of chickens and sacks of vegetables that Marilia had prepared the previous afternoon. She had worked a long day while Tritan was off searching for Pietrich in the woods. They had not spoken since then and Tritan knew he deserved her anger. Given tonight was the only night of the year she really drank; he did not doubt that he'd play audience to her frustration when the evening came.

It was a busy morning despite the early hour as lots of the villagers gathered and conversed happily and from this Tritan was excluded. He had several deliveries and collections to make and decided to get the worst of it done first and so he headed to the small wooden structure where Eira was helping her mother by handing out pre-arranged packages to the regular customers.

Kayla had been appointed the collector of all the villagers' produce for the festival. She also traded a good number of desired exotic foods, those that could survive the long travels from the islands whence they came. Trade had only recently begun again with the Maluabian islanders and so these goods were a rarity. The war had caused the islanders of Maluabaw to retract into their own lives and only a few of them had resurfaced since. Of the fruits from the islands, papaya, plantain and pineapples were amongst the favourites. Tritan usually cared nothing for these and always collected apples by the dozen, in part for he knew it was a particular treat for Diablo, an ally worth spoiling.

Tritan dismounted the back of the cart as Diablo's trot came to a halt. He picked up two cages of live clucking chickens and walked past Eira at the front of the stall unaware of the fact she had intended to greet him kindly.

Tritan dumped the cages down onto a table in front of Kayla, intruding upon her conversation with another villager. Kayla ignored Tritan and turned her attention back to the woman.

'You've been more than generous, Bethan, and I'll see to it come tomorrow that the children share the sweets in equal measure, they'll not learn greed from the likes o' us.'

'Thank you, Kayla, Treat that little darling of yours to a sample y'hear. I must away. We all have a long day ahead.'

'Aye. that we do.'

Kayla took a breath as Bethan left the enclosed stall and turned to Tritan. The two met each other's looks but Kayla diverted her attention to the chickens instantly.

'Couple short, looks to me,' Kayla said as she moved the cages behind her counter.

'I can't force a chicken to fuck any more than I control the size of the clutch.'

'That aside, us've all a responsibility to provide for the festival.'

'I'm not suggesting you short change the festival provisions, take it out of your personal share if you must,' Tritan sneered.

Kayla considered this and went off to grab a few sacks of vegetables and fruits.

'Not getting your serving maid to wait on the likes of me?' said Tritan.

'She's under strict instruction to stay well shot of you. If only all of us could afford such luxury.'

Kayla dropped the sacks in front of Tritan before removing several of the apples. Tritan looked at her and his eyes cast a disapproving stare.

'Tritan, my intention is for you to take it out of your own share, I'll not have it said that I held out on an animal as fine as that steed out there.'

Tritan, indifferent to the course of the exchange, took the sacks and turned without another word, stopping only to catch eyes with Eira. For a moment he felt sorry for the girl.

Tritan cursed. 'Better to be an orphan, than the daughter of a whore.'

Kayla slowly reached for a sharp knife and her fist clenched tightly around it. But the look from Tritan was like staring into death's own gaze and she knew she would have had the pleasure of the meeting if she moved another inch. A moment later Tritan was out of sight at last.

The bustling streets were at their busiest. The ordure encouraged Tritan to move swiftly and he concluded his trades as quickly as possible. He was thankful for the cool breeze and cloudy skies as he sat on the back of his cart, gulping from a wine skin. He spied an ostler's stable where several horses were tied just inches from each other. They looked cramped and uncomfortable and Tritan patted Diablo with a caring hand, pleased that he had such a dear friend.

Without warning a cramp began to build in Tritan's body. The feeling in his stomach was agonising; the wine had worked its way through his liver and now his mind was screaming. It happened from time to time, and Tritan supposed that as all the earth's creatures had protested against him at some stage, why not his own body? The cramps began to have their way and a pang of intense pain shot across his entire body. He grabbed at the bridle around Diablo's neck, pulling himself to his feet and stretching out his lungs so that he could draw his breath with less strain. It was a temporary relief and was soon answered with another pang. The putrefaction nestled deep inside him was no doubt worsening with every gulp he had had these past months. The lack of supply had accounted for his good health whilst at war. The wine produced in the islands accounted for the majority throughout the lands and when it ran out, that was it. All a drunken soldier like Tritan could do was to fill his heart with want and ignore the headaches caused by the withdrawal of his addiction. Tritan had often wondered how many soldiers had been under the clasp of the drink. He convinced himself not to care; at least for the moment, his was the only addiction that mattered, for it was the only one that stabbed at his guts as another pang rattled him.

A loud snapping of wood sounded down in the high street below and Tritan, barely able to stand, turned to watch as the wheel of a cart worked its way free. The wood buckled sending splinters flying in all directions and as the cart turned the man riding it fell to the side before attempting to pull the cart straight again. The passenger, a young woman, managed to jump free as a second wheel buckled and the cart toppled upside-down trapping the man beneath. Tritan recognised him as Theo, a local musician, one of the few men in his mid-twenties that hadn't perished in the war. Tritan put his own suffering to one side and ran down to the cart where a useless crowd had now gathered. The young woman, Joanna, was leant against the cart trying her best to topple it back the other way; she caused it to rock but it was too heavy for her alone.

A few villagers were eyeing up all the goods, that had spread out across the pathway, with guilty temptation. They resisted the urge to enrich themselves but none of them ran to help Joanna. Tritan locked himself under the side of the cart and took a strong stance with his knees bent, pushing hard with his back, and slightly lifting the cart. The pain in his face was unmistakable as Joanna helped pull Theo free from beneath the cart and shouted.

'Thief! Put those down, thieving bastard those belong to my brother!'

Tritan pulled himself up and stood beside Theo and his sister to confront the thief, Jon, who was stood with the prize in hand. But before he could drop what he had stolen Tritan was on him like a newly-freed caged animal. Jon tried to push Tritan away but how does a sparrow fly against a storm? Then emerged Peter, the second of three brothers, who clamped his hands around Tritan's shoulders before bundling him to the ground. The two men spun in circles, arms kicking and flailing. The crowd drew away and Jon circled the brawling men, trying to time his strike. He dived forward as Tritan's boot met the underside of his jaw sending him reeling to the floor. Badly timed. Peter had now grasped Tritan in a bear hug but this was nothing more than a nuisance and after the third attempt Tritan cracked his shin with the heel of his boot.

'Stop!' A voice carried from the distance beyond the gathered crowd.

Tritan recognised it at once, for of the three brothers he had only bested two. Tritan crouched and held Peter's arm in a lock.

'Let him go, Tritan,' Thomas shouted as he passed through the crowd and stood in front of Jon.

'One step closer and I'll snap his arm and use the severed bone to spear his throat. Move quickly and you may just make it close enough to have a shower in his blood.'

Thomas daren't move. He knew a shallow threat when he heard it and this was not one. The healer took a pace backwards.

'Smart move, just the sort I can always rely on you to make,' said Tritan.

'Let him go for God's sake,' Thomas rebuked.

Tritan tightened his grip. 'You don't take another man's property.'

'Jon, not Peter, is guilty of that crime. I saw the whole thing and you have my word I'll see him punished.'

Tritan suddenly wondered why he exhausted himself on the younger brothers when it was Thomas who plagued him and so he let go of Peter's arm and allowed him to run back to join his brothers. He stood there staring at Thomas, no longer concerned with the petty theft. Theo and Joanna had managed to turn their cart back upright to inspect the damage before beginning to gather the surviving produce. But they soon realised that they would have to intervene as they saw Tritan unmoving. Theo and his sister gave each other a worried look as Joanna stepped forwards.

'I thank you, sir, for coming to our aid, but we consider the matter closed. I hope you'll feel the same,' she said.

Tritan spoke without addressing her.

'Forgiveness given too freely can come back to haunt you.'

Thomas considered the words and replied with his own.

'I would not speak so ill of forgiveness, given the amount

that you yourself need. For now, let us put aside our differences, it is not the time or the place to unbridle whatever is brewing inside you.'

Tritan swallowed hard as the pangs returned; how he wanted nothing more than to eradicate this lineage of brothers. But on one point he could agree with Thomas, now was not the time to pursue his grudge.

From the crowd that had gathered around the scene emerged Jonah. He faced the self-indulgent men who stood amongst the debris of the cart.

'Thomas, get your brothers out of here, now, before you talk yourselves into an early grave.'

Jonah stood his ground in front of Tritan until the brothers had left and then he addressed the crowd.

'Nothing more to see here, you lot. We've a festival to prepare for dammit.'

Tritan felt a sudden pang, worse than any previous, and it grounded him in an instant so that he doubled over and vomited. He lay there for a while, shivering and incapable of controlling his body. Jonah, Theo and Joanna surrounded him and held out their arms. Eventually they managed to help him to his feet.

'Theo, help me get him to his horse, I'll make sure he gets home.'

'He was trying to help us, all this is my fault. I shouldn't have ignored the rotting wood on my cart.' Theo looked appalled at the mess he felt responsible for creating but Jonah merely shook his head the way a kind teacher does when trying to figure out the culprit in a disagreement.

'No, lad, he went too far, and you were as good an excuse as any for the fool to throw fuel on the fire.'

4

A crimson veil hung overhead where the night sky slowly extended to flood the village in darkness.

The cart was laden with tools, the sign of a busy day's work in the fields. Marilia pulled the barrow through a pathway, collecting the final implements, and headed towards the barn. This was the moment she always dreaded; to lock away the day's work with the sight of Tritan curled up in his corner. Though this time was different. She had heard about the fight in the village square from a neighbour who thought it best to give her forewarning.

She took a deep breath and recoiled at the sour odour that hit her as she pulled at the barn door. The door creaked open and Marilia dragged the cart inside. The stable was a mess. Diablo was resting in his stall and hay was scattered everywhere. This was truly how animals lived, and were they not to have shared a common kin, Marilia might have believed Tritan was not of her species either.

She slowly approached Tritan as though he were a bull. His figure was illuminated by the light of a single burning candle.

Marilia grabbed it instantly and placed the exposed flame inside a lantern and then hung the light back onto a hook that protruded from the beam above where he sat.

She looked him over and saw the bruises and cuts on his shoulders where Peter had clawed at him. His torso was peppered with scars, each recording their own story. Most apparent was a long thin line right across his chest. It looked almost surgical, not the kind of rough wound soldiers received in battle, and just beneath it a more vicious jagged ridge ran around his abdomen. This scar was a mess and had obviously been crudely stapled at first by some field apparatus. Marilia knew Thomas had done it to keep him alive through the harsh journey south to the village.

'You'll be so laden with scars one day no one will know you.'

Marilia took a damp cloth to the exposed wound on Tritan's shoulder.

'If that were true I'd throw myself into a fire.'

Marilia had entered the trapfield and to return would show weakness. She would navigate her way through somehow.

'Your son drew a picture for you today, perhaps you should thank him for it?'

'He ought to be helping you in the fields by now, he's old enough. He'll soon outgrow his interest in sketching; once he fights for himself he'll abandon the practice in an instant.'

Tritan winced as Marilia picked the grime from the slit on his shoulder to prevent infection. She leant in close to whisper in his ear.

'Perhaps that's why you let him run off into the woods, so he could learn to fight for himself?'

'I was younger than him when I first drew blood.'

'You were born in a war, that war is over.'

'No, it is dormant, the slightest thing, a scintilla, would resurrect the feud and end this current purgatory.'

'Many would call it peace, not purgatory. If this is hell's garden we're living in, then I have nothing to fear again. The villagers laugh by day and sing by night; we barely have enough food to get by, I know, but, our son lives. Are these not the gifts the skies send down to us?'

Tritan stretched out his back and chest. The impact of hitting the floor had stiffened his ageing body. Marilia ignored his discomfort and continued.

'Tomorrow evening must be special for Pietrich, please concede me a compromise in that matter.'

Tritan held out his hand and spat into his palm, offering it to her. Marilia looked at him disgusted though she refused to let it show; for a moment she almost smacked him across his bruised cheek. She chose another course; hawking back her own thick phlegm she spat into her right hand and shook his. The agreement was done; sealed in the manner of vagrants more than lovers, she would play him any way he wished, for now. Marilia threw the cloth into the water bucket and stood to leave. She paced to and fro driven by love and exhaustion.

'Loving you is a fool's game, how long can I play the part...?'

Tritan's reply came instantly for one so tired. 'Love is at least a game to be played, war is a way of life. You can live without loving but you cannot love without living.'

'You treat love as though it were a curse, even though you are blessed with the love of your son. That is the kind of love worth living for. Would you spurn mine too?'

Marilia flung a piece of paper to the ground in front of Tritan and waited impatiently for him to unfold it. He saw before him a rough sketch of a man on horseback overseeing a farm. The horse was clearly Diablo on account of the empty eye sockets. Though Tritan's likeness was questionable, the depiction was complimentary; his back straight and strong and his face almost held a look of pride.

'I don't know this man,' Tritan said. 'It is you who tends the fields, not I.'

'He remembers fondly the days when you used to help me, as do I.'

Tritan flicked her a look as though he too longed for that spring to return. Marilia had seen it in that moment, a mind tormented but a deep torrent of some human emotion existed beneath the cavern. There was goodness there and she wondered if she could ever dig to such depths to retrieve it. For tonight, reproof was enough and with that Marilia whipped around on her heels and left, offering no chance for further reproaches.

Tritan folded up the sketch and tucked it away beneath his damp shirt as though he meant to treat it with care. Alone again in the flickering amber candlelight, the isolation grappled him. He had made his point and she hers, though he knew not if he believed his own sermon.

THE NIGHT WAS warm and Tritan headed out into the moonlight. He carried the flickering lantern with him, although the blue floodlit fields were bright as always with each full moon.

He headed around the corner of the barn and saw them there, sat in a large iron tub. It was a pleasure that Marilia and Pietrich shared together on occasion. The freeness of bathing in the moonlight comforted them both, surrounded by the singing birds of the night and the gentle winds that ruffled the trees playfully and with softness. It made Tritan uncomfortable, because he was jealous that the other men of the village might see Marilia naked as her name day, or because the other men had families of their own that they weren't detached from. Tritan thought perhaps she did it to provoke him but stubborn as he was he meddled in her diversions not at all. His real anxiety would have been if Thomas had stood nearby. But Thomas hadn't dared, either out of fear of Tritan or respect for Marilia. Tritan didn't care which reason drove the healer to stay away so long as he remained distant.

Marilia was washing Pietrich's back with a strong scrubbing brush. The boy enjoyed it though he was ticklish and struggled slightly with the rough bristles. She took a cloth to his ears to clean out the wax and this made him giggle. The sound reverberated around Tritan's head like a heavy church bell. The joy she brought their son was immeasurable and Tritan had no right to share these moments.

Tritan's mind wandered off into a fanciful world where he'd never been at war and death was a mystery, the way that love was to him in this life. He imagined endless nights of laughter and how it might have felt to hold his son the day he was born, cradled him on his first birthday and cleaned him when Pietrich was young and incapable. All those summers lost that could otherwise have provided his salvation. Does love not heal the soul as water quenches thirst? Perhaps Marilia was right, maybe the war was over. Time for peace... His mind wrestled in its own disorder and he forced himself with all his strength to stay with this dream. Tritan gazed back to Marilia and Pietrich. They were so beautiful and for the first time he allowed himself to realise it. He felt a sentiment inside him that had hibernated, he had assumed indefinitely, until this moment. Her back was an alluring sight of curves and exquisite flesh, the bumps of her spine protruding to the centre of her majestic posterior. It tormented Tritan. It was as though the entire world existed just for him to delight in her beauty. The moment was a gift and nothing else mattered nor would matter again. The trance embraced him fully. The intrusion came instantly.

Two men staggered drunkenly across the field behind Tritan and their night torches billowed brightly, casting his shadow across the farm. Marilia saw Tritan's form flicker before her eyes on the rough soil.

Tritan withdrew in an instant for fear of her knowing of his presence but he knew he had been too slow. Love had abated his reflexes. The drunken men carried on and paid no mind to the bathers or the thief that stole his looks. Of that crime Tritan was guilty and he would steal again, though as he peered around the corner the feeling had passed. The world was again as before and no longer designed for his purpose. He felt then that he would never again be able to love Marilia the way he had in those beats that his heart had skipped and darkness crept back into him as he paced backwards towards the barn, a silhouette in the night. No longer a lover or a father but once again Tritan, the boy who had killed his mother.

THE PARTY STARTED with a bang and the children gazed in wonder at the multicoloured exploding lights in the sky. The music was lively and many of the villagers had already gathered to dance. The finest cooks among them had prepared the feast with diverse food from all contributors and the aroma was intoxicating. Several tables were laid out with garnished meat, the grease glimmering in the firelight from the bonfires and children chased each other around the hog roast, screaming with joy.

Once the fireworks were over, the festival kicked into full swing. There were few who were sober among them and least of all Tritan who circled the outskirts alone with his skin of wine. He uncorked it and drained the contents. The music and the bustling crowds dizzied him and so he found a grassy bank to rest upon.

Marilia was conversing with many of the other villagers. She was happy and pleased, most of all by Pietrich who ran around with Eira, and although Kayla was keeping a close eye on the pair she had, for now, allowed them to enjoy each other's company.

Jonah called upon all the children to gather by his fire for a story and they ran to him like moths to a flame. Pietrich joined the other children though Eira stayed dancing alone, carefree and joyful.

Jonah spoke. 'In these woods she lurks, mourning the death of her child. But wander not into her grasp as she seeks another to replace it. She has eyes that could burn through your own like hot coals and skin like rotting bark. For many years, the forest has been her dwelling. She lives off the wild animals, feasting from raw flesh, watching, waiting, and anticipating her moment to strike. Go not towards her temptations and gifts, for you will join her child in the afterlife as she claims you for her own.'

The children sat captivated and did not notice as Jonah rifled in his pockets. He threw a handful of powder into the fire and an explosion of flames and sparks shot up into the sky. The children scattered and screamed, running in all directions. All except Pietrich who remained seated; Jonah saw the boy staring into the woods. He was filled with a sadness that only pity could instil.

'It's not true, what you said,' Pietrich said. 'Her skin isn't bark-like at all, she is just old and frail. They will all think she is a demon. But she isn't... she's just like the rest of us.'

Jonah smiled at Pietrich and sat down to join him.

'We can't always tell the truth, or there would be disorder. It's not easy to learn the balance but sometimes we must wrap ourselves in fear's cloak, for fear can aid us in the darkest corners.'

'I don't understand, I thought trust was built on truth?'

'Aye, oftentimes it is, but tell me, lad, would you expect your mother to reveal all her deepest and darkest secrets to you without fear of causing you hurt?'

'I don't know.' Pietrich shuffled uncomfortably.

'You can't show a shadow to a blind man and ask him to point out the light that casts it. You may not think it fair, and you'd be right, but we each must know what we can and play our part, and we're not all equals to each other, though we may believe it is so. Some must be sacrificed so that others can live in peace.'

'Like my father?'

'I'm not sure, lad. His is a tale shrouded in more mystery than any other I've known. He truly is a man apart.'

'He always seems so sad, but when he's near I feel safer, even though I'm afraid of him at times.'

Pietrich looked down at the ground and began to sketch in the dirt.

'Pietrich, let me ask you. Why did you want to protect that old lady? She could have hurt you, you do know that don't you?'

Pietrich replied. 'Mother says all people are born good, it takes the world to ruin them.'

'Aye, the war has ruined many lives. So you believe in second chances?'

Pietrich hesitated at the question, it held more weight than he could have imagined and Jonah saw that weight in Pietrich's expression. It was as though a great overwhelming doubt had descended upon his shoulders. Jonah opened his mouth as if to take back the question but Pietrich looked across the flames and saw the figure of Tritan sat alone in the outskirts and spoke.

'Yes... I do believe in second chances.'

Tritan glanced at the unfolding madness that surrounded him. Groups of villagers were comforting each other for the loss of their loved ones. Children were play fighting with sticks and one even speared the hog on the spitfire with a homemade trident; the three points were fashioned out of kitchen knives and the shaft was a broomstick. Across by the well in the centre of the square a man well into his fifties was flirting with a girl no older than nineteen. The war had made many such affairs plausible, as choice of a mate was scarce and many of the middle-aged villagers were widowed.

Tritan's eyes landed on Pietrich who had moved over to Eira; he was presenting her with a flower. From his vantage point Tritan could tell Jonah had been the instigator of this trickery, but Eira responded well to it and kissed Pietrich on the cheek before dragging him into the melee of dancers. The timing was apt, for Theo had begun to play a romantic paean and Tritan admired the skill with which he controlled his fiddle; the lyrics however he could do without. Though Joanna sang it beautifully, the song spoke of a fantasy of heroism for the deeds done in war. Such songs of praise sickened him and he tried to close off his mind to the words. The depiction of glory and bravery of soldiers doing battle and fighting for their homeland was exhausting; there were no songs to describe the smell of a skull whose contents had recently been pulped into a paste. No words could portray the sound of screaming children as they watched the rape and murder of their mothers, sisters and brothers. The songs were meant to comfort the soldiers, to celebrate their efforts but Tritan had no use for the pity of a musician, no matter how beautiful the sound.

Marilia was tipsy. She moved away from her crowd in search of her husband. She already knew to look towards the outskirts and there she saw him sat upon his solemn bank. The music was haunting and it sent shivers down the spines of the hardiest villagers. Marilia could not tell if it was the song that affected her thus or was it the desire she held for Tritan, now more than ever, that sent the icy tremble across her forearms.

'If I hurt you, it's not what I intended,' she said.

Tritan stared up at her as the song came to a close, the magical notes drifting into a distant past as Theo began to play another song, this time a lively folk tune with an upbeat tempo. Marilia turned to watch Pietrich and Eira dancing together, swinging around like crazed children and she knew all was as it should be, for this night was for their children. They were the future.

Tritan arose to stand at her side. He was formal about the gesture but had moved closer to her now than any recent time she could recall. She wrapped her arms around him. She had almost forgotten how big and strong he was. She let her head slip down onto his shoulder. He allowed it too.

'Would a soldier of Harmion dance with a farmer's daughter?'

'I'm no soldier, I have been retired.'

Marilia had not known what to expect, she had allowed herself to hope but perhaps it had been the drink that caused it. She wiped away the tears and tried to ignore the sick feeling in her stomach. She fought back the only way she knew how and turned to face Pietrich, dancing through the crowd. She smiled at him in all his glory.

'Your son is a braver man than you.'

With that she headed off into the crowd and Tritan stood alone again, the empty wine skin, now a burden, thrust to his side. He watched the world continue, a world in which he had no part to play.

Marilia entertained many of the crowd with her elegant movements; she was without a partner but she held the floor on her own. As the villagers began to clap and cheer, Thomas appeared and offered his hand, which she took. They danced together and smiled and looked into each other's eyes.

Tritan was locked to the spot like a statue, his feet grounded and steady. He felt himself drop slowly to the floor and without thinking he clasped a large rock in his right hand. His grip was firm and the stone was jagged, a lethal edge pointed outwards. He stepped slowly towards the crowd, entranced, enraged and delirious. The crowd barely noticed him as though he had left his body behind and it was his spirit pursuing the healer. The music peaked and the whole village now moved and Tritan felt as though time had slowed, he was invisible. Pietrich and Eira had stopped dancing but now held each other's hands and moved closer together. He paid them no mind, fixated only on Thomas. He picked out his mark; the temple of the right side of his head was the most exposed. He had killed stronger men with lesser odds.

The moments that passed seemed like a dream, all who played a part drifted as if on a cloud that would carry them each their own way and no man or woman was master of their own fate. Eira screamed, the music stopped, and the dancers halted. Marilia spun and pushed the blockade of bodies to the side as Pietrich fell to the floor. Eira held him in her arms and watched as the blood poured from his nose and ears. He convulsed and shook and white foam formed at his mouth. It was a moment of extreme confusion and Tritan would have barely noticed were it not for Thomas rushing through the masses towards Pietrich. Tritan turned and saw his son lying on the floor and he dropped the stone that instant. He barged through the crowd, as anguish broke loose and swept across the festival. Tritan's rough shoulders knocked several villagers to the ground as he ploughed through, desperate to discover the reason for this madness. He arrived at his son's side first; the others were still stuck in the crowds. Marilia and Thomas gazed at him as he pushed the onlookers away, creating a circle of space. Eira screamed another wail that pierced the night.

'Give him room!' Tritan bellowed. 'Move aside, all of you now, dammit.'

Thomas ushered the villagers to the side and tried to calm a hysterical Marilia, a torrent of uncontrollable shouts and cries passed from her throat until it became raw and she could taste the blood.

Pietrich was still. Tritan wiped the blood and mucus clear of his throat and heard his groans. Under the circumstances that was some comfort to them. Sound meant life and in this state, any sound would do. Thomas knelt down at Tritan's side to examine the boy but Tritan pushed him away.

'Tritan! Please. He can help,' shouted Marilia.

Tritan looked at her and then Thomas; she was right and God damn himself to perdition, he would let the healer pluck his harp.

Thomas listened to Pietrich's chest; a faint wheeze was discernible.

'We must get him home, at once,' said Thomas.

Tritan picked Pietrich up from the ground and carried him through the panic-stricken crowd and towards the cottage. Marilia and Thomas followed closely behind.

'Jonah, fetch my instruments at once,' Thomas shouted back into the gathering. The healer had a tune to play and his audience, he knew, was death.

Eira stood hopelessly alone in the circle of confusion that had reshaped the evening into a nightmare. She was hit by a bolt of terror and dropped to the ground in search of her flower, bawling her eyes out at the thought of losing it and, crawling on all fours, oblivious to the cuts on her hands and knees, she found the flower in one piece. She held it to her chest and breathed out a deep sigh, gasping for air and clinging onto a foolish hope, a childish hope. She prayed then, to what and whom she knew not, but she would pray for Pietrich from now until the end of time and if the world fell apart around her she would still pray. He needed her now and she knew it.

Many moments passed. Time became an illusion that Eira drifted through and like a feather caught on a breeze, she rose above it higher and higher as she thrust her hopes into the skies. It was silent all around her. She opened her eyes and aside from her mother who was knelt at her side, an empty village square was all she saw before her, but she cried no more for somehow she knew her childhood was over. It was time to be strong.

5

The room was quiet and eerie. All around them was a rabble of discussion, muted by the thick stone of the cottage walls. A crowd had gathered outside and the villagers fought to look through the small window slits. It was human curiosity at its worst. Had they been there for genuine care of the boy Marilia might have forgiven them, but she knew in her heart they were fighting for the right to be informed. The gossiping clutch sickened her, only one innocent among them, the girl Eira. She loved Pietrich and Marilia knew it.

Marilia stood forlornly and pained herself with the darkest of thoughts. Tritan could do nothing but pace about the kitchen causing her further stress and frustration. In front of them was the partition that made up Pietrich's quarters where Thomas was checking his breathing. The boy had settled but was barely conscious. His breaths were short and whistled and even the subdued light pained his eyes so all he could do was to squint them shut tight. Thomas draped a cool wet cloth over his head to help protect his weakened senses.

Thomas emerged from the partition to address Marilia. 'I've

done all I can for him for now, he'll be in great discomfort and he will cry out in pain from time to time as the aching of his eyes overwhelms him. I'll mix a tonic that should be taken twice daily, it will ease him and allow rest.'

Thomas was putting off the true diagnosis and Tritan knew it, but could see Marilia clinging onto hope as if some sedative would save the boy.

'If you've any sense, healer, you'll get to the point. Spit it out, now!' demanded Tritan.

'Very well; the boy is dying, it's a rare malady of the head and I've only seen it twice in my time, once in a soldier up north and once in another young lad half the age of Pietrich. If there's any hope it's that the ailment seems to do its work slower in the young but do not misunderstand me, it will consume him. Perhaps by the time the autumn leaves have fallen and the winter snows have settled, if he is resilient he may still know the first day of spring. He will need comfort until then, for the sickness will eat away at the vitals and the first thing he will suffer is the loss of the use of his eyes. You must care for him as though he were an invalid for that is what he will become.'

Marilia could not hold herself up and the strength went from her legs. She crashed to the floor and knelt over to dry retch; nothing came out except the streams of tears from her eyes and she screamed.

The whispers and conversations outside stopped for a moment and Eira caught a glimpse of Marilia through the slit and it thrust a panic deep inside her. She had worked her way to the front of the mob and stood atop a stool to reach the window. Even as the pushing and shoving behind her knocked her balance she remained resistant and spun around to glare at those beneath her. A lesson was learnt from her hardened stare; the girl had stirred shame in all their hearts.

Tritan had not broken his gaze from Thomas though the

healer had not even sent a flicker of attention in his direction.

Tritan spoke. 'So what are you doing here?'

Now Thomas did look, and as confused as he was, the fear was greater.

'If you cannot help him, what are you doing in my home?'

'Caring for our young is my sole intent, Tritan, please understand I wish you no ill on this night above all others.'

Marilia forced herself to recover, sensing the trouble was far from over.

'Tritan, please, listen to him, think of Pietrich and naught else, as we all must.'

Thomas began again. 'He will suffer these coming months, more than anything you or I could ever imagine. We must offer him something to aid that suffering.'

Tritan turned to Thomas. 'Your tonic will sedate him, I do not doubt, but he will not be himself.'

Marilia got up and grabbed Tritan's shirt and shook him.

'What are you saying?'

Tritan gave her a hard look. It was difficult to hold such a penetrating stare but she held it firm. 'Sometimes it's better to leave well enough alone,' was all he offered her and then he turned back to Thomas. 'Does it give you some joy to control how we feel? Whether we live or die? You say it was a miracle that saved me, but it was by your hand that I now stand here today. And yet you cannot save a nine-year-old boy. What shame that must bring you!'

'Tritan, that is where you are most wrong, that is not what brings me shame, mine is the knowledge that I allowed suffering to envelope this household the moment you drew breath in my arms. I had been taught to believe that all life deserves a chance. How grave a mistake I made then when I dragged you back to *my* village. A mistake I will never make again.'

Tritan had had enough of words, and lunged towards Thomas, surprising himself at how fast he could still move. Within an instant he had bashed Thomas across the head several times with his fists and the cracking sounds of knuckle against jaw did not cause him to falter. Tritan grabbed at Thomas and dragged him towards the door of the cottage, kicking it open and splintering the wood of the frame where he then faced the entire village who were still gathered outside. Tritan was barely aware of their presence as he threw Thomas into the dirt. He then ran down the steps and knelt on Thomas ready to strike again. The villagers were in shock and no intervention was made; to sedate such a ferocious beast at its zenith was a far greater risk than any dare to take.

Thomas gargled through the blood in his mouth. 'I should have left you to die!'

'So why didn't you? Why?'

Tritan spat in Thomas's face. Blood and saliva blinded the healer and dribbled down his cheek onto his chin; the ferocious ex-soldier struck his victim again and again.

Marilia ran down the steps and grabbed Tritan by the shoulder to pull him away. Tritan, unsound of mind, let his arms flail to cast off the pest who troubled him. It was only in a sobering instant after that he realised what he had done. Tritan stood and turned to face Marilia who covered her face, bleeding from the nose where he had caught her in his piteous moment of rage. She crawled away backwards, afraid. Tritan felt sick as he turned to face the crowd, and now he saw them. Every one of those judgmental pairs of eyes, glared at him. Only Jonah looked away for he could not accept what had ensued, but Tritan was already standing trial and he knew it. They all knew it. It was Kayla who spoke.

'You're done here, bastard.'

Tritan didn't hang around to hear the sentence, he would be

banished and outcast from the village, never able to return. He would not be afforded the last few months with his son. Marilia would never forgive him and he would not know home again.

TRITAN READIED his things in the barn and loaded up the saddle onto Diablo's back. He grabbed the stirrups and tied off a few provisions so that they might make it to the next town. He had enough full wine skins to entertain a legion. At the back of the barn he unearthed a dusty pile that had not been touched since his return from the war. There he found his armour, sword and shield. He packed the sword but left the armour and shield behind.

Tritan felt hesitant but for what reason he could not tell. He knew his time here was over and it was time to move on but one last task he must first complete. In his abandonment, he would attempt a small degree of mercy.

Marilia had barely left Pietrich's side and so Tritan had to wait, observing them secretly until she needed use of the privy. He could tell she had held on for as long as possible for fear of Pietrich passing in her absence. As she disappeared Tritan emerged from the shadows and approached the bedside where Pietrich lay. He stared at the boy who looked weaker than ever. Tritan held a thick blanket in his arms, folded tight. He wrestled with it to make it as compact as possible and leant over to smother Pietrich as he slept. For the first time he could remember, Tritan cried, and tears rolled down his cheeks and dropped onto the blanket which he still held just inches from the boy's face. The sweetness of the child was ever present as he slept, the dribble bubbling on his lips hard to watch for it showed such innocence. Tritan struggled with himself and cursed his weakness for he could not do it. Even now in this condition he could not set his son free from the suffering. Instead he softly wiped the excess saliva from his son's mouth, threw the blanket to the side and left.

Dawn had barely begun and Tritan was already leading Diablo down the village path and past his cottage; he looked at it for the last time. He thought he saw a shadow moving in the doorway; perhaps Marilia had not slept either. But he could not be certain. As he rode through the empty village square, Tritan spotted Eira by the mourning tree, its leaves had all turned a golden vermillion shade and some had begun to fall to the ground. It was these leaves that Eira was picking from the floor and skewering back onto the branches, as if to prolong the autumn.

Eira heard hooves beating against the ground and it sent a shudder down her spine. She looked up to Tritan who was a dark figure against the purple skies. He looked so fierce and she understood why she had always been afraid of him. But she was not afraid now.

'If all hope was lost, I still could not abandon him.' Her voice trembled as she spoke, but the sentiment was clear enough.

Tritan stared back at the girl and he realised she was braver than he. Yes, he had been outcast, but was it not an invitation he had hoped for so long to receive? Eira continued to look at him, and if he could have read her mind he would have been certain she was begging him to stay. But he knew he could not; better he disappear and maybe finally he would be granted permission to die. Perhaps only in death would the world forgive him for all that he had done. And with that lingering thought that would stay with him for the rest of his time, Tritan turned Diablo towards the village gates and they rode off into the distance leaving a trail of dust in their wake. Eira held her forearm over her eyes as the dust blinded her and once it had settled she could see Tritan was gone.

6

The grating sound of metal scraping across the ground was accompanied by the rattling of chains and only the burden of the sun beating down on them was worse. Each of the chain gang felt as though they carried half their weight in steel around their ankles, wrists and necks. They passed heavy rocks and debris from the hole they had dug in the ground across a field. The earth was dry and the hot orange soil reflected a burning glow, and none amongst them could escape the savage light. The strongest of the twelve captives, Fieldes, had been tasked with smashing the largest rocks into smaller pieces so that the weakest could more easily manage their burden. He grunted as he bore down with the mass of a large hammer that scorched his sweat ridden and blistered palms.

A landowner loitered in the distance keeping an eye on those at work. He was in his early fifties and had the appearance of a seasoned brawler; excessive muscular arms and veins that jutted out like worms under the skin; numerous scars that marked the brow of his head and a jagged ridge that ran around the nape of his neck where a sword had once near taken his head off. He traded now in the lives of criminals, bandits and anyone who committed a crime serious enough to warrant punishment by loss of limb or life. He put them to work on his land, a deserted patch in the lower midlands of Harmion, where no fertile soil existed and water was scarce. It was for these reasons he had chosen it, as he knew no one else would work such tortured wilderness. The effort to create something of this land was immense and he was the man for the job.

At the edge of the field was his cottage, which was little more than a shack with a rusted metallic roof, made of scrap sheet metal once used to fortify a ditch during a nearby battle. It sat at the top of the hill that overlooked the nameless town below. One day he would name it, when it deserved a name. The pairing was fitting he supposed, for though he had been born Wendel, all knew him as the *landowner*.

The town was nothing more than a dirt track sided with huts and a sewage gully that overflowed with urine and excrement. But to the rabble of townsfolk it was home and it afforded them greater comfort than the wild they had escaped from. It boasted a wooden cabin that doubled as a tavern and a brothel, where most of the diaspora spent their time. Almost half the itinerant populace slept on the streets that were patrolled by guards, under Wendel's partial employ, trying to keep some semblance of order. The town was made up of survivors from all over Harmion and some had come from as far as the eastern coasts that had seen the destruction of most of the warships; there were a dozen languages spoken amongst them but no common tongue. Wendel was the only man with a vision in this town; his ambitions were his alone regardless of the benefits to the others. Life ran its own course in spite of his influence though he was occasionally able to save a man's life by buying him into slavery, shackling him in chains and setting him to work.

. . .

THE SCREAMING BEGAN as it did most mornings, Wendel turned to face his home from whence the noise came and strolled towards it dejectedly.

Born a bastard, Wendel had been forced to serve his father's three legitimate sons. Taught in many trades, he would become their horse keeper and food servant, healer and laundry boy, but most importantly he would fight each of them daily on the practice field where the art of swordsmanship was cherished most. It was during a time before the war when aristocracy ruled and the common folk would each serve a master; a way of life long forgotten in the turmoil which now flourished throughout Harmion. Wendel had seen the fall of politicians and the rise of leadership through force. It was his wife, Brynhildr, who had saved him from his servitude, a well-respected proprietor of an embroidery shop. She pitied his mistreatment by his half-brothers and had agreed Wendel's employment with his father who no longer cared for his position within the family. Wendel was emboldened as a trader to travel the lands in search of the finest materials and to sell Brynhildr's evermore popular gowns and dresses to the richest women. He left behind his old life and started anew with her but the war had already begun and he was soon drawn into its clutches. He had never known a day in his life without work but nothing had prepared him for the strain on his life as it was now. The delirium and anguish of his wife was a daily reminder of what they had lost; she woke each morning to discover anew that their son was no longer with them. She had suffered a severe stroke when Wendel had brought the boy back home, dead at just seventeen. At the sight of his lifeless body she had lost control of her thoughts and her mind turned inward.

As Wendel entered through the makeshift swinging door he

saw her lying on the floor with her hands held high in the air. She had soiled herself and Wendel knelt down by her side, oblivious to the rancid smell. He stroked her cheek and as she calmed he began to undress her until she stood beside him, naked, but with no sign of shame. Wendel took the clothes outside and threw them into a bucket filled with water and made sure they were deep soaked before returning to wash down the rigid, dirty woman he had lived with for so many years. She barely moved the entire time as he restored her dignity and wrapped her in a gown so that he could walk her outside into plain view.

The slaves knew better than to pay heed to the goings on in Wendel's personal life, although it was inseparable from his charge over them, for Brynhildr was an immense responsibility.

Wendel smiled at her; she almost flickered a look back to him. 'My Brynhildr, I envy your days; they start anew as each sun rises. Do you see anything of my temporal loop as we dance the same dance from dawn until nightfall? To learn such things as I can teach you, only to forget them again whilst you sleep. I wonder if you are aware that I love you and do not need to learn to love you again each day, as you must learn to see that it is so.'

Brynhildr muttered no sound in response. Wendel expected none, he practiced such poetry on her daily, but she always replied the same way: with silence.

'Today, my love, we shall visit Jason where he rests.'

Wendel awaited some objection.

'Very well, let's get moving, a long day awaits.'

Wendel often avoided the gravesite of their son, as he knew it caused her pain, for it caused him pain too; a pain that no parent should ever know.

They walked slowly up the field and along the brow of the hilltop where the grave stood proudly. It was the result of

Wendel's effort and workmanship; by any standard it was a stone, nothing more, but to Wendel it was a monument to the lad he had lived for, and who now lay resting beneath it.

The gravestone still looked fresh; violet and rose flowers covered its base. Wendel knelt beside it and brushed his hand across the engraving to loosen the dust that had gathered in the cracks. The engraving was simple, stating only the forename of the boy on account of Wendel refusing to pass on his bastard's name. Beneath it read:

Jason herein laid to rest. He fought bravely by his father's side in the forty years war until his last days.

He hated the mention of the war, but he knew his wife had been proud of their son for the part he had decided to play and so knew he must include it in the engraving.

A chill came with the truculent breeze that unsettled them. Wendel caught Brynhildr shivering and wrapped his arms around her. A black crow flew down and landed on the grave then squawked as if master of the stone. It tapped its beak against the solid rock and its cries echoed across the valley. Wendel met the eyes of the black-feathered bird and for a moment they seemed to read each other's thoughts. Wendel thought that perhaps the crow was his son's protector in the afterlife and silently he blessed the skies.

The visit was over and they strolled back towards the digging site where the dozen men and women were resting; Wendel knew they'd earned the moment. He strolled over to the well and the hole that went deep into the ground. He descended the rope and tested the soil at the bottom. It was dry and coarse. No sign of water.

Later that afternoon, Wendel headed down the hill into the tatterdemalion settlement. As he strolled through he saw acts of lechery, unashamed and as public as the hangings that took place at the gallows by the end of the street. Not his idea, but to retain order he had to allow the people what they wanted more often than was good for them. This he knew was the definition of the complexity of ruling. The people must be free to choose for themselves, but as a spoilt child does, they will choose for themselves more often than for others. He glanced towards the noose, which was currently wrapped tight around a young woman's neck. She appeared feral and dirty. Dried and crusted blood ran down her thighs. Wendel watched her swinging corpse, limp like a strangled snake, her gown billowing in the wind.

'Just some whore, wouldn't do as she's told.'

The wine merchant was dismissive as though Wendel ought not to care for her. But the sight of a small child crying and alone, wandering in the distance at the foot of the gallows, riled him.

'Is death to be the punishment for all disagreements now?'

'It's not for me to say, Landowner, I'm merely an observer, and here to quench the thirsts of those in need.'

Wendel looked about at the traded goods held on the merchant's stall.

'That ring, where did you get it?' Wendel pointed to a silver etched ring, faded with time.

'Just some thief I expect, this is a captain's ring after all. Fool didn't know its worth, traded it for a skin of wine.'

Wendel picked up the ring and read the engraving.

'No mere thief would survive lifting something of this importance.'

'Mmm, no stranger would pass through these parts unless he were truly lost,' said the wine merchant. 'But curiously, he would not part with his wedding ring.'

Wendel nodded, intrigued, and carried on through the town, acknowledging those who knew him. He judged the condition of the place that was of his making, analysing every aspect.

Filthy and wretched, he thought to himself. But better to be father to this wasteland than a beggar on the outskirts of paradise. Wendel had always had trouble with obedience, especially when demanded from gluttonous, prissy old men who had never held a sword in their life except at some worthless ceremony where new titles were conferred. Hollow titles, the kind bestowed by pompous turds that hid behind their cloaks and sermons. Wendel had rubbed shoulders with such pious religious types in his youth and offended as many. The remembrance brought about a smile as he suddenly felt a flush of pride flood across him. This was all his. The naked children running in the filth, the wenches selling their oversized bodies to the guards who could barely afford their rising prices. The outhouses and crooked stables, fashioned together by unskilled workers, and the tavern that served putrid wine and sour ale. Even the gully overflowing with sewage was his. It was a start, a spark of life he had ignited. Did anyone appreciate his efforts? It hardly mattered. Wendel vowed to continue his work, to dig the well on his patch of land and bring fresh water to the rabble. That was his goal, one small step at a time.

Focused and driven, Wendel turned about to head up the hill to the digging site to see the progress made by the twelve-chained criminals. He owned them too.

THE NIGHT PASSED as it did most nights, quietly and with a sadness lingering in the air. But Wendel had slept uncomfortably, rolling and dreaming of an uncontrollable rage that made no sense to him. It was not his own rage, or the rage of a particular man, just rage itself. He awoke suddenly at the moaning sounds, cries and shouts coming from the town below. Wendel felt his back wrench as he rolled out of bed and he struggled to his feet. He bent over to put on his boots and the cracking and tearing sounds beneath his flesh that he heard each morning reminded him of his age. The disturbance that had awoken him so early could only mean one thing. Execution. It wasn't a rare thing, but to happen so early... the locals must be out for blood.

Wendel dressed quickly and laid a blanket over Brynhildr who still slept. He prayed her dreams were as peaceful as she looked and headed off into the field. The workers were still stirring as the sun glimmered over the horizon. He'd leave them be for now, time was likely short if he was to make his move.

He carried with him an old sword and donned a thick leather jerkin that had seen years of use. His boots were sturdy and heavy but they hardly slowed his pace. Wendel approached the high street and saw that the crowds were out in full force. He had to push his way through the men, women and children who roared at the gallows before them. It was a rough crowd, the rowdiest Wendel could recall having seen. The populace of the slum seemed to have doubled from its usual numbers. Every drunken creature, wastrel and whore had gathered for this occasion.

Wendel was now clear of the bulk of the crowd and saw two men and a woman, covered in bruises and cuts from the stones that were hurled towards them by the onlookers. Three on the gallows was quite a rarity. There had never been the need to put two men or women to the noose at one time let alone three. No wonder the crowds had gathered; this was a one-off show to marvel at and Wendel knew that to purchase their lives would be a hard task. One of them was damned already, that was a certainty, for there would have to be some blood spilt to appease the audience. The crowd would never allow all three to walk. In fact, if they conceded to only one death it would be a miracle. He would have to act fast to save any of the accused today.

A horse neighed and buckled the wooden stake to which it

was tied. The timber gave way and collapsed but the horse remained tethered to the foundation, which held strong. Wendel turned his attention to the horse and saw that in spite of its protests it would likely remain tied. It was like no horse Wendel had ever seen, so large and black and scarred but fierce and strong, a beautiful creature. Most intriguing were the two empty sockets where its eyes had once been. Wendel wondered what kind of a man would let an animal live in such a state. This was a man after his own heart and he knew then that he must find the owner for he would be a rare man indeed and likely he was amongst the three with nooses around their necks.

The guards tested the timber structure to ensure it could handle the weight. They reckoned a quarter ton would be swinging from it within the hour. It was made in the same rugged fashion as the rest of the settlement but it seemed satisfactory for the task at hand. The width was plenty to fit the accused side by side and three wooden stalls about two foot high were placed under the slack ropes. One of the executioners had to signal to the crowd to halt the throwing of their rocks as one of them cracked into the side of his shoulder. The crowd obeyed but the shouts were not diminished. A screaming mother, holding her young daughter tight, seemed to be rallying the loudest cries. The girl dare not show her face as her mother pointed at one of the accused, calling for his demise.

A guard spoke. 'These three bastards stood before you have been brought forward to pay for their crimes. You will see justice done today.'

The crowd cheered as a guard approached one of the men who wore a strange wedding band. The guard took out a knife and went to cut the finger off and claim his prize. It was then that Wendel chose to make his presence known and he stepped onto an upturned bucket to raise his position.

'Hold! Guard, you'll ruin my goods. Tell me, what crimes

have been committed that we should see three of our children perish before midday is upon us?'

As though a speaker at a pantomime, the man replied. 'Landowner, we all here respect you and what you have done for this place we call home. Some of us never knew a home until you united this rabble. But today I would urge you not to interfere, these are three devils the world will not miss.'

The crowd roared and shouted at Wendel where he stood, but he remained strong, unwavering amidst the passion for violence. 'I do not question the validity of these crimes you put upon their necks, I merely ask to know what are these crimes, surely no man, woman or child here would deny me the knowledge you all seem to share.'

'A fair request, one that goes hand in hand with the custom of announcing the sins of the committers prior to their deaths. The dirty bitch to your right is guilty of murder, of not one but three. She admitted as much herself fully as she was brought forward at the waking hour,' said the guard.

'And here she stands now, gagged and impeded so she might not argue her case in reply to your accusations.' Wendel spat back at the guard.

'The fat turd of a man you see before you,' the guard continued, ignoring Wendel's reply, 'raped and abused the girl who stands at your side, see how ashamed and tormented she is.'

The mother pulled her daughter's hands from her face and spun her to Wendel to show him the marks upon her face. Wendel studied the brutal wounds and then the mother pulled up her daughter's dress to show her bloodied privates. He grimaced and looked away.

'Enough, I see the evidence plenty clear, allow the girl her dignity, she has clearly suffered enough. But what of the third captive, we do not know him. Has any of you seen him before? Has he committed any previous offense?'

'He tracked an elderly woman to the town. Drank himself into oblivion and as the sun broke the horizon he made his move. Were we not there to save her, her throat would have certainly been cut.'

'And where is this elderly woman now? So that we might hear her account.'

The crowd shifted at Wendel's request, looking about them for the woman to come forward. She did not.

Wendel readied to speak again. 'It's a tale you've heard from me on more than one occasion, but workers are hard to come by, and I have plenty of work that needs strong and able bodies put to. As always my version of justice does not arrive without payment.'

Wendel dangled a bag of coins as he jumped from the bucket and approached the gallows. The crowds gaze was now upon him, but he moved in such a commanding way that it was hard to see the ageing, fragile man that he was becoming as each season passed. Nor did he show signs of fear at the depleting supply of coin that he had saved all those years ago.

Wendel circled the criminals who were stood on their stools, the loose ropes hanging around their necks. He kicked them in the backs of their legs and smacked their arms, testing their strength. As he faced the suspicious man at the far end, Wendel was met with a look that held hatred, suffering, pity and guilt all rolled into one spearhead gaze. Wendel knew at once that this was the man, the owner of the blind horse. He noted the scars that were peppered over his body and the tone of his muscles. This was a fighter and no mistake; Wendel took a moment to admire the wedding band he wore.

'I see promise in these three. We are short of water. Many in our town are sick, too sick to work. Would you not let me put tools in their hands, their punishment would be gruelling I promise you. And at the end when it is done, they will bring you water. No more half-day hikes to fetch the piss we all drink from the next town. Then we can reconsider their position. Today their deaths will bring us nothing.'

Wendel's speech was met with a stunned silence; he looked around at the townsfolk below him, no longer shouting and crying out for blood. Not until the mother stepped forward with her daughter. She would bring down fury upon them all and nothing less.

'Listen to this man, he thinks he owns us all because he bolted a few iron slats to wooden struts and called this place a town. How many times have we seen him rescue criminals with these so called acts of kindness? My daughter was raped and beaten, how can a man capable of such things appeal to our supposed landowner. We should string him up there with the rest of them.'

This ended the silence of the crowd, and to Wendel's horror he knew her words had struck a chord with the hearts of all who were here today. Their intention was to see Death swing his scythe and Wendel knew the shadowy ghost of the afterlife lurked among the crowd. The landowner's next play would either be his undoing, along with the three accused, or the finest moment of self-preservation he'd have ever achieved. He saw the looks of the crowd; his first instincts had been right, they would not leave satisfied until blood be spilled.

Wendel paced towards the murderer and the keeper of the blind horse. He untied their nooses and knocked them both to the floor. The guards, confused, secured the prisoners as the crowd broke into near madness. The audacity of Wendel's actions was sure to insight a tremendous rebellion. He walked next to the final criminal; the rapist smiled at him, already thanking him for saving his life. The crooked smile through black teeth was met with a sharp tug as Wendel tightened his rope, pulled hard and fast and secured a knot against the wooden block at the base of the gallows. Moments before the mob was able to surge forward and prevent Wendel's mercy, he kicked out the stool on which the man stood and watched him drop. The cracking sound as the neck broke silenced them all. The rapist wriggled for several moments before his body went limp and Wendel threw down the bag of coins to the guards. The chinking sound of coin landing on wood was heavy and rich and a roaring cheer followed it. Wendel had won over the crowd. The mother and her daughter were so relieved and tear-stricken they had no more reason to challenge him. The murderer on her knees looked up into the skies and prayed and thanked the gods of the world for the mercy bestowed upon her, and as she looked down she saw a face in the crowd that beamed at her, a young woman who had remained quiet throughout the ordeal held her hands over her heart and cried.

But in the shade of the gallows, where no light shone, a man hung his head low. Dejected and crestfallen, he felt only disappointment. Tritan had only a moment to consider the implications of the clemency shown to him before the butt of a spear cracked him across the head and knocked him into unconsciousness where he would meet the demons of his dreams. The nightmare he had come so close to leaving behind was not yet done.

7

The last structure standing was a humble slate roofed cottage that claimed the shadow of an old oak tree positioned proudly at the centre of the town. It was adjacent to the river that now flowed red. Smoke billowed across the rubble of the fallen homes and lying in the dirt were the remains of the cadavers that were once the lifeblood of the settlement known as Port Melees. The small town had once been home to smugglers who used its position on the trade routes; waiting in the night to cut the ropes of the large ships' cargo holds, their boats lurking in the gloomy darkness to off-load the stolen goods to the mouth of the port at the edge of the town.

It was nearby up river, in the sole standing cottage, that Castellar Dell'Anima was being held captive. In his youth, he had worked hard to bring education and prosperity to the town, and rallied for the construction of the lighthouse that lit up the port. Eventually, through peaceful means, the smugglers had all left and over time the town grew into a haven. He was famous for this as no other settlement had ever been liberated without bloodshed. It was this that made him most dangerous to his enemies as the town had managed to withstand the pull of war that was now twenty years through its course.

Now, the sole survivor, he had seen all that he had built destroyed by the wrath of Augustus, who was busy planning a large push to the east where the resistance was still strong. The decision of what to do with Castellar was not yet made.

It was almost fourteen years to the day that Augustus had ridden out to certain death with his crippled 11th Legion. The sun had saved him that day, as the vicissitudes suffered by his enemy had been fierce and final. The forces against Augustus had ridden into battle without foresight or care for the rising sun that would blind them at the moment of combat. In a matter of minutes the orange dawn turned into the blistering white of day and Augustus realised the advantage was his. He could not have foreseen how the rising dust would catch the light, and the glare of a furnace was cast into the eyes of every man who had stood against him. His injured soldiers, many wounded and maimed, fought feverishly as they massacred the blinded foe. For Augustus it was a moment of ecstasy; trained soldiers turned into fodder against his vengeful madness. An impossible victory, it had earned the 11th Legion the name *The Cripple Army*.

A rider galloped through the desecrated village and quickly jumped down before entering the single standing home. Inside he met the looks of several of the 11th Legion that guarded a thirteen-year-old boy who was shaking where he stood. Blood trickled down his sword and dripped off the sharp point onto the wooden floor. The boy stood mesmerised as he watched the blood seep through the cracks as if seeking some refuge from this carnage. Was this the lesson that had been intended for him to learn? the boy wondered, as he glanced at the family he had massacred single-handed. A mother lay dead between the two lifeless children she had been trying to protect. Near them sat Castellar on a short wooden stool facing the boy. He made no attempt to overwhelm him for three men of the 11th would be on him before he left his seat.

'You *must* send me to join them, surely you can see that? You've already taken my life, there is only death for me now.' Castellar broke the silence by addressing the rider who entered, pulling off his helmet and setting it on a side table. The room ignored Castellar.

'What news?' spoke the highest-ranking soldier, Kal.

The rider responded. 'He's still not made up his mind, but I was sent to tell you that we will have his answer within the hour.'

'I see.'

'Perhaps he wants him as a bargaining chip, he may be of importance to the bands of guerrilla fighters.'

'No, this one's methods are rare. If nonviolence goes unpunished it will remain an inspiration.'

'You'll get nothing for sparing me,' implored Castellar.

Kal finally turned to acknowledge their captive. 'Caste, you old goat, you'll not bend my deaf ears with your magic tongue.'

Castellar turned to face the shivering boy. 'This one's ears aren't deaf, he is still young enough to learn the difference between the darker actions and the lighter ones that a man may commit, or not,' he rebuked.

The room filled with laughter, except for the boy, who was silent and confused. Why would the captive be concerned for his soul after watching him butcher his loved ones and leaving him with nothing in this world to continue living for?

Kal spoke through a wide grin. 'Our young companion here is a special case; he's seen and done things most men in their late twenties would cry themselves to sleep over. What say you, Tritan? Should the man live or die? Should the ringleader of the peace alliance be shown mercy? After all he's killed none, nor did any of his followers, but this you see is what makes him dangerous, for he is a visionary to his people. Though I am afraid for our old friend, Caste, most of them will never re-awaken from their slumber.'

Tritan stared at Kal, searching for an answer but none came. All he could do was look back to the dripping blade.

'Speak, lad, words have their place when the killing is done, you need both blade and wit in this world.'

Still Tritan could find no words and Kal, bored of the matter, left the home in search of other amusement. Castellar leaned forward, trying to get Tritan's attention.

'I see you're confused, boy. You know that taking their lives was the wrong course, but now to take my life would be a mercy. You mustn't worry; I've already forgiven you. All that is left now is for you to do it.'

Tritan shifted uncomfortably, transfixed by the captive's words. The other members of the 11th had turned to idle gossip in the corner as they awaited orders.

'Let me tell you something my grandfather once told me when I was your age. All matters of good and evil in this world exist only in the world of men, for all else is nature. The action of a bird that catches its prey cannot be considered evil, for it is its nature and without that action its own life would soon be forfeit. But we men like to believe we think freely, that we are not animals. This makes our actions those of choice and not of nature and therefore only in humanity do good and evil exist. In truth, child, your actions are not of your own choosing, they are the will of one man, so you are still therefore as if a product of nature. Men have spent centuries convincing themselves they are a higher form of being but have also mastered the trick of delegation and therefore expunge themselves of guilt and responsibility. Which is guilty of evil, the king who orders a death or the executioner who kills?' Tritan looked up to meet the man's gaze as he searched for some sign of acknowledgement. Satisfied, he continued. 'I cannot answer the question for you. Each man must learn from his own actions, as you must learn from yours. Actions can be commanded but not feelings, for feelings are involuntary and you are powerless against them. You may take my life or not. Either way you will feel the weight of that decision, as you may promise your love to another, though such a promise be hollow, as one day you may fall out of love. You cannot claim that who you are now will agree with who you will one day become.' Castellar leaned back.

Tritan felt awkward, the sense of being so intensely scrutinized bothered him in a way he had never known. He had been watched before, committing other atrocious deeds for his father. But never before had he felt that someone other than he could be aware of the thoughts rushing through his mind, that his feelings were so transparent. Did the rest of the 11th Legion know the hatred he felt for them, or the guilt he felt for all those deaths he had been ordered to carry out? Was the truth so clearly written across his brow for all to see? He knew he had no choice though, not really; he was responsible for his mother's death and so he owed everything to Augustus. He was reminded daily of the suffering his birth had caused.

'They have taught you to kill, but not to speak it seems?'

Tritan shuffled his tongue at the base of his mouth, wetting the dryness and preparing himself to address Castellar.

'I'm not sure I know what to think,' mumbled Tritan.

'You are already thinking, child, and those thoughts are not yours for the choosing, for they come to you from a deeper place than you can reach. Now, to the task in hand, be merciful and kill me. How you feel when the deed is done, only you will know.'

Tritan didn't have time to consider his decision as moments

later Kal returned with his orders and he bent over to reach the boy's ear in order to conceal his whispers. Seconds later Tritan stepped forwards and plunged the sword into the belly of Castellar; he aimed low so that he could then slip the sword out with ease, as no powerful muscles would clutch the blade. He then followed up by stabbing at the same point, this time in an upward motion so that he would pierce either the lung or heart. Judging by the blood that was instantly spat out of Castellar's mouth, Tritan guessed he'd cut the lung. This time pulling out the blade was a strain, but he managed it and the final blow was a downward plunge through the shoulder at the nape of the neck and through the centre of the chest, avoiding as many bones as possible as the blade cut through flesh and organs. Castellar hit the floor like a stone. The anatomy of a man was no mystery to any member of the 11th Legion. It was one of the first things they were taught; Augustus had made sure of that.

Kal ran his hand across Tritan's head and ruffled his hair as though he were some pet who had performed a long practiced trick with aplomb. Tritan could not tell why this simple gesture disturbed him, for in itself the act was inoffensive, but he resented the sentiment. He had killed a good man and the feeling of disgust he felt for himself was not his choice. He vowed to make some of his own choices from that day forth, even if he were punished for them.

The strength of Castellar's words circled around Tritan's mind. He had been schooled in many things in his life. In a way, Tritan was already a man who carried twice his true years, but no lesson, however hard, had touched so deep inside his soul, where a part of Castellar would live on forever. The thoughts dancing in his mind like a firefly were in sharp contrast to the sight of his victim's limp body being hauled out of the cottage, where the shadowy figure of Augustus looked on, standing silhouetted in the doorway against the smoking village fires.

8

It was said that the 11th Legion could best any army throughout the lands of Harmion. The Cripple Army, as they'd become known, had won perhaps the most crucial battle of the war and Augustus had become the leader of a feared and terrifying group of soldiers. But in a moment of madness, so enraged by the nickname of his 11th Legion, Augustus had ordered that all the maimed soldiers be sent away so that only able-bodied men remained. Having won his battle, the courage of the injured men was rewarded with exile. Augustus grew his 11th Legion again and harshly trained the new recruits so they would live up to the name. But they would never shake off the name of The Cripple Army. The years that were to follow along with Tritan's bloody education found the war drifting into a two-sided conflict. Fought between those who feared Augustus enough to side with him and those who would sooner die than be ruled by this monstrous dictator. The two sides would fight for a further twenty years before an exhausted stalemate grew out of colossal losses on each side.

The population throughout all of Harmion had fallen by more than half. Merely hundreds now inhabited towns where once there had lived thousands. Many of the surviving soldiers had become nomads, wandering in the wilderness.

Tritan rose to fame amongst the 11th Legion and at the age of nineteen he was their fiercest soldier, driving terror into those he fought against and some of those who fought at his side. Those who did not fear him respected him. Any who were ranked higher allowed him some independence but he would never disobey a direct instruction from Augustus. Carrying such guilt for the death of his mother, the teenager dreamed almost nightly about her screams and had visions of a white robe soaked in her red blood. Her hands always stretched out towards him, desperate to clutch him in her arms, the sticky drops of blood for which he was responsible, running through her shaking fingers. He had killed this woman, who was so desperate to love him, or so he believed, for none had ever allowed him to think otherwise. It was a leash around his soul that Augustus held firm, the truth locked tightly in the cage of his mind.

BUZZING flies and mosquitoes filled the afternoon air as they floated about the heads of the sweaty and fatigued workers. They were on a break and the cruel heat ensured that their rest was almost worthless. One of the weaker men wriggled and cursed the burning steal that seared his flesh; the more he struggled the more the chains scalded his skin. Fieldes sat still, and defiantly looked up to the blue skies with not a cloud in sight to shield them. Beside him were two new additions to the chain gang. The woman from the gallows could not rest and was ready to work, embracing this new life. Tritan however struggled to settle, writhing in pain from a deep agony in his gut. His thick leathery skin had tanned in the short time he had been the landowner's captive. Some of the others had severely blemished white patches from the months of peeling and blistering skin.

Wendel strode over to the chain gang and handed them each a sip of water, one by one, from a large canteen. Finally arriving at Tritan, Wendel drank from the canteen and then offered him some. Tritan accepted at first but then spat out the contents on the floor in front of Wendel. The scene caused many of the chain gang to perk up.

'Wine!' Tritan demanded.

Wendel took the man's request as a joke and smirked. '*This is* your wine from now on.'

Wendel offered Tritan a second chance to take some water, but Tritan turned his head away in response. Wendel thought nothing of the slight and made to walk back towards his shelter.

'Back to work, on yer feet now, the lot of you,' he shouted as he left.

The gathered crew grumbled but slowly began to rise, the murderer and Tritan both joined at the end of the line by the long chains that bound them all together. Tritan, however, refused to move and the chain that was linked to the others pulled against him.

Fieldes spoke. 'You must work, farmer, your life is cheap, he will take it if he must.'

Tritan met Fieldes' glare with a hard cold look, the kind that would silence a room of the hardiest warriors, but he made no sound.

'You are a farmer? You look like a farmer...'

Tritan slowly rose, much to the relief of the rest of the gang whose movement he inhibited. He picked up a pitchfork that lay by his feet and dusted it down. Fieldes nodded his approval;

were they finally to witness this creature's obedience? Moments later Tritan tested its weight and balance and then in an instant shattered their hope as he threw the pitchfork as though it were a spear and he was hunting wild boar. It cruised through the air in the direction of Wendel who was now almost out of sight. The pitchfork carried at an impossible rate, especially having been thrown by one so bound in steel. It landed just inches from Wendel's feet and he nearly fell at the shock. He spun around furiously and saw Tritan standing there with his chest puffed out.

'You missed,' mocked the murderer.

'No, lass, I'd say that was a pitch-perfect throw,' jested Fieldes.

Tritan held firm to where he stood as Wendel marched back, releasing a wooden baton from his sleeve. The rest of the slaves staggered backwards onto the floor, denying any sign of complicity in Tritan's defiance. Wendel arrived and stood a foot in front of Tritan, noticing again the obvious strength the man possessed, though Wendel himself was not so small against the hulking soldier.

'I saved your life, lad; the least you can do is get in line. We've a well to dig and I've wasted enough time on you already.'

Tritan smiled at Wendel in a way that would flatter a maiden, though in this context it riled Wendel so that he beat Tritan with the baton, a furious blow to his chest that forced him to take a step backwards. But Tritan held the smile and stepped forwards again.

'It must take a sick man to be able to laugh in the face of death,' accused Wendel.

'*Those you can't control, inflict pain upon them,*' recollected Tritan.

'Is that so?'

Tritan looked around at the men and women beside him, a sorry bunch he thought, but something familiar about their situation amused him. 'I once knew a man who lived by those values.'

'Indeed, and what happened to this man?' Wendel queried.

Tritan shook his head. 'It's too early in the morning for sad stories.'

Wendel had had enough of the arrogant slave before him. Now was not the time to play his game, so he walked to address the others.

'Get to work, every one of you. You want food and drink today? Then you work.'

He hoped it was enough to restore the authority that had never before been questioned. At least not until this enigmatic man, who so intrigued him, had happened upon his land. Tritan had angered him certainly, but had Wendel really expected thanks from such a man? *Only a fool would expect a smooth ride from an unbroken beast.*

Later that afternoon Wendel emerged from his home with Brynhildr and they headed towards the top of the hill to the place where Jason's grave lay. Wendel squinted to accommodate for his blurry vision and saw the workers carrying on about their business. Tritan was sat facing away from the well, but he had at least moved to a position that allowed the others to dig. That, thought Wendel, was a start.

The evening meal was simple as usual, sticks of meat from the livestock that had been slow cooked on a fire and a handful of stodgy rice for each man and woman. Wendel dished out the food to those who were now fastened to large boulders at the edge of the digging site. The steel chains held them all together through strong hooks. Tritan lay uncomfortably at the side; he had no food or water. Wendel made a point of passing him by while he himself took a large satisfying bite of the fatty meat.

It was the chill of night that surprised Tritan the most; the days having been so hot. He presumed the lack of water and food had left his body incapable of keeping warm. The other slaves had been afforded the luxury of blankets to keep the chill at bay and nets to protect them from some of the relentless insects that feasted on them while they slept.

All Tritan could do was shiver, wiping away the flies that sucked at his warm blood and praying for starvation to end this charade. But, as he considered the cruelty of being chained like a dog waiting for its master, Wendel appeared with a flickering lantern in his hand. He held it close to Tritan so he could judge the paleness of his skin and the goosebumps that covered his body. Wendel threw down a blanket over Tritan and turned to walk off into the moonlight. As much as Tritan desired to throw the blanket aside, to refuse the peaceful offering, his will failed him and he wrapped himself up and curled into a foetal position.

That night Tritan slept well and when he woke he had almost forgotten the pangs of hunger and thirst. In fact it was the first morning he had woken in years without the thought of wine and the desire to wet his lips with the cool medicine. The other slaves were already at work; he was now bound by a longer chain he noticed, allowing the other slaves to continue their task.

Tritan tried to hate Wendel, but he knew his reasons for doing so were unjustified, petty and childish. In spite of his captivity and condition he held a bizarre admiration for the man whose crusade was turning a cesspit into an oasis. He reminded him in a way of Castellar, in spite of his more brutal methods.

Wendel slowly approached Tritan. His steps were purposeful

but hesitant. Tritan could sense his trepidation but also felt a lecture was imminent. Tritan wished he could become invisible, or crawl down the darkest hole and be forgotten by the world. Like Castellar, Wendel represented hope in a way he had never known, and it was an uncomfortable, unfamiliar emotion. To cling to hope and fail was to fall into the darkest of places.

Wendel sat himself parallel to Tritan, facing towards the men slaving away at his grand ambition. It was Tritan who spoke first.

'For days on end I've watched this gang, searching for water beneath the dry dirt that fills their lungs daily, yet I have still to see you with a tool in hand alongside them. They say the best masters lead by example.'

Wendel nodded. 'Aye, they do say that. But you flatter me. You must see a younger man than is before you now.'

'Surely it's the mind that defines our age.'

'For me it's the other way around, I've a mind as able and ambitious as any youth. But age has spoiled my body.'

Wendel shuffled stiffly where he sat, as though to demonstrate his point. Tritan watched him until he found his spot. Silence fell upon them for a short time, but the discomfort of each other's company had abated. Tritan only spoke again on account of the curiosity he had kept hidden all this time.

'They all respect you; I sense they fear you too but only a smidgeon. Has no man tried to escape this place?'

'Only once, one man tried; it was long enough ago that most have forgotten it. It wasn't easy having to cut him down as he ran. All these men and women are here because I want them to be. I try to appear strong and ruthless, the guards in the town would never follow a weaker man, but they obey me and so the rest follow.'

Tritan felt he was being gifted with something that the other men were not privy to, and wasn't sure he liked it. Wendel carried on his reasoning.

'I'm not sure I could claim that any of them share my vision, but enough that I can slowly fashion this place into something worthwhile. I don't want to see four seasons wash us from existence. What has no past, just may have a future.'

Tritan doubted the chances of his intentions. 'Is that why you must find water? Before this flash in a pan is forgotten?'

'It may not look like much. A man's life starts as a blank page. What is written on it determines his future. What I write here can improve their lives. What is written on your page, Tritan? Will you etch a future for yourself or will you continue to live as though a base animal? These people crawl in the gutters, piss into the winds and sleep under the stars in their filth. It may be that what I do here can change that bit by bit. I have to believe it. They have never known better and would not change of their own accord. In the evenings when they all come together to sing, it is as strong a community as I have seen, but the season for rain is months away and our reserves of water are almost gone. And when the rain comes, it comes with fury. Each man, woman and child here will work together to protect what little they have. But unlike animals, people can be taught more than just tricks, they can be changed. This revolution cannot happen overnight; it must be introduced slowly. So to simply provide water, for now, is enough.'

The cranking sound of a sharp tool, digging at the foot of the well, screeched and grated. Wendel was concerned for a moment, allowing himself a brief hope that there could have been some progress but found that he was more occupied with Tritan and their rare discussion.

'You assume they yearn for more; maybe they are content with their lot; have you not seen the troubles of those living as though their life has more meaning than those who serve them?' asked Tritan.

Wendel, who had been keeping a keen eye on the slaves, snapped away from the troubles of the workers and decided he should steer away from their current conversation. 'What was it that brought you to this place? I don't fancy it was your calling.'

'My calling was to take life, before I even knew what that meant. I was never old enough to make the choice, my page was written for me. Tritan shuffled and looked long and hard at Wendel. 'You remind me of a man I once knew. I considered him my greatest teacher for a long time. Though my time with him was fleeting, he helped me to think for myself. Before that I followed orders blindly.'

'What was his name?' enquired Wendel.

'Castellar Dell'Anima.'

'Ah, yes. The greatest teacher of peace this world ever knew. What became of your time together?'

'I slaughtered his entire family before him and then I killed him.'

Tritan spoke the words clear as day but his shame was more apparent than he probably intended. Wendel was shocked, though he knew better than to show it. He held both pity and disdain for Tritan. His lips trembled as he tried to produce a response but no sound came. Wendel decided to pursue his previous line of questioning.

'What has brought you here, Tritan? I understand every one of the men and women here, each cut from the same cloth. But you I cannot figure out.'

At that moment they heard the loud stomping of hooves. Both men turned to see a boy running up the fields towards them from the town below. He was possibly as old as thirteen, quick and skinny, but his speed was no match for the three horse-backed raiders that chased him.

Wendel stood instantly and positioned himself in front of the well and the chain gang as the boy ran behind the wall and ducked down as the riders approached. The leader, who was the youngest of the group, stopped to address Wendel.

'I've no quarrel with you, Landowner, it's the kid I want.'

Wendel looked over his left shoulder, careful never to lose sight of the three men. He saw the boy cowering behind the well.

'He's just a lad, can't imagine he's done much to upset the likes of you three.'

'That's none of your business. Just move out of our way,' snarled the bandit leader.

'Tell me his crimes and I'll see to a suitable punishment. You have my word.'

'You can write your promises on the winter winds for all the good they'll do me. The boy is a thief; his head will be on a pike by nightfall. You want yours beside it?'

Tritan sat silently throughout the entire disagreement, slowly nudging a hoe lying on the ground closer to him. He was careful not to let any of the bandits see his movement. He casually leant forward and felt the chain that bound him to the other slaves tightening. It was not the best conditions for a fight. The young bandit leader dismounted his horse and pulled out his sword, which glimmered in the sunlight and he reflected the light into Wendel's eyes to taunt him. In a mere instant, Tritan launched the hoe into the air and stretching out as far as he was able, swung it in a long arc catching the young bandit leader on the side of his face, splitting open his cheek from jaw to eye. The bandit reeled in pain as his skin flapped uselessly in the air, spitting blood onto the desert soil. The next two bandits approached and readied themselves for the fight but the more eager of the two, failing to anticipate the speed with which Wendel could move, was immediately disarmed by his power and speed. Before he knew where he stood, the landowner had driven his sword through the bandit's shoulder. Tritan took this opportunity to rush the final bandit before he overwhelmed Wendel, but the chain around Tritan's neck pulled taught as he ran and the combined weight of the slave gang, who remained unmoving, was too much for Tritan to overcome. He was snapped back, strangled by the chain, and slammed into the floor, the impact winding him. The final bandit had now managed to grab Wendel in a body lock and the two men grappled with each other like wild animals. The loose clothing they wore made it hard for either man to get a good hold on the other but the bandit managed to work the tip of his sword onto Wendel's chest. The pressure of their wrestling caused the blade to break his skin and he cried out from the pain it caused him.

'Move you fools,' cried Fieldes as he tugged forward the entire gang with his colossal weight alone. The chain dragged along the dust and the gang scrabbled forward as Tritan staggered to his feet, now freed from the burden of the chain that had held him back. He grabbed a rock from the ground and pummelled it into the face of the bandit, smashing time and time again until the skull was a bloody pulp. The bandit slumped downwards, the sword against Wendel's chest scraped and persisted to cut into his flesh and then released as the dead man fell. It was only a surface wound. Tritan helped Wendel to his feet and the two men locked eyes in a moment of tension. Pulses were amplified and the taste for killing coursed through their veins. Suddenly they were distracted by the bandit leader, screaming as he scrambled away with the three horses, holding his hand to his slashed face as the tearing winds of his escape ripped against him. Riding one handed, the bandit leader left behind his slain companions and their killers. All that was left for Tritan and Wendel to do was to turn their minds to the kid; surrounded now, he had nowhere to hide and nowhere to run.

He sensed the judgment that was due him. Excuses flowed thick and fast through his mind; he was well practiced at deception. Caught between a swift handed old man and the angry slave who had slaughtered the bandit as though he were pulping fruit to quench his thirst, it was the slave the boy feared most.

9

'Bastard! Fool! You would have us all slaughtered for your prize.'

Tritan raged at the boy, his sticky palms stretched out, searching to appease their ferocious lust. Wendel wrapped his arms around Tritan's puffed out chest, holding him back as best as he could whilst the boy darted and sprang around the well like a cornered hare.

'Hold back, man. Hold back,' bellowed Wendel as he spun Tritan about to redirect his fury onto himself, 'Let me deal with the kid, walk it off.'

Tritan paced back and forth, seething. The chain occasionally tugging against his throat as the slave gang all stood stunned and bewildered by what they had witnessed. Wendel approached the lad calmly, stretching out his hand, his expression that of a cautious friend.

'It's true that you stole?' he said. 'Show me the spoils.'

The kid looked about him, unable to tell if this was some sort of trick. He eyed up the gang in chains and glanced at Tritan who still paced about, oblivious to the rest of them.

Slowly he took a pouch out of his pocket and handed it to Wendel. Wendel slowly looked through its contents, mostly there was nothing special, just a few silver coins and some rolling herbs for smoking. But at the bottom of the pouch was the heaviest item, a golden crest that bore the mark of the 11th Legion. Wendel nearly dropped it from shock and glanced over at the two dead men lying face down on his land. He approached them in haste, checking their vitals as if they might suddenly spring back to life; though the fact they would not was what troubled him most.

'Boy, do you realise what you've done? Do you know who they were?'

The kid shook his head. 'I only wanted enough to survive,' he pleaded, 'and they'd barely notice it was missing.'

'So how did they catch you? You can't even lift a small purse, is that what you're saying?'

At this the kid perked up, angry now, for he had been accused of theft more times than he could count and rightly so, but to be accused of being a bad thief? That was a fresh insult.

'There's nothing wrong with how I went about taking it, only that the fatter one there woke the next day and noticed it had gone. I thought they were just messing around, as though it was some sort of game, but they tracked me south for three days. They wouldn't give up.'

Wendel hung his head. 'They were men of the 11th Legion lad, The Cripple Army.'

The kid stood still; he'd heard the name before. But it was Tritan who suddenly paid an interest in the dead bodies.

'Landowner,' he said. 'How can you be sure who they were?'

Wendel held out the crest and Tritan took one glance at it before walking towards the closest corpse. He couldn't quite reach it so he shot a look back to the other slaves to slacken the chains by stepping in his direction. Tritan knelt down and rolled over the head of the older of the two bodies. He recognised him that instant. He was one of the three who'd stood watch over him the day that he had killed Castellar in the smugglers' town as a teenager. The man was perhaps fifteen years his senior, it had been ten years since he had last seen him, the day he was left to die in the mud by his father and The Cripple Army.

'More will come, I don't know what they'll do,' Tritan lied.

'I do,' replied Wendel.

Later that afternoon, Wendel fed and watered the boy as the slaves lay resting in the sun. They spoke for a while about the kid's journey to this place and he told them of the dire need of his family and village for food and coin. He belonged to the smallest settlement in Harmion, a humble place called Krali that had relied heavily upon the larger surrounding towns for its livelihood. Krali was made up of about a half dozen homes and many of the men and women from the village would travel at the break of day to the nearby fort similarly named, Krali Fort, serving the aristocracy and armies that had once lived there. After the army had left and the fort became a ruin, the boy's father, who had worked as a stable master, found himself without a livelihood and spent his days wallowing in self-pity. In desperation the lad had taken it upon himself to learn how to hunt the nearby forests that surrounded them. But the harsh weather had driven much of the wildlife away from their lands and so he travelled south, away from the icy fields that bore no fruit or grain, in search of richer soil.

Tritan noted the closeness of the conversation between the kid and Wendel. Even as Brynhildr wandered around the hill, spouting senseless words, Wendel remained transfixed by the lad's story. Tritan was again chained up alone. But the chains around his neck were gone and replaced by a bandage where the steel had chafed him and left a nasty sore. Fieldes was sat closest to him, drinking water from a tiny flagon. He offered it out to Tritan who gratefully accepted.

'We've not been afforded this much rest in all the years I've worked this land,' said Fieldes.

'That's because he knows what is to come,' Tritan whispered under his breath.

'Say again, farmer?'

'Nothing.' Tritan hadn't intended to be heard at all.

The strong man felt slightly offended that Tritan was not joining in this conversation. He tried again to engage the man who he had earlier watched split the skull of a legionnaire.

'You have a family, farmer?' Fieldes asked, but no reply came so he continued. 'I have a son. I do not know if he is alive or dead. This haunts me every day.'

Tritan took a deep breath, but no words formed, instead he rubbed his sore hands in the soil to take his mind off the pain they caused him.

Fieldes spoke again. 'You know why he saved that boy?'

Tritan nodded, he knew all too well. A look of remorse came over his face and Fieldes wondered what thoughts passed through his mind. For once Tritan would not keep his mind a mystery.

'I used to watch my wife, Marilia, from a distance; I wouldn't let her know I was there. I'd think to myself how lucky my son is, to have such a woman for a mother. But then by the riverside, I'd crouch down to touch the water and I'd see my own reflection, distorted by the ripples as it flowed, and I'd realise he's not lucky at all.'

'You have wronged them?'

'Yes.'

'So you must find them, and make it up to them.'

'There is no forgiveness for what I have done.'

A butterfly fluttered above them, an anomaly in the

bloodied and desolate desert landscape. It landed on Tritan's hand. He could not help but smile at its beauty; he had almost forgotten what magnificent colours nature held in her palette. Fieldes also admired the painted beauty of the fluttering being that had once been trapped in a cocoon. Now it floated free and almost solely justified all living things. It was a joyful moment.

'Every free creature only knows it is free, if before it knew a cage,' he said, holding up his chains to Tritan and smiling.

Tritan smiled back before responding. 'Not all cages are forged by steel.'

Wendel paced over towards the two men. He patted Fieldes on the shoulder. A slight gesture of his thanks, but it was Tritan he had come to see.

'So, just a farmer after all, I've never seen a farmer who bested two men of the Eleventh.'

Tritan nodded a silent reply.

'Either way, I owe you my thanks. I know that much,' said Wendel.

'Why stand up for the kid? You owe him nothing,' questioned Tritan.

'I seem to remember you striking the first blow.'

'Call it self-defence.'

Wendel chuckled. 'An amusing prospect for someone who seems not to value life.'

'Not my own perhaps.'

Whether Tritan had meant it sincerely or as a sarcastic rebuke he could not tell, but moments after he said it he recognised the look Wendel gave him. Marilia had often looked at him this way during his drunken rants and it made him feel like a child. After a time they forgot the course of the conversation and both Tritan and Wendel returned to fearing the consequences of what had passed this day.

Wendel bent down to unhook Tritan's chain from the rock. 'I've something to show you.'

The view was something he had not considered since arriving at the town. Tritan had thought only of the fact it was a hovel, filled with filth and scum. Now he saw the rolling hills and the drifting mist of the clouds that tickled the tops of the rocky peaks. The two men walked for a while as equals, admiring and appreciating the land. This gift had never been offered to any of the other slaves.

Tritan looked over the hilltop and saw a river, which split into three. He knew immediately where he was. It was unmistakable and he understood now why Wendel had chosen this place to start anew. For a moment Tritan was stunned, he'd visited this place in a previous life. Before him, over in the distance stood a single home, the only one standing in all the land that sprawled out beneath them. It hadn't changed much in all these years but brushwood had smothered the rest of the old port town.

'Port Melees.' Tritan wondered; he was further from home than he had realised. 'I see now it was no accident you chose this place. But why build on the other side of the valley, away from the river?' Tritan questioned.

'A wasteland, once run by smugglers, then destroyed in the war. Who would want to claim such a place? I do not consider myself a superstitious man but the history of Port Melees is too shrouded in darkness. But I don't need to tell you that, do I?'

Tritan realised then that Wendel probably did not know half of the truth about the land he had settled upon. He came close to explaining all that he knew, but his earlier admission was enough.

The men settled upon an overturned tree amidst a tussock, with the two towns visible on either side of their hilltop position. They turned to face Wendel's town with their backs to Port Melees.

'It's not much but it is all I have to give,' said Wendel. 'You see now why I know we will hit water once we dig deep enough. Having the well above the town will allow us to create an artificial waterway down to the main square.' He knew his methods were obscure but to him it made sense. He paused to take a breath and Tritan filled the silence.

'From what affliction is it your wife suffers? She seems so lost from the world around her.'

Wendel had wondered if anyone would ask him about Brynhildr; he figured Tritan had earned the right to do so now.

'I, like you, have seen many deaths in my years, but none has affected us a fraction of that of the death of our son. It is grief that took her senses.'

Wendel stood to walk forward and pointed into the distance. 'That is where Jason fell, to the north beyond those mountains where the earth turns from brown to white as the bitter cold frost captures it. He was just seventeen, too young to be a soldier. After he fell his wounds began to fester and the fever set in. The physician could do nothing for him so I abandoned my post in search of one who could. I travelled north and in time came to a place where there were rumours of a healer who had saved many a soldier. One hopeless case in particular interested me for it was said he was beyond life. By the time I arrived the healer had left and taken his patient south. It was here, at the edge of the mist, that I first encountered Augustus Léon. I was captured under suspicion of spying on him and his Cripple Army. In his prison, I learnt that the ageing tyrant had travelled this far north in search of immortality, said to be the prize for any man who could make it through the hundreds of miles of mist-covered labyrinth that lay ahead of their camp.'

Tritan had heard the stories of the land beyond Harmion.

The old world beyond the mist where the language was unknown and the people lived as close to nature as the wild animals. But in truth he expected there was nothing but miles of impassable terrain, shrouded in a freezing cold cloak of fog that never lifted. In his lifetime only a dozen men had braved the journey, none had returned.

'I gave everything to hope so that I could find a way to bring back my boy from his condition and I told my captives as much. But time pressed on and I knew he could not have survived. I was not executed, as I would have expected. Instead my punishment was to spend six months in a dungeon, with the knowledge I had failed my boy.'

Tritan felt for Wendel, but was intrigued by the story of his encounter with his father.

'You knew Augustus, and today you still draw breath; that in itself is a miracle. The man does not make a habit of leaving prisoners alive.'

'I did not say I knew him, only that our paths had crossed once. Life for a father who has failed his son as I have is a half-life at best. If you had children of your own you'd understand that, as he did. Sometimes the appearance of mercy is actually the cruellest action. But you speak as if you knew him... How did you survive your meeting?'

'I wish I could offer you something for that question, but there's nothing really to be said.' Tritan was keen to keep his secrets his own. 'Only know that I am beginning to understand you. If you'll permit me to say so.'

Tritan didn't know why he had said this to Wendel. Maybe he felt it was a sort of final confession. He wondered if Augustus would be among the returning 11th. He thought of all those years of separation and wondered if he would kneel down to the man once more, maybe it was here in this forgotten place that his journey would finally end. He knew weak men were a curse to Augustus, and a weak son was worst of all.

Tritan ended the discussion there and then before heading off down the hill towards the well digging site. Wendel lingered a while longer, all the energy and drive he had mustered these past months flattened by the mysteries that were unfolding all around him.

TRITAN GRABBED a sharp pickaxe and descended the well. Curious eyes were upon him as he began to swing the axe into the ground, breaking the soil and loading the bucket with the debris he created. For hours he worked alone, tirelessly. Foot after foot he dug deeper into the ground. Sweat was pouring from his entire body. The slaves could not understand why he'd chosen now to begin to work. Wendel returned finally to discover the scene; amidst all else that was happening, he felt he now understood something more about Tritan too.

The day grew long, time dragging so slowly for the rest of the chain gang they believed it was running backwards. Tritan continued his digging through the fading light of the setting sun, demanding a lantern at night, as he would not sleep until at last, he finally broke deep into the well and water spurted out and flooded his feet. Wendel awoke and ran to the well and leant over the wall, watching as Tritan hauled the bucket filled with water to the surface before climbing his way out. They looked at each other and no words were spoken; the look on Tritan's face showed he knew it was only coincidence, the men had been digging for weeks now. Wendel knew this too but, sensing the satisfaction he must have felt, he decided to share in his moment.

'I was right after all; a good strong worker is what you are. It is a shame it will all be for nothing.'

Tritan laughed; he knew it too but the truth could not steal his pride just yet.

'Sometimes we just have to act without thinking, thinking has caused me more pain than any blade ever did.'

Wendel nodded in agreement. Not a single scar on his body had hurt like the scars his heart carried. The two men were then as equals, basking in the success of a plan fulfilled. Thinking of their private suffering. They drew out the moment for as long as it could stretch. The freshly found water was shared amongst all the slaves. Their purpose satisfied. Nothing could harm them as they shared the spoils of their efforts. *A parched mouth enjoys water more than he who has it in surplus*, Tritan thought.

'Listen to me now, lad.' The words shattered the glass of their shared dreams. Tritan expected the storm to follow. 'I must beg your obedience in something, it's crucial you do not object. There is no knowing when, but soon, there'll be nothing left for us here. You must go now, and take the kid far from this place. If there is to be only one order of mine you obey, let it be this.'

'Why is it so important to you? How much can this boy mean to you?' Tritan asked as if Wendel needed to reply; but they both knew he didn't and as they stood in silence the colour of the sky changed from the dark blue of night to a fiery red. The word that was playing on both their minds was then spoken to confirm the allegiance of their minds.

'Everything,' said Wendel.

'Why?'

Silence.

'A son must survive his father.'

The words struck Tritan like a slap from a dazed dream and he aligned himself completely with Wendel's intended retribution. He thought of his home and family, the kid and those he had been stealing to provide for, he thought of Wendel and this land that he had worked so hard for that was now certain to fall. He thought about it all and at once and before he knew it the sound of hooves was building in the distance; the waiting for this moment had been shorter than expected. This time there were at least a dozen horseback riders, men of the 11th Legion, armed to the hilt and thirsty for blood. Tritan had no time to think, no time to argue. He readied his horse and Wendel aided him with supplies and the kid mounted its back behind Tritan. The sound of galloping hooves grew ever nearer.

'What about you, Landowner? What about these men and women?' said Tritan. It was hardly a moving farewell but they were the only words that came to mind.

'We are all free now.'

Wendel watched as Tritan and the boy rode off towards the distant forest. After they had disappeared into the woodland he ran towards the slave gang and broke their chains. For so long he had wanted this moment to come though he'd never thought it would be under these circumstances. He spoke the words he had dreamed of saying for so long.

'You're all free, there's nothing here for you now,' he bellowed.

But to contradict Wendel's moment of resolution, they simply slipped out of their chains and grabbed their tools as the twelve riders appeared at the bottom of the hill, their swords raised high above their heads. Fieldes spoke.

'We'll not flee and leave you all the glory, Landowner.'

Any who had felt the urge to run now stood firm with the others. Their first decision as free men and women would be to fight for the land they had slaved over. It would be a worthy death.

10

T he overgrown pathway spiralled through the forest like a gothic stairwell and contorted roots jutted out of the earth making the riding hard. The effort was doubled with the lad at his back. Tritan figured the boy weighed no more than a sack of rice, but his horse was old and blind and this addition was a noticeable burden. In spite of the horse's strength the sharp twists and turns slowed them far more than Tritan could stomach but they pressed on.

Tritan's arms and back ached fiercely. He had worked himself to within an inch of his ability and for what? A moment of splendour? It had seemed so important then but he cursed his actions for now he may have to fight for not just his own life but for the kid's as well, and against the very men who had trained him. No. Raised him.

His senses intensified as the forest echoed the sound of four horses behind them. As the noise of hooves grew louder and stronger he knew that these men were on fresh steeds, likely stolen from some poor villagers who had bred and nurtured them. Tritan had thought they'd made a clean escape but these four must have diverted from the core crew to search the forest and had managed to pick up their trail. Tritan was carrying an extra load and was out of shape. So was his horse. He considered for a moment dropping the boy from the saddle and riding away hard and fast. But he heard Wendel's words ricochet inside his skull. Maybe the kid had hoped for a brute to hide behind, to protect him. The boy had come across them at the shack of a town and chosen Wendel as his champion. But Tritan was all he had now. His former allegiance with the 11th might be the only thing that stood between the fleeing pair and the end of a sword. But it had been many long years since those same companions had decided that he was better off left for the crows.

He heard the name resounding in his mind, drowning out the echo of the approaching riders. The name was Augustus. Augustus… Father. Tritan realised he had closed his eyes but could do nothing to open them as he drifted into a conscious dream. He was lying in a patch of soil holding his midriff; blood was spread across the dirt, painting the dry fallen leaves with lustre. The sound of riders drifted away until calmness surrounded him. He listened to the singing birds, which at first was a comfort, but the sound morphed and thickened into the sinister cry of crows, circling above their pending feast. He saw above him an injured tree that held a wound not unlike his own, cut deep by a sharpened axe. The shape of a man towered above him and an instinctive reflex caused Tritan to lash out with a pocket knife before the shadowy figure tumbled down upon him.

Tritan came to his senses with a start and opened his eyes. He sat astride his horse in a clearing, the kid tugging at the back of his shirt. Four long swords pointed towards him, held by men of the 11th as they sat atop their stallions.

'Thieves and fucking ghosts today, boys,' cried out the

leader. It was Kal. 'My age must have made me blind or at least I have become demented.'

Tritan felt the recognition boring through him. Aside from Kal he noticed Jaz, a beefy man and the jolliest of The Cripple Army he had known. The other two he had never come across in the years he rode with them. But he had known the youngest of them recently, the gash across his face, now held together with crude stitches and the hatred emanating from his sharp gaze revealed him as the front-runner of the previous morning's raiders. This was Sy, the newest recruit of the 11th, which also made him the most arrogant.

Tritan wondered why the four men had not cut him down already. Hesitation was not a trait of his old companions. He suspected Kal needed to give the order first.

'So much has become clear to me now,' Kal chuckled. 'You sent this one back to me with his face half opened.' He gestured to Sy to clarify the point. 'I couldn't believe it when he told me a slave shrouded in chains with naught but a garden tool as a weapon had caused so much fuss. But there you sit. You either truly are the toughest bastard I ever knew, or a witch has been at you. Well, never mind that now. Hand the boy over.'

But Tritan had nothing left to lose.

'Either we both walk away or the forest will claim six lives. I'll start by finishing off this one.' Tritan pointed directly at Sy and he could see the hatred rising, overflowing the capacity of even his dark soul.

Sy spoke through what must have been agony as his jaw pulled at the freshly bound skin. He used only necessary words.

'Let me end 'em both, be done with this foolish play.'

'Tell me, Sy, how do you kill a man who's already dead?' It was Jaz that spoke now. His grin was of some comfort. Tritan almost felt that Jaz was happy to see him alive. The two who knew Tritan laughed. The others remained silent.

'The punishment for deserting the 11th is death,' Kal offered.

'I ought to slit all your fucking throats for your part in my *desertion*.' Tritan rebuked in a sudden eruption of rage that he knew he had long buried deep but he followed it with action and made the sight of his short blade, hidden beneath his jerkin, clear for all to see.

Jaz lowered his sword and signalled to the silent legionnaire to his right to do the same. Kal and Sy kept their guard up. Jaz rode forward without threat to study the son of Augustus.

'There's no coming back from the state you were in. No man can survive such a thing.' Jaz slowly lifted his sword and used the sharp edge to raise the material covering Tritan's scar.

'Like what you see? I can give you one of your own if you like.'

All of them bellowed with laughter this time. Tritan joined them. Only the kid remained quiet.

'Give it up, man, the lad is already dead. Why stand in our way for a thief?'

'Kal, you forget, I too am already dead.' Tritan didn't look at Kal as he spoke. His concern was with Sy, in a moment of mad haste this situation could turn into a bloodbath.

'Very well, I have a better idea.'

Kal rode behind Tritan's horse and winked at the kid.

'Reed,' he shouted at the silent legionnaire, 'fall in behind me, we're off to pay our respects to the landowner.'

They rode a slow pace back through the forest. Tritan and the boy were surrounded by the four riders who were guarding them. Not a word was spoken between them. The boy was clearly fearful and also confused at the familiarity between Tritan and these men. How could he have known them? He himself had spent limited time travelling around Harmion but he knew enough to know the odds of this coincidence were slim at best. Tritan struggled to guess at what Kal was thinking; why lead them all back to the landowner? Surely he should either kill them both in the woods or let them go? The latter was an unlikely outcome. He could only imagine that they would be handed over to Augustus to do with as he wished. Tritan wondered then at the absence of his father. Kal had always ridden side by side with Augustus. Why now did he not? In his prime Tritan had been a better fighter than all of them, save for Augustus. Augustus's brutality had never been equalled; his simple talent for taking life almost made it a marvel, not a travesty. But ten years had gone by, and Augustus had been approaching old age even then.

As they broke through the forest boundary the blinding light of the sun reminded Tritan of where he had been these past weeks. Even an hour riding in the woods had adjusted his vision. The coolness of the shade had made him more aware of the tingling of his reddened skin. They approached the well digging site and as his sight returned to normal all that Tritan could see was red.

Bodies were strewn about the place like a carnival show. But this was no performance, every one of the chain gang who had been in chains that very afternoon had been butchered. Kal led them through the wake of death and studied the bodies. Only one man was still alive, knelt down and surrounded by the six riders who had made easy work of the slaves. Wendel's hands were caked in blood but it was not his own. He dropped his head low as he saw Tritan and the kid approaching with the other men of the 11th.

Sy noticed there were two of their own men dead. They had clearly been killed at the hands of the landowner and Tritan suspected Fieldes had played his part before he fell. But there was still one of the 11th missing. Then came the screams, the familiar screams that cut a hole in Wendel's heart. He did not need to turn to look as the man pulled his wife from their home. Her screaming was incessant and the legionnaire elbowed her, breaking her nose to silence her.

The boy noticed the attention was on Wendel. He and Tritan were now a sideshow. He whispered to the man whom he clutched tightly and with fear.

'You must do something. You have to do something. Please!'

'Quiet, boy. Or we will all be killed for your foolishness,' Tritan rebuked.

'You can't just sit here and watch this happen!'

Tritan didn't reply this time. He surveyed the scene and took note of the dead. Wendel knelt before Kal, his wife, her nose pouring with blood, was being held by one of the remaining ten men of the 11th. But where was Augustus? It was out of character but he must have sent his minions to do his bidding for him. Tritan dismounted and approached Kal slowly. Outnumbered, he knew he must outwit the man, he could not kill them all. Tritan used a softness in his voice to which he was unaccustomed.

'This doesn't need to happen, Kal.'

'That's where you are wrong lad. Two birds with one stone.'

Sy eagerly approached the two men, listening into the conversation.

Kal continued. 'Reallocation of land—'

Sy broke in. 'And a dash of revenge.'

Tritan was at a loss. He thought hard about his next move. But he was out of options. He noticed the ring on Wendel's hand and was met by an incriminating stare from the landowner.

'One simple thing. I asked you to do one simple thing.' Wendel shook his head, forgetting all else around him for a moment except Tritan. Tritan looked away, shamefully.

'Good afternoon, Landowner,' said Kal.

'I'll give you ten seconds to crawl back down that cesspit hole you came out of, or let's finish it now,' Wendel replied.

More screams from Brynhildr came next, a sickening sound, prompting the man holding her to strike her hard. Wendel tried to stand to rush him but was instantly blocked and held down by two of the 11th. Wendel bit and wriggled, throwing his head wildly at the men but they were too strong and Wendel was too tired from fighting.

'Bastards! Let her go, she's got nothing to do with any of this mess. You fucking cowards!'

Kal struck Wendel, drawing blood from his mouth and causing him to choke. This silenced him but Kal was not satisfied. He kicked Wendel between the legs sending him back to his knees and gasping for air. Tritan could do nothing but stand and watch helplessly. He had never felt so useless as he did now; he had rarely been just a bystander. But from this new perspective he saw the violence for the brutal cruelty that it was. To cause another man pain seemed less natural when it did not come from his own hand. Wendel spoke again through bloodied teeth, his resolve turning to desperation.

'Please, please, what do you want?'

'Landowner, what's yours is mine. That much should be clear to you by now. Which means I have no further use for you.'

This was it, Tritan could tell. The play had reached its final act and he was nothing more than an onlooker, making up the numbers on the stage. He found his mouth opening, his voice croaked.

'You can use him; why not make him an asset? Your numbers are fewer than when my father culled the injured soldiers all those years ago.'

It was Sy who responded. 'Bastard thinks he can give us orders!'

'Nine years dead and you presume to influence our course?' Kal questioned.

'I owe this man nothing, I was a captive here remember, bound in chains when I gave your prince his smile.' Tritan threw his look to Sy who stormed forward to retaliate with force. Kal held out his sword to block Sy's path. He shook his head slowly.

'Tritan, you were fleeing, unbound, when we found you. Prove this man is not your ally.'

Tritan froze. He could sense the old feeling of judgement from Kal. The same he had experienced in years past when he had stood before Augustus.

'I expect you're right, however,' Kal continued, 'he must be a good fighter to have sent any of our men to the grave.' Kal approached Wendel who was still cowering, fearful for his poor Brynhildr.

Wendel held up his hand to shield his face from the sun that beat down upon him so he could see Kal eye to eye. But in a swift flowing movement Kal swung his sword and cut off the hand that had sheltered him. The move was sudden and it was a moment before Wendel realised that his hand lay in the sand beneath him. Blood spurted from the remaining stump, covering his eyes and blinding him. Tritan's head dropped in defeat. Kal turned to walk back, smugly beaming at Tritan.

'I'd say he's more or less useless now.'

The 11th roared with laughter. They'd not had this much fun in months. Tritan could not look away from the dirt and saw only the pattering of feet as the kid ran to Wendel in a senseless move to protect him.

'Stop! You can't do this,' he said.

'Don't be stupid, kid. Move away from there or you'll get a knife in your belly.' Jaz spoke as if he was actually concerned for the lad. The same boy they had ridden all this way to kill. But the tables had turned. None of them had expected to find Augustus's son still alive. Tritan admired the boy in that instant. How was it that this boy was braver than he, to argue for a stranger at his own increasing peril? Tritan composed himself and went to grab his sword but Wendel, ignoring for a moment his extreme pain, shot a glance at him, shaking his head. Kal moved towards the kid slowly, pulling out a knife and handing it to him. He nodded to Wendel and all knew what was being asked of the boy.

'Gut him like a fish.'

The laughter that had died down from the men of the 11th rose again. This they could not wait to see. The lad panicked, he had not expected this. It was the worst outcome he could have imagined, though he would never have conceived it. The kid turned to Tritan, desperately searching for some mercy. Kal offered his thoughts to the pleading eyes that glanced past him.

'Why look at him, boy? He can't help you. Gut the landowner, or I'll take your manhood.'

Kal raised his sword between the kid's legs. The boy began to shake, tears streaming down his cheeks so Kal pressed harder as though he had to prove he held no sympathy for the boy's predicament. The 11th waited in anticipation. The finale was due. Brynhildr was quiet now, ignoring the blood dripping from her nose and staring into the distance. The solitude of her own world that no one else, not even Wendel, could enter, was now her greatest gift.

The kid helplessly walked towards Wendel, who looked at him as if to say, *It's okay.* The knife plunged forwards with such weakness that it barely broke through Wendel's skin. The boy pressed harder and the blade dug into Wendel's chest just half an inch. Sy found the pathetic effort hysterical and moved in to finish off the charade. But Kal held him back.

'Give the boy another chance.'

Wendel winced as the blade came out and he gave the kid a firm look, seeing the distress in his eyes. This was a good boy he thought. Not a killer.

Kal screamed impatiently. 'Again, harder... harder!'

The kid took a step backwards. He needed momentum. He did not know how to take a life. He wanted only for Wendel not to suffer. It would be death by a thousand cuts if he could not muster enough strength. The boy hated his weakness. He began to scream, gripping the blade tight. Wendel turned his head to Tritan as subtly as he could. They gazed into each other's minds where their thoughts ran parallel and an unspoken pact was made. Tritan knew what had been asked of him and he stormed forward, his sword drawn, and before any could contemplate what was happening, he brought the sword down in a clean and just strike, decapitating Wendel instantly.

The kid staggered backwards and the 11th were now silent, disappointed and confused. All except Kal, who smiled. This was exactly what he'd wanted. Tritan stared at the mess he had created as Kal strode over and looked right through his soul.

'There he is, boys,' he paused. 'There he is.'

11

The feeling was of weightlessness, but not like the dreams of flying he'd had before. It was more a gentle tugging of the mind and no wind drifted over him despite the ground beneath floating past. It occurred to Pietrich that he could sense the earth shifting. Whispering sounds from every direction flooded his thoughts and as hard as he tried to close off his ears they would not obey his timid demands. Were these sounds real or had his mind simply lost its focus he wondered. Lately his sight was almost completely gone and he felt only the sense of a soft warm light around him, a candle his mother had lit he presumed. Each day had felt like an age these past weeks, confined to a palliasse with unseen voices dictating that he should *eat this* and *drink that*. Disgusting herbal concoctions that Thomas would bring him thrice daily that made him want to vomit. Only once had Marilia attempted to take him outside to enjoy the fresh air, but he had stumbled and fallen, for the light of the sun was too great for him to bear. It had been his tenth birthday, but there was little to celebrate. The only comfort was the sound of Eira's voice, which he now seldom heard due to the limitations imposed on her visits to his bedside. Each morning his throat was coarse and dry and he wiped fresh, crusted blood from his lips that had formed whilst he slept.

Trying to escape the day that drifted closer to him as the white light grew stronger, Pietrich forced his thoughts to the stranger that had visited him nightly in a waking dream. The visitations had occurred several times now and although Pietrich could not understand their purpose, each felt increasingly real. He had heard that in losing one sense often another was enhanced and as his sight deteriorated, he believed his hearing was keener than it had ever been. He focused his thoughts and pictured the stranger; an old man who bore withered grey hair and loose leathery clothing that hung from his wiry body. Pietrich had tried to speak with him but no sounds passed between them. Instead they sat together in a wilderness staring at the scorched lands of an unknown vista, a world, perhaps, not belonging to this one. Black charcoal ash covered everything in sight and the stranger used bizarre gestures to communicate with Pietrich. His arms flapped and twisted and he drew in the ground beneath, scratching a shape that was indiscernible. There was frustration between the two who were alone in this internal prison. Pietrich felt his lips parting as his words dwindled between them. The man was drifting more and more into the distance. The reply was just as silent and the stranger's mouth opened, a gaping black hole staring back at Pietrich.

Pietrich was woken suddenly with the feeling of a cool damp cloth on his brow. Or rather not woken but his mind brought back to his body and he was once again no longer able to see and could barely move. He recognised his mother through the touch of her soft fingers as they offered him comfort, stroking his sweaty hair back away from his brow. He was upset by the banging sounds outside that were pounding in his skull.

'Mother, please, tell them to stop. Must they work so close to the cottage walls?'

Marilia was confused and shook her head though Pietrich would not have known it, save for the change in the flow of air around them. 'There is no work, sweetheart, the day is young.'

'But I can hear them, breaking rocks and laying them out. They're so close,' Pietrich pleaded, desperate for some reassurance that Marilia could not offer.

'I fear it is your dreams speaking to you still. Don't worry, Thomas will be here soon and his tonic will settle you into the day.'

Pietrich feared each visit from the healer; the intended tonic would settle him indeed. He would be sedated for the rest of the morning, incoherent in speech and for certain he would be too weak to walk. He often thought of Eira before taking this drug that so incensed him; the joy of running about with her and chasing the chickens about the farm. Challenging each other to cause mischief. How he dared to hope he would play such games again.

'Can I not spend today without it? It's a sickly drink.'

'Sorry, my love, we must do what we can to make you comfortable, I'll ask him to add some sweet herb to soften the taste.'

'What is wrong with me, Mother? I am being consumed aren't I?'

A tear ran down Marilia's cheek as the thought of not visiting Pietrich in any state saddened her. And although she knew that day would come, the question she could not face was when. She wiped away the tear for fear that he would see her sadness; impossible though she knew it was for him.

'Don't cry, please, I can't bear it when you cry.'

Marilia was startled. 'Pietrich, don't worry about me, I'm not crying. I'm here for you, for all you need of me.'

'I cannot see, Mother, but the sound of your tears rolling down your cheek is like a river running through a gorge valley to me.'

Marilia laughed and kissed her son. 'You are such a sweet boy. Your imagination is wild.' For this she was grateful. 'Rest now, and travel to a better place than this.'

Pietrich was angry that she dismissed his heightened sensitivity, but he knew not to argue. She had made daily excuses to try and convince him his mind invented his visions and the things he heard.

She left her son's side and headed towards the solid wooden door that was the entrance to their home, slowly pulling it open, hoping to make little sound so that Pietrich may fall asleep calmly. Marilia closed the cottage door behind her and made her way across the village square. Back inside, Pietrich felt the building shake and he shuddered at the banging sound it made. The spinning, dreaming sensation returned and he rolled away like a bale of hay tumbling in an autumn gust.

Marilia strode through the village holding her head up high as she felt the gazes of Knighton's people upon her. She must appear strong. Pietrich's passing would come soon. Only then would she deal with their fussing and fretting. Knighton had little gossip to fuel the empty minds of its simpletons and right now she could hardly bear the weight of their interest.

The wind had picked up, sending the fallen dust and dry foliage across the main street and into Marilia's eyes, forcing her to turn and wrap her headscarf around her face. Marilia saw Eira sitting by the tree, which she had kept a keen watch over ever since she had decided to reattach the fallen leaves. Marilia was still moved by the gesture to prolong the autumn as though she could prolong Pietrich's life. She was shaken from the thought as she passed by Thomas who was making his rounds. Marilia smiled at him. It was a smile for show; she had nearly forgotten the other kind. He nodded his head graciously as he did each day when their paths crossed. They had yet to talk in much detail of anything other than Pietrich's health. The wounds Thomas had suffered were healing well and he refused anyone fussing over them, wearing them with pride. He had not hidden away in the days after Tritan's banishment as other men may have, but walked proud among the village so that all would be reminded of what had been done to him. Combined with the limp that now seemed more pronounced, Marilia knew that the hatred towards Tritan had worsened. Marilia found herself locked in a daze and realised only after it was too late, how long she had been staring at the healer. As he stepped towards her she hurriedly swung about and raced off. She was blushing and felt the crimson heat rising; she knew how her daydreaming would be interpreted and dread enveloped her. It had been too long that this unspoken awkwardness had carried on between them and Marilia vowed to address it this evening when Pietrich was being put to bed.

After a while Marilia realised just how far she had walked through the many crop fields beside the stream that flowed around the village. The fields were now empty as the villagers awaited the grip of the long winter. She took a moment for herself and ran her hands through the water, which felt glacial on her fingertips. She had walked at quite a pace for she felt herself sweating and wiped her brow with her forearm. A little way ahead she became aware of a banging noise coming from the forest perimeter. Two workers were fixing a wall and a viewing post. One of them was using a sledgehammer to break up pieces of rock as the other mixed a thick muddy paste to build the foundation. She laughed to herself, disbelieving the sight and headed over to the two. It was Jonah and Kayla; she was pleased to see them both.

'Are we in danger?' she asked.

Jonah looked up at Marilia and smiled. 'A simple request from the mothers, no immediate threat.' He choked on his last breath, suddenly aware of the direction the conversation was heading. The two workers tilted their heads and averted their eyes as Jonah leant on the handle of his hammer, grateful for the moments rest.

'We're to set lookouts in shifts upon the tower. We've enlisted half a dozen volunteers already.'

'I'd gladly join the list of names,' Marilia said.

Kayla tried to sound as comforting as she could but her tone was not matched by the words she spoke. 'You need not concern yourself, under the circumstances 'n' all I mean.'

'I've raised my boy alone more or less since his birth and until recently I also tended to a drunken husband who barely lifted a finger. I trust you'll agree I am capable to take a turn at staring into an empty forest for a few hours a week.' In truth it was exactly what she needed, a few moments peace and nothing but nature's garden to look upon. She knew the construction was an overreaction. They were in no more danger now than before. It saddened her that such fear had driven them to raise the walls. It was this fear that had driven men apart before the war and for certain that very fear had caused it. She looked towards the forest where she had walked freely as a child and knew it was their own freedom that was being lost.

'I'm sorry. I meant no disrespect. I am no expert in what you must be going through. I didn't mean to impose a limitation on you.' Kayla hung her head at the last word.

Marilia looked at the part-finished wall and saw many hours of work still to be done. 'May I help you now? I would welcome the distraction, and I am already hot and flustered, I'll change into something more suitable and return.'

Jonah looked to Kayla and knew they could not refuse her. 'We'd be most grateful.'

Jonah and Kayla continued their work as Marilia made to set about but before she left she turned to ask a question that had been playing on her mind since her visit with her son. 'Tell me, did you work closer to the cottages this morning before heading out here?'

Jonah shook his head confused. 'No, what you see here is the result of an early start. We rose before the cockerels crowed to get to it. The sooner it's done the better. Why do you ask?'

'Oh, it's nothing, I thought I heard some work taking place outside my kitchen whilst I made breakfast was all,' Marilia lied, her mind playing heavily on what Pietrich had said to her. From this distance it could not be possible he had heard them working. She convinced herself it was a silly coincidence and nothing more and made for the stables to put on her work clothing. She thought of the boundary wall and nothing else. Marilia was glad to be doing something mindless and headed out to join in with the work.

The day grew dark as the tower and wall began to take shape but there was still a whole second tier of woodwork to be added. Marilia looked down at Jonah who had passed her the last cutting of measured timber. After laying it out with Kayla's help the three of them agreed it was time to call it a day and each set about their homes for the evening. Kayla spent that evening with Eira, grateful for the time she was given with her daughter and for her good health. Jonah had a good stash of barley wine that he saved for special occasions and treated himself to a nightcap as any worker would after exerting himself. Marilia returned home and washed herself and as the dirt left her skin she felt the joy of the day slip away. Her thoughts returned to Pietrich who was lying in the same place she had left him. He was still, pale, and sound asleep. It reminded her of the sight of her father on his deathbed. So many things had gone unspoken, the hatred she had carried for him for leaving her and her mother for another woman would never be resolved, but she had loved him dearly all the same. He had been her protector for much of her life. It made her think of all the things she wished to say to Tritan as she harboured a similar hatred for him that she knew must be released. *How could he be so cruel?* Her love for him assuaged the pain he caused her but for him to be defeated so easily and flee like a whipped dog was unbearable. Leaving his son without the strength of a father. Yes, he had been banished she knew, but a real man would fight for his right to stay and protect his own child in such a state. She willed him to return, as if by some miracle he was still alive and could hear her thoughts. She yearned for him to be here and to see him say goodbye to Pietrich before it was too late.

A gentle knocking at the door brought her around and she realised a water pan was whistling. She quickly pulled it off the stove, fearing Pietrich might be awoken by the sound, but he still appeared to be fast asleep. It was Thomas at the door, with his set of tonics and drops and instruments. Marilia greeted him as she did each night and took him through to Pietrich.

'He hasn't slept so well at this hour for days,' she said. 'Perhaps he will rest unaided tonight?'

Thomas shook his head. 'I do not think that would be wise. If he were to wake in the night without this medication he would be in great pain.'

'Leave it with me then, and I shall stir him in an hour, for now I wish to see him resting.'

'Of course, you are right. Perhaps then we could talk a while, if my presence does not burden you?' he asked sweetly.

Marilia thought she heard Pietrich shuffle but convinced herself it was not so and remembering the promise she'd made to herself earlier that day, she led Thomas through to the kitchen, poured glasses of wine, one for him and one for herself.

'Thank you, I did not realise you had taken to drinking again.'

Marilia gave him a telling glance. 'With the past weeks as they have been, how could I not?'

'Indeed, a toast then, to wine well deserved.' Their glasses met and a ringing sound chimed before they each sipped their drink.

Not far from them, Pietrich screwed up his face in pain, the singing water pan had been hard enough to bear but the pitch of ringing glass pierced his skull like a needle. He had not slept at all but was pretending to rest to avoid the tonic. Suffer though he must, he wished to have his remaining senses in his control. He heard his mother talking with the healer about all the things that had been left unsaid since before he was born. Thomas was trying to appeal to Marilia's weakness and to take his father's place and for this Pietrich hated him. He knew Tritan was a damaged man but had learnt very young that even troubled men had some good in them and Thomas was evidence that a good man could also be wicked.

The following minutes felt like hours as Pietrich tried to make sense of all he heard. When at last silence fell, he heard the soft meeting of wet lips between his mother and Thomas and sensed the subtlety of their arms embracing. He cursed the weakness of human desire and in despair forced himself to rest and to find solace with the voiceless stranger of his dreams. He resolved to find a way to communicate with the man and knew he could not use his voice even in his subconscious seclusion. Pietrich focused his energy on drifting deeply into his mind's eye and tried to control his enhanced sense of hearing to listen to the thoughts of the stranger. Suddenly he was floating again across the endless landscape to the place where he sat with the silent man. He channelled all his attention into his hearing and it was instantly flooded by a barrage of sounds of crying animals, creaking woods and flowing waters, despite the surrounding black landscape that contained no life at all. The stranger stared deeply into his eyes as if aware of what Pietrich was trying to do. He opened his mouth and the same gaping hole where a tongue had once been was all Pietrich could see, black as the dying world around them. Screaming sounds hurtled towards him, but they felt distant, as though a memory. It hurt his mind to be bombarded by such a vast array of sounds but he would not close himself off to it. His control steadied and then somewhere amongst the waves of noise that invaded his concentration he heard a voice. *Yes, you are right to have faith in my son.*

12

More often than a morning bird sings did Brynhildr vanish from sight, evading the care and supervision provided by her husband as he worked and struggled to keep track of his contradicting lives. It had become a game that she played, though she knew it only as her life, as she was an involuntary player. This life without her son and without the stability of a sharp mind made it hard for others to read her feelings. She could not understand why clear thoughts evaded her. Perhaps it was because she did not even know she was confused. She lived each day without recalling the events of the last. Once recognisable faces became strangers and their familiarity towards her frightened Brynhildr into a state as if she were a feral cat trapped in a dark street corner. Once she had walked thirty miles in the direction of the village where she'd spent her childhood, a small and quiet settlement called Llande, a beautiful place full of artisans and buzzing with trade in its prime. It was here as a young girl she had learnt to weave from her mother.

Wendel did not know what had prompted her disappearance

and word only reached him of her whereabouts after stories of a mad old maid, sick and thirsty had come to his town. He rode out instantly to rescue her from the tavern crowd who belittled her. He had found her, soaked to the bone in ale, being spun like a top on a large oak table. Wendel drove a knife into the hand of the man that spun her. Many of the tavern folk had claimed that she had been searching for her sister who he knew had died years ago. Brynhildr had believed they had arranged to have afternoon tea, so they claimed. But Wendel had not heard Brynhildr speak a word for many years and did not believe them. Given his wife's condition, Wendel and Brynhildr were allowed to return home the following morning after paying a handsome sum to the blacksmith who would no longer hammer steel. At home, Brynhildr would often sit, emptily staring across the lands of their settlement. Her daily activities were habits rather than deliberate actions and to this day Wendel had seen to her every need. Unknown to her was the reason why, but he would care for her no longer.

STEP BY STEP Brynhildr plodded through the barley fields and the bristly ears of the wheat brushed against her bare thighs. She was completely undressed and the breeze caused her to shiver as she covered her breasts and felt her nipples harden from the gelid chill. There was an orange flicker somewhere about the night sky and it seemed a curious invitation though unsound of mind as she was, she couldn't understand, where was the man who she saw daily? Each day Wendel had tended her, fed and clothed her. Now here she stood as naked as her name day, dried blood crusted over her chin and chest. But today he did not come. She wondered who was this man that he would spend so many years by her side only to vanish. She had not remembered the sword that felled him and felt the longing akin to an infant whose mother had turned her back for a second.

She staggered towards the glowing oasis, becoming increasingly aware of the pain that pulsated through her nose. As she neared the flickering orange glow she admired a low cloud lingering in the sky. There had been no clouds in this dry valley for weeks. It was as though it was Wendel's spirit refusing to abandon his home, refusing to abandon her.

A rough sound flooded the evening to accompany the crackling of charred wood and whining of expanding metal. It was the sound of brutality and celebration. Drunken men of the 11th Legion were applauding their own actions in the small high street that was being torched. Helpless men, women and children were huddled together and remained as quiet and hidden as they could, watching all that Wendel had built for them destroyed. These were not casual raiders. The kid had been tied to a horse and dragged around to witness the barbarism. It all seemed so pointless to him. Why would mindless destruction against a far weaker people be something to gloat about? He could understand the victory in defeating an unlikely foe, much as he fantasised about how good he would feel were he able to kill all these men for what they had done. But like most dreams that come to us so freely, to listen to the encouragement they give us and take action would be futile. The boy pushed his mind onto something more real, more tangible. Suddenly he felt the hatred for all these men become concentrated into a single being. Tritan. He thought long and hard about how he would rejoice in his suffering. The feeling would be regal and just. He had never known of such cowardice and in such an unlikely form for he had seen the man fight whilst chained. Perhaps it was Tritan's arrogance or maybe the kid simply resented him for living when surely he deserved death as much as the landowner. Thanks to his brutal intervention Tritan had been spared. The boy was tormented by his whirling thoughts and knew that he had also been spared and worst of all, Tritan had played a part in that.

Brynhildr had now approached the burning street. It was a tunnel of fire. One way in and one way out. The lad watched her stagger through, as though possessed by a strange spirit. The men of the 11th laughed at her as she passed them, mindlessly heading into the blazing gulf. The searing heat caused her brow to sweat and her whole body began to blister. Confusion formed itself upon her face, though the billowing smoke that shrouded her masked the bewilderment. Her mind wandered as she stared through the blinding golden light and she saw a figure standing there before her. It was Wendel. He was youthful and strong as the day they had met. Gazing deeply, his eyes bore into hers and she knew he invited her to join him. For the first time in an age, Brynhildr recognised him. She knew it was her husband that stood before her and she spoke to him at last.

'Yes, my love. I will come.'

A smile crept across her face, it was a rare smile and she approached the flames so close that she could kiss them, and she did.

13

T he echoes of tortured cries subsided like the dancing shadows cast by a once blazing fire. A deep blue shroud hung in the night sky as if the forthcoming day had whispered its promise. *Everything would be different now,* the scraps of morality Tritan had clung to vanquished by the tepid exposé of a former self. Maybe he had never ceased to be the boy who had killed his mother, never escaped the guilt and fear that had been his life for so long. Even though he had not yet seen Augustus, Tritan felt his presence in the air around him. His father's smell lingered in the breeze, his voice hidden in every sound and the promise of fear resonated through the child inside of Tritan. He clung to that fear desperately, overwhelmed by the despair of the man he was now.

Tritan didn't rest that night, he only watched the dying embers of one man's efforts fade into a quiet and sad vision; a clear and brutal end had befallen this place. Suddenly the roughness and the bickering of its people seemed like a haven compared to the havoc that had been wrought here by the 11th. He longed to see Wendel pleading with the townsfolk over trivial matters, knowing with hindsight that they had a greater, more privileged life than any of them had ever considered. Tritan thought hard about all the places he had seen, reliving the journey of his life to this moment in a rapid whip of lights, flickering inside his mind. It was like watching a wrecking ball destroying everything in its path. He longed to see his son again. He longed to tell Marilia how sorry he was for all the anguish he had caused her family. But it was his family too, and maybe forgiveness was beyond him, but was there nothing more he could do?

As the sun broke across the horizon, the 11th began to stir. Tritan had not been the only one who had not slept. He knew that the kid too had wandered aimlessly, enraged and helpless, through the dark hours. Sy had bound the boy's hands together and fastened him to a strong timber rope that was locked to the foundation of a stable. The lad still paced back and forth as far as his bindings would allow, his head slumped due to the fatigue of sleep deprivation and thirst. Tritan sat and waited as Kal approached him. He brought with him a strong broth that contained a ground herb, hot water and sugar. Kal offered a cup to Tritan before sitting beside him.

'You'll be needing this inside you with the day we have ahead of us.'

Tritan took the cup and sniffed the contents. He blew gently on it to reduce the heat and sipped it carefully. 'Willow leaf,' he said. 'Seems fresh enough, though I doubt you picked it from around this barren land.'

'We have travelled far and fast. Jaz keeps the herbs fresh with a plant oil. It works well. Gives us an extra day or two with most things that grow from the ground. It takes the edge off the rich flavour but sacrifices must always be made.'

Kal joined Tritan in sipping from his own cup. The two of them sat in silence for a while, watching as the Legion readied itself for travel. The men bundled their bedding and food and pans together into sacks and then tied them off onto their horses. For a small band of men they carried a great deal. Clearly many of their possessions had been inherited from those who had once travelled with them.

'Do you plan on allowing the kid to travel with us? If so, he'll need a good share of the brew. He's been sulking and expending energy like a flogged horse all night,' Tritan said.

'Yes, he'll come with us for now. We are few in number and one so young, maybe he can learn.'

'Do you go to report?' Tritan finally dared to ask. The real question in his mind was *Where is my father?*

'Report? No. What were you expecting, that Augustus would leave us to drag our heels with you whilst he waited with anxious expectation? If he were with us you'd have known it long before now. That one was born to lead by example and no other way.'

'So he has finally found his grave?'

'I can't be sure it's so simple as that but he took his fate into his own hands. We were left with less than a hundred men by the time the real fighting was done. Villages we passed through were left barren cemeteries, the stench of death fierce. We picked up fewer and fewer supplies as we continued following your father from one hopeless task to another. He became enraged by his increased weakness and slowing due to age. Time was finally catching up with him, so he headed to the misty plains to the north and made the journey through.'

'Can it have been so bad to have driven him to near madness?'

'He wanted strength and power, the kind that does not come from wielding a sword. The kind that comes from chasing myths. So we began chasing those myths, speaking to the winter dwellers who live near the impassable mist. But I fear most of what we learned there was rumour and lies. Something you can't see or touch is not a thing to seek out. But when he finally decided to make the journey, Augustus allowed most of us to stay behind.'

'So now you lead them?'

'Lead? No. We have a common purpose and many still await Augustus's return. But none of the men he took with him have returned either. When you head into the darkness, the darkness heads into you. For now we must seize greater opportunities. Local clans will grow from the pits of destruction, forged in the forty years of war; any man with strength and foresight will recognise it and take advantage. As did your captor, the landowner. We can't allow such unallied communities to flourish, or control will be lost forever.'

'Without Augustus, people will have less to fear.'

'Yes, but before me sits the next best thing.'

Tritan felt the words cut deep inside his throat and as he attempted to swallow he believed he tasted blood. Jaz approached the two men where they sat. He was sweating from loading all the horses.

'Well, the men are ready for travel. Sy has insisted the boy walks. Thought you should know that. It'll slow us down something fierce.'

'He will ride with me,' Tritan rebuked.

Kal looked unconvincingly at both Tritan and Jaz. 'Well, I suppose there's no use him slowing us down. Give the kid a cup.' Kal handed the canteen of brew to Jaz who nodded and left them.

'Be careful you don't get too close to the boy. He may yet betray you. I see how he looks at you. The same way you look at me.' Kal smirked as he spoke his final word before looking sincerely at the younger man and nodding. He rose to ready his horse. There was a challenge embedded in those few simple words. Tritan deliberated the terms of his entering once again into this pack of wild men. He wondered whose trust was the likeliest to be betrayed among them.

The simple formation of the 11th manoeuvred to make for the northern path heading out of the valley. Crows circled overhead, waiting to begin their feast for they smelt betrayal and the promise of blood. It would be a king's banquet, unlike any they had seen these past months. The war had made them as greedy as men and now they craved the meat of corpses.

Tritan offered his hand to the kid and Kal whispered in Sy's ear to soften his rage. But the boy surprised them all and spat at Tritan's hand, preferring to struggle behind them all on foot than accept help from such a man. After all, and although the kid did not know it, from Port Melees to the landowners town, Tritan had ruined the settlements in this land not once now, but twice.

THE RIDE WAS long and slow, due mainly to the kid who, though fit for a lad his age, had no hope of keeping up with horses such as these stallions. They travelled for miles and miles and stopped only to set up camp when it was dark, covering as much ground as they could during the waking light. Their provisions held them in good stead for a time and occasionally they hunted in the woods they passed. Jaz was the overseer of their stock and made the daily bread from the remaining sacks of wheat flour. He allowed the boy to help him and learn the culinary methods required on the road. To his surprise the kid was accomplished at many of the skills required to survive in the wild. He became one of the keenest hunters that Jaz relied upon, his lightness of foot allowing him to gain a closer proximity to the animals.

Tritan barely spoke to any of the men for several days, not

even Kal who led them further and further north. They had left the river that flowed to the old smugglers' town and entered into a granite rock mountain range. Due to the barren narrow path that was a major detour and likely held no provision for food, Kal sent a couple of the men off the long way around the mountain with the horses and made the rest of them scale a sheer rock face to the summit. From here they could spy the closest forest or settlement with hopes of scrounging some food.

The climb was long and arduous, each man's life was in the hands of the one ahead and the man behind them was their concern. The height of the climb had meant they would camp for two nights on the ascent, tying off cradles made of material with the ropes hammered into the crevices by large bolt pins. It was hardly safe or comfortable and the howling gales that bowled over them at night prevented them all from gaining proper rest. On the third day they managed to reach the top but the razor sharp rocks had shredded much of their hands. It took them most of the morning to wash and bandage themselves before they were able to set off towards a ramshackle wooden cabin that looked as though it had not been touched for years. It was fortunate that inside was a growth of a rich mossy grass, disgusting to taste but full of nutrients and the only green substance they had seen all day. The forest in the distance appeared to be unreal, a mirage on the far horizon. The original perimeters could be seen from the summit as though a scythe had slashed right through the land and taken the natural earth with it. This destruction was man's doing; ironic that now it was man who needed the aid of the forests.

They continued ponderously, miserable and moaning at the state of their hands. It would certainly make hunting harder. It was only the kid who had managed to come away with relatively minor wounds and doubtless he would heal more quickly than most of these older men. Maybe he would be useful to them after all.

It had been years since Tritan had travelled this way and his senses were dulled but the dropping temperature proved his suspicion correct as to the direction they were headed. Now in the shadow of the mountain, the nights became increasingly harder to bear. Even with the thick straw mats and wool Tritan struggled to get his body to a temperature that would allow him to rest. He saw the boy shivering as he was barely covered at all. Sy had seen to it that he would suffer and Tritan, ashamed and pitiful as he felt, was not yet sure what place he held among these men. Each petition he made on the kid's behalf only drove Sy to become more suspicious.

One night in particular they stopped and burned much of their firewood to provide warmth. Even those with the thickest clothing were chilled through to the bone. 'Break out some drink, lads,' shouted Jaz. 'We'll gain an extra layer or two of heat with our senses tamed.'

They had stopped close to a river. The night was already upon them and their horses were weary. Tritan figured they had been on the road for a week by now. Their supplies had diminished heavily and they hadn't come across a single settlement for three days. Tritan, as per most nights, had kept to himself and sat in the shadows. It was as though they'd never found him at all. The boy was more visible. Always forced to wait upon Sy and remain in the light. But this was the first evening his share of the food had been so heavily cut. Tritan supposed they could afford to let him starve, in spite of his newfound usefulness. He also suspected that the main reason he had been kept alive was to help tame Tritan into some sort of submissive state of compliance. Tritan was a boy again. Following a band of killers, to what end, he knew not, though he feared his purpose was already preordained. The liquor that was now run dry had allowed many of the 11th to pass out, the fires began to dwindle and frost settled in around them. Tritan rolled over, agitated. The cold was too hard to endure so he got to his feet and wore his bed sheet like a cloak. He knew the only way to warm himself was from the inside and he took to walking briskly around the camp. He listened eagerly to the sounds that emanated around him. The disparity of the world at such a time to the way Tritan usually perceived it humbled him. He listened to all the nocturnal creatures living out their lives and felt belittled. His race was always obsessed with the notion of being at the centre of everything, the top of the food chain. But Tritan knew as he listened to the songs of the night and saw the lights of the stars that they were merely guests and he was the most insignificant of all. He remembered the words of Castellar who'd once shown him compassion, although his actions warranted no forgiveness. Tritan was a prisoner again, only this time he carried baggage; he was leading the kid into a life worse than death. If he could learn how to negotiate with his old Legion he might at least save the lad. For his life was surely drawing to an end as certainly and slowly as was that of his son Pietrich.

Tritan took to resting awhile against a tree. He leant back and relaxed his senses. As he began to drift into a waking dream, a young fox approached him and snuffled. At first the fox was cautious but Tritan made no sudden sounds or movements. He thought that the fox must be intrigued by the bundle of soft layers that he was wrapped in. Tritan unrolled his outer layer very slowly by his side and then drew back and waited. The fox came closer and sniffed the rolled out bundle curiously and with an eye trained keenly on Tritan, lest it be a trap. Slowly it stepped onto the soft and warm cloak. It was a joy to watch as the fox rolled and wrestled with the cloak until it was firmly around him. Tritan wondered how such animals survived this harsh season so far north. Suddenly he felt a hand push against his shoulder. Tritan leapt to his feet and the fox, startled, sprinted off into the distance. Tritan spun in circles looking for the intruder but there was no one there. The sensation had felt so real that fear now rose in him. The physical tingling on his shoulder was still distracting for he knew it had felt like a boy's hand. But there was no boy here with him. Tritan rolled up the cloak that still lay on the floor and decided it was his conscience playing tricks on him and he made his way back to the camp where he found the kid curled up in a position that did not suggest comfort. It was like watching a fragile and helpless newborn.

Tritan laid the cloak over the boy and tucked the sides in to better insulate the warmth it would generate. As he walked away he thought he sensed the twinkle of an open eye watching him but thought better than to show it. His body almost felt looser and Tritan decided to visit Diablo. *Better to rest together than apart at this hour*, he thought. Diablo welcomed the familiar smell and weight of the man he held dear. Their bond had been proven two days past when Sy had decided to try and ride Diablo, disbelieving the skill that Tritan held with this blind horse. After the miserable charade, Tritan insisted it was no skill at all, only trust, something one could earn from any species but Tritan realised that Sy had probably never known trust from or for any creature in his entire life. The two men were keen to defy one another and Tritan knew that great damage had been done to this man. There would be no alliance built between them, regardless of Kal's intentions.

Tritan's mind slipped into a daze with the warmth of his horse pressed against his back and he dreamt that he was an infant being cradled by a mother that he had never known. It was a good dream.

14

One of the many recurring dreams Tritan had suffered as a child was of Rose, a village woman who rescued her son from a fearful prophesy that would have otherwise ended his life. Tritan had been told the tale by one of the 11th Legion when he was very young. Augustus had seen to it that no one made mention of it again, as any such tale could encourage one so young to believe they may choose their own path. But such a legend was entrenched in the history of this world and it was impossible to ignore. Tritan often wondered why he should be guarded from such a story. He thought it might be due to his part in the death of his own mother and the retelling of such stories awoke the pain Augustus suffered. But that would not stop the boy legionnaire dreaming that his own mother was Rose and he was the son who had been sentenced to die.

In the ancient time when nothing was recorded and only folk tales survived, a great plague swept across the lands, infecting the young with a malady that caused death in the womb. Such febrile torment caused hundreds of thousands of stillbirths, an entire generation wiped out. All that is, but one. Rose was the mother to the sole survivor. At that time a lineage of kings ruled the land and the current king was Elucifice. Elucifice heard of the boy and believing the miracle to be a bad omen, ordered the presence of the family in the high court. A rapacious king, Elucifice feared anything that might threaten his wealth. Men and women had lost their heads to simple ideals whispered in the taverns of the common folk. The king sentenced the boy to death at once but pardoned Rose and her husband, Chalstice. The condition of their pardon was that they make no intervention in their son's fate. A cavalcade was ordered to escort them far away until the baby had been examined and disposed of. Rose and Chalstice wept as they were taken away for they knew it was madness to abandon their boy. That night, out of desperation, they killed their sleeping guards and stole the horses to return to the dungeons where they sought out their son. Chalstice fought to the death protecting Rose as she escaped with their baby who, with great fortune, still yet lived. Rose named their son Maldus, a word from the old tongue once associated with the love for the distant lights in the night sky. Rose and baby Maldus journeyed north for weeks before the king's private army caught up with them. A thousand men had tracked them down and were now only a day's ride behind. With no other options she descended the snowy peak on the borders of the north and headed deep into the mist that separated the known lands from those that were feared and shrouded in darkness. Knowledge of this other world, branded as Orldin or 'unknown' in the old tongue, was scant; no one had ever seen it or at least had never returned alive to describe it. But Rose had no intention of returning and strode forward, Maldus cradled in her arms, through the thick and mysterious fog.

Out of the thousand who had left by order of the king, only a dozen had dared to follow her and they were never seen again.

It cannot be said exactly what passed in the days that followed. Tritan's dream always faded as fast as the image of Rose disappearing into the mist. It was where the story ended.

A METALLIC CLANG rang out like an alarm though there was no urgency in Tritan's rising. He had rested so deeply that it was a wonder he had woken at all. Above him stood Jaz, a proud look upon his face and a steaming brew in his hand.

'Morning, lad,' said the welcoming hulk of a man.

'Jaz, you're too kind,' Tritan offered ironically. 'What is the sense of that noise at this hour?'

'Training the kid is what that is.'

Tritan threw aside his idleness and arose quickly at this revelation then downed the brew, patting Jaz on the shoulder before making off towards the ringing sound of swords.

Tritan approached calmly and with no intention to make any kind of fuss, but he also wanted to make sure that it was in fact training that was taking place and not an unjust beating. He suspected it was the latter and the sight of Sy prancing around the kid like a royal fool confirmed Tritan's fears. Many of the 11th had gathered together and offered shouts and cheers celebrating the performance; they disguised their gloating as advice for the boy. Only Kal kept silent and Tritan placed himself just in front of Kal so he could not avoid his disapproval. The stage had been set amidst a circle of trees where the audience leaned and watched the unravelling performance. Tritan couldn't hold back his thoughts any longer. 'Your methods haven't progressed I see.' Kal fidgeted behind him but did not reply. 'Easier to get another to give the beatings than do it yourself is it? After all that one has no moral centre, even compared to us.'

'Better to refrain from sharing your pithy observations,' was all that Kal offered as reply. But Tritan could sense in his voice that Kal was unsure if he believed in these methods anymore.

More than twenty years ago it had been Kal himself dancing around and making a fool of a young boy who was barely capable of wielding a sword. Tritan's first real lesson had left him with bruised forearms and a broken shin. His knuckles had been so raw from dragging across the soil that he hadn't been able to grip his sword for days after. But the fact that Tritan had been younger than ten at the time was the only solace he found in the sight before him now, the kid squirming with each beating stroke of the flat of Sy's sword falling upon his body. No doubt under that jerkin he was a purple mess.

The boy was now weaponless and barely able to stand. He fell backwards hitting his head on a stray rock which dizzied him and looked around to see the crowd laughing at him. There was no smile on Sy's face, only pure wrath. A warm and wet sensation trickled down the kid's arm and although he had not felt the slow and deliberate cut from Sy's sword, he could see his own blood dripping from the metal tip of the blade. Shortly before passing out he witnessed Tritan leaping forward into the ring, grabbing Sy mid-swing and tossing him into the dirt.

'Enough!' bellowed Tritan. 'You'll kill the boy!'

'Out of the way, you bastard! Or shall I teach you a lesson too?'

Tritan didn't need a second invitation. He spun around and went to the closest man and unsheathed their sword before charging Sy with a heavy swing. The power and weight behind the blow was something Sy had only felt once before, but this time he was ready and parried the blow sending Tritan's sword into the trunk of a tree where it stuck. Sy forced a fist into Tritan's face as he struggled to release the blade from the wood but Tritan barely flinched and used his anger to summon strength enough to pull the sword free. He ducked underneath a rapid brutal swing that came from his adversary. Tritan was surprised at the speed with which Sy was now attacking him, and barely able to keep him at bay. He remembered he was fighting a far younger man whose greatest ally was speed. With that in mind he used the only option available and grabbed Sy in a bear hug, forcing him to take tiny clutching swings that merely broke Tritan's skin. Tritan raised his head backwards whilst using his sword as a clamp and aimed his forehead for the festering cut on Sy's cheek. It split open instantly but the cost was dear, as Sy had worked a knee into Tritan's groin, sending him to his knees.

At this Kal stepped forward, witnessing the blood lust but he did not intervene. It was fortunate then that Sy threw his sword to the side, though the lesson had not yet run its course. He plunged his elbow down into Tritan's face, sending him to the ground. Tritan was a bloodied mess and the fight was won, or so Sy had thought. Moments later as Sy turned his back; Tritan slowly and defiantly rose to his feet. 'Now let's see what you're really made of!' Tritan screamed as he hobbled forwards, still disabled heavily by the blow he'd been dealt between the legs.

Sy scoured the area for a weapon and found it in a large branch that had been used to beat the dust from their cloaks. He took aim and swung it into Tritan's stomach. Tritan lurched backwards but his face showed no sign of pain.

The 11th were no longer laughing. Every man among them was a hardened soldier. But no man willingly asked for such a beating. Kal hesitated and flinched as the next blow came, forcing himself not to interfere. It was a crippling shot to the shoulder that sent Tritan back to the ground. All watched as he rolled around in the dirt, wrestling with the pain. Sy threw the branch onto the crippled body of his victim. Strange for him to have felt the pleasure in killing defenceless innocents just days past, but to attack now, one who welcomed the pain, left him with an empty, used feeling.

The next insult came shortly after. Tritan placed a palm onto the ground and forced himself into a squatting position. He was like a flogged hound, scrabbling off the floor for no reason other than to know it was possible. It was. Tritan stood there for all to see. He wavered and stumbled but he still remained standing. What is one to do with such a thing? Sy knew he had been bested by sheer will and to kill Tritan now would only deepen the hollowness of his victory. The two men simply stared at each other and Tritan, thinking only of the kid's condition, added another debt to the account he held against Sy.

Sy turned away and pushed his way through the silent crowd. Never had he been seen with his head hung so low. Tritan turned back to where the boy lay unconscious on the ground and with the strength he did not deserve to muster, he picked him up and carried him towards a tepee where he lay him on a soft sleeping mat. Kal followed him and stood over his shoulder. Tritan worried at the consequences of his actions and turned slowly to hear the sentence for his crime. No sentence came so Tritan spoke.

'Had your day's entertainment I suppose? Or are you simply too old to join the fight now?'

Kal smirked at Tritan for a moment. 'They had to see you were still you.'

Tritan realised then what he had done, this was not an act of defiance against the 11th. It was a show of leadership. For Kal to do anything other than stand and watch would have weakened Tritan's authority. Slowly but surely Tritan was becoming the thing he feared the most. He was rising from the darkness of the past Augustus had left in his wake and stepping forcibly into the light of the future these men had been seeking.

15

Thick slabs of stone supported the oak beams that ran across the ceiling. All around were stacks of hessian cloth filled to the brim with seed. The atmosphere was dry and cool, suitable only for the seeds capable of withstanding a long winter in near freezing conditions. Beside the storage barn was a hearth being tended by an elderly lady. She was one of the many workers that lived in this stony settlement of barracks set amidst a cold northern valley. She occasionally billowed the flames to keep the air from frosting.

Kal strolled back and forth inspecting the sacks and approving their quality and quantity. He clutched a handful of seeds and took them towards Jaz who nodded in agreement.

'Aye, they've dried well against the odds,' Jaz said optimistically. 'They'll make the next harvest, even if we lose a tenth of the stock there's enough seed here for well over five hundred acres.'

Kal considered this. 'And what are our chances they won't germinate? For this to work we can't afford for them to seed.'

'Well, last spring the only plants that produced new seed

were in the fields I kept aside for that purpose. This store contains the ones treated with the spiced oil and if I were a betting man I'd say they'll only yield one harvest in their lifetime.'

'Let us hope so, ay.' Kal patted Jaz on the shoulder for a job well done. All the while Tritan observed the men, still surprised he had been brought to see what was transpiring in these barns. He had never seen such a store of seed in all his life. It would not have been such a shock to him normally for he was no accomplished farmer but neither were these men.

They had endured many long nights riding, Tritan's wounds had caused him such discomfort that he passed in and out of consciousness continually. He had suffered a broken rib on account of the branch that Sy had swung into his body and clutching the stirrups to ride Diablo was like welcoming a mountain to rest upon his lungs. The relief had finally arrived at the sight of the fort. The garrisons it contained had been here for several years. It had housed many soldiers throughout the war and had been the workplace of many of the surrounding village folk. Now it was just a place for the recluse settlers and the 11th Legion to call home. The old stone storage barns to the north side of the perimeter were Kal's devising. Tritan had recognised the place at once upon arriving; Krali fort. This was near where he had fallen and later been discovered by Thomas with his innards as visible as the roots of the upturned tree he had crawled under for shelter.

In spite of the simplicity and basic construction of the fort, Tritan could not help but feel overwhelmed by its presence. To know you had once met death in a place was reason enough never to return. But his path had now led him back to this domicile, to inspect a room full of seed. For what purpose he had yet to discover. He knew at least, from his limited knowledge, that the seed had been sorted into types for there was rice, corn, cotton and wheat in this one barn. Altogether there were four barns.

Tritan continued to watch as Kal and Jaz made their rounds from one enclosure to the next. By the time they had inspected the quota the rest of the 11th had settled into their barracks. None of them had known such shelter in weeks. The southern dry blistering heat of Wendel's basin land was a distant memory.

Kal turned to see what impression they were making on Tritan. Though he remained silent his face betrayed a certain measure of intrigue. Kal smiled and gestured towards the barns behind where he now stood.

'This is the beginning of something we have never seen, it requires no magic nor do we have to travel through an impassable mist to reap the benefits.' Kal took Tritan by the shoulder; it felt awkward at first but soon became strangely comforting. 'I've been building this for some time. But before long I will be too old to see the benefits of the work. There was a great deal of scepticism at first, as I'm sure you can imagine. Fear alone can no longer control the course of this world. Water, grain and shelter are the three things that play on all our minds. Homes can be built with the vast expanse of woods and slate from the mountains. Water is there for those who would work for it, the landowner played his part to prove that. Seed and grain is the only thing we can really control. After all, the coin in your pocket is only as good as the resources you can buy with it. We will supply a new form of seed, and within a matter of years it will be the only seed the farmers can yield. Every grain that surrounds us will germinate no further seed. And so the demand will rise as we continue to produce it exclusively from this secluded stronghold.'

Tritan gave Kal a stern look. 'How will you convince them it is not some form of witchcraft? Assuming you're not wrong and no new seeds grow, or more to the point how will you convince so many to disregard the seed of their own lands? Some farming families have used generations of seeds over centuries.' Tritan thought of Marilia at this moment. He had never really listened properly when she spoke about such matters, but even so he knew she had spoken of her father's ancestors who had farmed their land and never was there any meddling from outside the village of the kind Kal was intending. It was a wicked plan, and as did all wicked plans, it sounded dangerous.

Kal stroked the newly formed beard that had grown thick these past weeks. Tritan awaited his dictum.

'Therein lies the rub, but you came back to us, and brought with you a talented young thief. It is plain to me now that had we taken the boy's life we'd be short a measure of stealth for what must be done.'

Tritan felt the invisible shackles tighten and off he wandered, a rabbit roaming deeper and deeper into the wolf's lair.

That night he felt a change about the camp. More of the men greeted him with interest and a form of respect. He would struggle to remain so concealed from now on. A large fire was lit at the centre of the barracks and fresh trunks were laid out in a circle for them to sit upon and feast. The fort boasted shelter from the harsh conditions that surrounded it and the populace that lived and ran the domain busied themselves with hunting, cooking and all the other needs that a community required. It was the first time that Tritan had seen anything resembling a community in weeks. Several of those that resided here were efficient at all things; music, farming and hunting. In fact it occurred to him that none of the men he had journeyed with had lifted a finger to contribute to this evening's festivities. In a way it bothered him, for it reminded him of how he had lived under the protection of all Marilia had offered. He had truly contributed little, and now to make matters worse he'd left her alone to watch their son's passing without a companion to share the grief. He shuddered now at the thought he would not be free to return to them. Once again the desire pulled at him like a taut rope that could sometimes be ignored but never forgotten. How had he ended up so far from them and with little likelihood that he would ever be free to return.

Tritan had hardly seen the kid or Sy since the altercation days past. Both avoided him with an equal disgust and Tritan knew he had been blamed for the punishing injuries the boy had sustained. Although he did not know where Sy had taken himself this evening, it was obvious the kid was resting nearby. He had been hurt badly and the cold had not allowed him to recover quickly. Tritan's own injuries were worn like a stain and he endured any pain as only temporary, something he had learnt as a soldier. It was this that allowed him to continue fighting at full strength. Tritan knew the boy did not have this skill.

Jaz, who had sat himself next to Tritan, passed over the canteen of wine. To the surprise of both of them Tritan handed it straight to the woman who was sat on his other side, a fairly tall and toned lady of Tritan's age named Sal. She was taking a break from her harp and welcomed the drink gladfully.

'You'll not be bitten so fierce with regret if you drink,' she said.

Tritan wasn't in the mood for idle talk but felt that to remain silent would have been the worse course. 'What should I regret?' he said, but he thought himself a fool for asking the question. He had opened the door to gossip and she was about to come bounding through it with a silver tongue.

'From me? Nothing. And you can avert those puppy dog eyes immediately. Send them flying elsewhere.'

Jaz gave him a knock to steal his attention for a moment.

'She's a mystery is our Sal. Not just the best musician here but also our best hunter. Don't let her size fool you, she's quick as a fox.'

'Shut up you giant oaf,' she rebuked. 'So will you not drink?' She gestured to Tritan with the raised canteen. He shocked himself at the lack of interest he held for the red elixir.

'I'll have more to regret if I do.'

'Suit yourself then.' With that Sal turned away and didn't offer Tritan another thought the entire night. Jaz was amused by their interaction, like a caring uncle jesting at the expense of a nephew trying to learn the ways of women.

'You've truly not changed in many ways, lad.'

'Truly I feel as though I have returned to my childhood.' Tritan did not mean it as a joke; this time Jaz did not laugh.

'It's that sort of talk will get you into the shit with your ass hanging inside out. You should not throw away the kernel of respect you have gathered these past weeks for such pithy self-loathing.'

Tritan did not need to reply to that. He knew the words Jaz spoke were true. As much as he hated the position he was being forced into he would have to ride the storm for now; no other option seemed possible. He had considered sneaking off in the night and fleeing with Diablo but he knew the boy would be killed without his presence. The kid hated him so much he would not likely travel with him if he suggested they run together. And to return south to Knighton, well he would simply draw a band of bloodthirsty warriors down on the people he had already wronged beyond repair. He wondered at what stage the kid's life had become important to him. Tritan had never held much stock in the relationships of those he loved and that needed him most. Now here he was full of worry for the boy and to make matters worse, he was allying himself further and further with the men who had imprisoned him.

'Cut me a piece of that deer meat, will you.' Tritan instructed

Jaz as though he was entitled to. Jaz obeyed for the same reason.

'Where does the kid rest?' Tritan asked next. It was met with a willing gesture to a small lean-to adjacent to the furthest barracks. Tritan nodded his thanks and headed off to it leaving Jaz to quietly hum to himself.

The lean-to was not well sheltered. The entire south facing side was open and exposed to every element of the weather. Thankfully, the wind had died down for the time being. The lad sat in the corner, hugging himself and shivering, his fire now dwindled, coughing up the final splutters of amber light. The pale blue of the night made him appear sicklier as Tritan's eye struggled to adjust from the bright warm glow of the fire that he had left behind.

'Why do you sit alone? There is a place by the fire for all of us.' Tritan threw down the hot meat and saw the lad consider it. But he made no move nor did he speak. Tritan moved slowly, closing in around the boy. 'You should at least eat it while it's warm. It'll be cold by the time I've given up on you and you will wish you had not made such a protest.' He wondered if Wendel had felt this frustrated when he had visited Tritan in the cold of night. To be refused aid by someone who needs it could be the most maddening situation to endure.

The kid didn't waste any more time, but his frozen hands could hardly tear at the meat. Tritan squatted in front of him and carefully pulled out a knife from his waist so as not to appear intimidating. He sliced the meat into manageable portions and then handed them to the boy who began to ravish his way through them.

'Well, I'll leave you to your meal, but don't forget you have a place should you wish. No one will harm you tonight.' Tritan got up and readied to leave.

'Were you able to see through my eyes, you would laugh at

yourself. You think you are changing and perhaps you are pretending to grow kinder. But when you realise you're worse now than when I came across you at the landowner's town, you'll hate yourself to death. At least then I might pity you.' The kid struck a deep nerve with the words and this time it was Tritan who remained silent. He had not thought about changing or attempting to be kind. In fact he agreed with the lad, he had become a coward again. So why had he found himself so concerned for this boy who hated him? Months previously he'd have left him to die and not thought twice about it. He realised now how one-sided the relationship was and knew the longing for some reciprocation was a feeling he must have forced onto his own family time and time again.

The crowds had mostly departed to their barracks now though a few who had drunk too much remained beside the embers of the dwindling fire. Tritan could not sleep and walked around the fort perimeter to visit Diablo. The horses had been tied to a set of posts and gated in. These other beasts must be wild and untrustworthy, he thought, for he had never needed to tether his own horse. Tritan arrived to find a tetchy and aggravated Diablo.

'I am sorry, boy. These men fear anything that runs free.' Tritan knew the sentiment really applied to him and all of the 11th. Not even Kal was free from the memory of Augustus. Kal's plan to use Tritan to fill the void of leadership amongst them was not certain to work and if it did, Tritan would be merely a puppet. The memory of his father would pull the strings that dangled him like the weak marionette that he was.

Not far from the makeshift stables was a place Tritan had come to know all too well ten years before. He found the tree, which still carried deep scars from the axe that had been wielded against him and leant his weight on the strong trunk. A pain suddenly shot through his chest. It carried down to the pit of his stomach and he felt beneath his garments to the scar that now held him together. It felt tight and sore, the area of skin that stretched had bothered him ever since he had been struck that day but this was something new. The pain came from his mind, not from the old wound. Memory truly is the greatest adversary, he considered.

THE FOLLOWING morning was a disordered affair; the stench of hangovers and quenched lusty thirst was all about the camp. A quick broth was put together and then Kal began to organize a few of the 11th who were the most clear-headed. Sal was amongst them. She was dressed in her hunter's garb, bow strung and quiver of arrows already flung across her shoulders. Resistance to the drink seemed to be another talent she was blessed with. Sy was to stay at the fort with the remaining members of the 11th. Only a small deputation had been picked for this delicate work.

The few were to set out in the guise of a travelling band and rabble of farm folk for Baurticeford, the largest remaining town within a day's ride. The landscape this far north had become so sparse that you could admire the hills in all directions and see no sign of men. Baurticeford still boasted a trade market for the northern agricultural communities and though not in season, the market town was home to many during the winter. Its central attraction was a famous tavern named "The Oxen". It was here they would check-in as simple travellers and musicians, with a sample of seed that they carried from the stores of Krali fort. Kal had conceived the plan, to send the kid out in the night to ascertain the extensiveness of the seed supply that was held in a locked keep to the north of the town's perimeter. Once they had been rejected by the local traders they would leave amiably and wait for the right moment to send the boy back inside to destroy the supplies. To avoid suspicion of their actions, Sal agreed to play her part, for this was her town. She was born and bred in Baurticeford and once played at The Oxen as a regular in a group of folk musicians before her companions had been killed during the raids on the town throughout the war. After burying them she had taken up her bow and joined the 11th as a means of avenging her friends, for it was the less peaceful members of the resistance against Augustus that had killed them. With the dwindling numbers within the legion and her skill with a bow, she was welcomed.

If the plan went through without a hitch, the town would fall into despair once the fires were dowsed. Kal would wait patiently. It would be only a matter of time before riders were sent to them on behalf of the farmers, willing to make a trade.

Sal rode beside Tritan, who led the journey a short way ahead of Kal and the kid. Just the four of them made up this grouping. Three men also followed them half a day's ride behind to avoid suspicion, for the residents of Baurticeford were well organised and would have watchers throughout the forests and rivers that flowed east of the town towards the main entrance gate. Sal had loaded her harp into a cart that her horse and Diablo were jointly responsible for drawing.

'You've a beautiful creature there,' she remarked. 'Though I've never seen a horse without eyes. Some would say it is cruel.'

'We go through life assuming the world is known through our senses alone. Trust between one living thing and another is more important than any of them.'

'Oh joy, a would-be philosopher in our midst.' Sal was not one to be schooled. Tritan had forgotten the pain of being mocked. It reminded him of all the times Marilia had berated him for his drunken behaviour. Ostensibly this was to be endured in the same vein, with silence. Sal did not allow the quiet to linger. 'I heard the men talking about the things you had done; it makes it all the harder to believe that Augustus left you to die. Perhaps that is why he returned to claim the fort for his own after the fighting was done. But by then you were gone, supposedly eaten by the crows.'

Tritan sniffed. 'I've heard wilder stories.' And so their parrying continued as the journey progressed into the middle of the day. It was a while before they stopped to rest and when they did, Tritan and Kal discussed the details of the plan and awaited their meal as Sal and the boy went off to hunt. They returned in no time with a hare that had been struck with two arrows. Sal paid great compliments to the kid for his speed and agility. He appeared in much better shape today, the meal the night before had done him good and his injuries were less prominent now. As ever though, he moved like a being that had no drive. Surcease for him was rare as a jewel flowing down a stream.

Dusk was setting in by the time they approached the town gates. The palisade was impressive and entry was only possible at the south-eastern entrance of the town. All others had been blocked off. They wandered through without any trouble as Sal nodded to the guards and gestured towards the harp they towed. The streets were laid with cobbled paths that ran up and down a series of winding hills. The town had been built on what appeared to be a number of mounds. It was hard to navigate such a place without getting lost but Sal knew the streets well.

The light faded and a vast array of lanterns lit up bringing the town to life with anticipated excitement. There was little sense of danger here and that alone was enough to make Tritan find the place curious. He had visited here only once as a teenager, and his mission at the time was not dissimilar to the one he embarked upon now. Baurticeford had changed very little. The streets were littered with children and market stalls and the smell of food drifted through the alleyways from the roasters selling cuts of choice meat. To dream of such possibilities weeks back when they were travelling north through the wilderness would have been torture. Tritan was grateful now that Kal had not thought to mention their destination previously, still recognising the smell from his time here all those years ago.

Kal bought some meat and a tray of boiled vegetables that they all enjoyed while watching the townsfolk settle into the night. Sal proudly described her home, recounting a litany of history and geography until she was sure her companions knew the place well. The sermon was exhausting and Tritan was glad that they eventually departed to head for the tavern. The only thing he had learnt of value was the existence of the rare arable land that surrounded Baurticeford; something he had already gathered to be the case or why else would they want to infiltrate the seed supply? It was surprising that Sal was so blindly in favour of this plan given this was her home. Musicians were a fickle bunch, Tritan thought, as if he deserved to judge another.

'This is the place,' Sal announced as they rode towards the inn. It was a tiny construct given its infamy. The Oxen was hardly a fitting name for it. 'Kid, take the horses to the stable and ask for a man called Eyon. See that they are well settled before you join us. The other animals bred here are extremely wild. They do not know a soldier's discipline and could rouse unwelcome attention.'

The lad wandered off with the straps clutched tight. Kal followed him and nodded for Tritan to go with Sal. Neither of them were trusted alone, Tritan noted.

'Tell me. How are we to avoid attention since you know the town so well?' Tritan suggested sarcastically.

'It's been a long time since I was truly known here. The owner I trust with my life and he is not a man prone to gossip.

Besides, our best form of camouflage for such a task is to remain fully in the light at all times. Suspicion here is only given to those who lurk in the shadows and say little. We will make a troubadour of you yet.'

'Then you'd best gut me now and use my organs as bagpipes, I'll never sing a tune while I still draw breath.'

Sal had expected as much encouragement from him, but it did seem to concern her that Tritan may not suit the part he would have to play. If they were to pass as a travelling band of farmers they needed more than one musician. But these were merely details she mused over as she rapped on the door to the side of the tavern. 'We'll have to build you up slowly then, at least be gracious and enthusiastic. We're tradesfolk remember. Never has a cynic sold a bean yet.'

The face that came to the door was weathered, but kindly and comforting. He looked at Sal as though he had expected her all along and instantly flung his arms around her. They kissed on each cheek twice as appeared to be the custom here. The wrinkled glinting eyes turned to acknowledge Tritan, who bowed his head like a child in the presence of a teacher.

'A' right, laddy, don't fret, I'll not kiss you too.' The old man extended his hand and Tritan shook it at once, offering the minimum smile required. 'And what might they call you, my boy?'

'This is Toby,' Sal interjected. Tritan had almost forgotten what his name was supposed to be. He owed Sal for that reminder.

'Toby is it? Nice, well pleasure of course, they call me Roberts. I did away with the other names, one is enough for any man.' Tritan agreed with the sentiment and was pleased, for it meant Roberts would have no interest in his latter name. Léon was a dangerous name to carry around; Augustus had smeared it across all the lands and its infamy had stained many lives.

They piled into the tavern and up a set of steps as though the whole affair had been pre-arranged. Tritan realised then that it had. Sal had sent word days before Kal had even brought Tritan to Krali fort. That meant she could not have expected them to bring him with them or in fact, the kid. Such a late change could not be wise. But Tritan suspected Kal had convinced her the lad carried less risk given his life as a thief and besides, if anything went wrong he was easily discarded. Tritan could sense the insecurity that Kal was suffering from with his own decisions, they were reckless and the risks were great. But here they all were now and this was the plan that had been set in motion, so they must follow it through.

The rooms were small, but warm and well insulated from the noise below, which meant they stood a fair chance of their clandestine activities remaining hidden. There were two large beds in the room, enough for the four of them to share. The idea of sneaking out to sleep in the stables with Diablo crossed his mind but he knew he must still tread carefully. A knock came at the door. It was Roberts.

'Come in,' shouted Sal.

'Pardon the intrusion, I trust all is in order?'

'Aye, it is, thank you, Roberts.'

'Very well, there's supper and drink downstairs for you all when you've settled; I'll have the harp tuned for you whenever you're ready. Oh and lest I forget, we've had an issue with one of the grain suppliers, he's had to tend to a personal matter so you'll be one short at your meeting come the morning.'

'Very well, we'll make do.'

Roberts left and the pair sat in silence for a while. This was not the news Sal had wanted to hear. For a change it was Tritan who broke the silence.

'Given the purpose of the meeting, one less trader will not harm the overall decision to send us on our way. News will spread as far and wide as it needs to amongst the traders.' A town such as this cannot hold secrets well, Tritan thought as he looked at Sal. If any of the townsfolk were half as inclined to gossip as she was then most of Baurticeford already knew they were here.

'Yes, I suppose you are right, nothing is lost. Come then, let us put on our very best for the evening's entertainment.'

16

You're in grave danger. You may be passing beyond this life but there is a new life awaiting you and it must be claimed. You must live!

Pietrich did not understand the urgency with which the tongue-less man spoke, such was the force of his words. He attuned his senses, forgetting his physical self and replied with the first thing that came to mind. *But if I am dying then the danger is already gone. I'm just waiting to be collected. I am a child waiting at the market for his mother to return.*

No! It is not that way at all. You must live! Again the power Pietrich felt from the tongue-less man was fierce but it was also kind.

How? asked Pietrich. There was no cure for his affliction, just herbs to steal his mind and prolong his suffering.

You are young and I must remind myself of this, but you are old beyond your years and time is not your ally. Eira, that girl you often think of, the one whose name you scream when your fever is high. Pietrich felt suddenly a line had been crossed; his privacy had never been invaded in such a way. Or had he offered his thoughts so freely? *She must help you.*

Help me how?

I do not fully understand it but of all the places you could send yourself, you came to me. You have something special inside you, Pietrich, ancient as the tales of old. Your heart is strong and your mind is keen, but we must save your body, for all we must accomplish there is little time.

I feel so tired, the longer we speak the worse it gets.

You shall rest soon. But first, try to see me where I am, not the place where your mind places me. Tell me what you see around me.

Pietrich opened his eyes, the ones that could see within his dreams. The tongue-less man was perched beside him on a rotting trunk. The very same one they often found themselves conversing on. *I see you in the place we always meet, the rotting trees that surround us are all fallen, the air is not breathable, ash floats past us like a swarm of bees.*

I am not truly here, as you are not. I wonder perhaps if it is the projection of the force guiding you that bring us to this place. There is so much to understand, but think hard about where I am, if the air around us is so spoiled I could not survive long in such a place.

Pietrich tried with great effort to see something new that had not been here before. He sensed a small fire, though he could see no light. Smoke billowed from the ground in a way that made no sense and suddenly he cast his gaze back toward the tongue-less man and saw he was no longer resting upon a rotting branch but was sat against a small wall, but it was so dark he could not tell what kind. *You are somewhere dark, a wall surrounds you and a small fire that keeps you warm casts the only light. And it's cold, much too cold.*

The tongue-less man shuffled and threw more wood on his fire, smiling to himself. *Yes, you see, it is something you can use as a tool, it need not be the case that it uses you. We must find your father.*

Somehow we must find him. The answer lies somewhere within him I am sure.

Maybe he would know you if he saw you? I could tell him all the things that you cannot.

No, he would not understand the voice he heard, it would not sound like his son, but a memory tormenting him. Neither does he know me, I would be an old man to him, without a tongue and incapable of speech. He would think me a beggar, nothing more. We must watch him from afar and influence his path. Pietrich's confusion grew stronger. *Why? I don't understand. You knew me when we first spoke.*

I have learnt many things in my sixty years. My son is, I fear, less informed than his own child.

But what if I merely see him in this place, the way I see you? Pietrich was afraid of his own limits. He was already tiring from this conversation.

Then we must learn to break down the walls of this energy. You are so close. But I am concerned for the care they give you. They sedate you to reduce the pain, but we need you to be sharper, not dulled. I am sorry, Pietrich. You will have to be strong and brave, we need your mind to be strong. I wish I did not have to ask you to bear the weight of this burden. Let me draw the place where I have settled. Try to see it and know that it is real.

The tongue-less man began to draw a mountain in the soil. A river ran across its left side and formed a wide ravine that carried down towards a small town. There were only six homes in the depiction. Crude though it was it did not resemble the black forest where they had sat all those times in the waking dreams. He settled beside his grandfather in the cold hovel by the fire and started to search outside to see the town for himself. Pietrich began to feel a strong pounding sensation in his head and the familiar orchard of charcoal trees began to swoop in around them. The dust thickened and rose from the ground where it had settled. The wind blew in towards them like an angry battalion charging swiftly into battle. It was as though their words had awakened a fierce power that was hungry and they were both lost to each other. Blinded again in his mind, the vision was now lost to him.

Abruptly, Pietrich awoke and in the darkness that he saw as he opened his eyes, he knew that he was back at home. He was being shaken like a doll.

'What are you doing?' he cried.

'Pietrich? Are you alright? You were sweating so hard and flailing your arms in front of your eyes as though you were in a sandstorm.' Marilia was panicked and beside her stood Thomas and Eira. They both stood silent staring down at the incapacitated child before them.

'It was just another dream, I think I had dust in my eye,' Pietrich said.

Thomas nodded as though this made sense to him. 'Yes, it is clear, I have often seen patients cling on to lost senses in their dreams, the mind cannot so easily let go of what the body has lost.'

Eira spat out at Thomas. 'He's not your patient to analyse so freely! He is my friend.' Eira bound towards Pietrich to try and comfort him. Marilia was proud of the girl in that moment. Thomas hung his head shamefully, he knew he got carried away when analysing the condition of those he treated. He had forgotten he stood beside the boy's mother and a girl who cared for Pietrich so deeply.

Marilia joined Eira at Pietrich's side, who had now settled his breathing. 'You have a guest. Eira has insisted that she helps tend to your needs to take the pressure from Thomas and myself, if you would like that, my love.'

'She is allowed to visit me?' Pietrich asked, a smile appearing on his face.

'All has been settled. No more hard feelings,' Marilia said comfortingly.

'The catalyst for all our problems, thankfully, is now far from this place.' The words that Thomas spoke were of no comfort at all. It was a cheap attempt to appear bold but cowardice was all that Pietrich heard in the healer's voice then. No one spoke for a short while until Pietrich decided it was time.

'Mother?' The questioning tone was soft and subtle. 'May you leave Eira and I by ourselves? It has been so long since I spoke to someone my age without an audience.'

Marilia sat up startled to be dismissed so soon, but she understood the need her son had and his time was growing short. Thomas left a small vial beside the bed and rested his hand on Eira's shoulder. 'Once you leave make sure he takes this, it will help him to sleep better.'

Eira nodded and watched as Marilia kissed Pietrich on the cheek and then left with Thomas.

Alone at last, Pietrich thought. But it was not to play the games of their childhood as they once had. Now the two of them, so young, must deceive an entire village and somehow relinquish the remedy in place of a more potent linctus. Pietrich was far too weak to leave the house now. He was useless in many ways and Eira must take on the full extent of the burden. *The only one I can trust*, he thought, for a moment believing the tongue-less man was with him, but he heard nothing. He wondered about all that he was going through. He wanted to tell it all, and now. But he knew he must be careful, this was not an easy thing to express. Not even his own mother would understand.

'You're looking to the walls,' Eira chuckled. 'You never did look me straight in the eye. I'm sorry it took me so long to visit. I have been fighting all sorts of battles to see you.'

Pietrich responded with an inspired glow, tilting his sightless gaze to the sound of Eira's breathing. 'The fighting has only just begun. I've something to tell you and at first you will struggle to believe it. But you must listen to everything I have to say.' The smile that Eira had come to love so much widened before her and Pietrich spoke again. 'We have a mission you and I.'

17

Tritan looked longingly at the window as drops of water pattered against the glass in a soft percussive rhythm and he lost himself in the torrent's song. It had been steadily raining since last night's performance. Tritan had met and sat with many of the farmers whilst Sal lulled them with her voice and the strumming of her harp. Kal had intended on taking the boy outside, unnoticed, to ascertain the seed supplies but the rain had settled in and restricted them. It was far from ideal but they would have to stay another night. They all knew the longer their presence was known, the greater the risk would be, but they had no choice. On the plus side it seemed Tritan was a greater performer than even he would have believed. After his third drink he had almost convinced himself he was the cultivator of a new, cheaper form of seed and had fully embraced his character of Toby. No one paid any interest of course, as had been expected, but the important information had been planted. Smiling faces had reflected back at him, wishing him luck as he thanked them and thought of the lives behind those smiles that would be ensnared should the plan come to fruition. It struck him then how far from the path Augustus had led the 11th Legion they were now leading. The intentions were still as dark and controlling but he had to give credit to Kal; the man knew what he was doing, in spite of the mess in which this ensemble had come together. But Tritan was distracted even still by the absence of his father. He never would have believed he would feel this way but he wished for his presence, he had so many questions that were unanswered. He thought about the suicidal mission Augustus had ventured upon. There was a part of Tritan too that wondered whether something really existed beyond the impassable mist. Was there something hidden away that might save Pietrich? No. That was impossible. He cursed himself for the thought. In truth he believed that Augustus attempting to traverse the barren landscape was as futile as a leaf trying to float upstream.

The rain had been singing its song now for hours. The sky was showing signs of light at last but the soft chorus of water splashing had become drones of warning snarls. There was suddenly a sense of panic amongst the group; this was not the kind of deluge that visited fleetingly.

The rest of the townsfolk of Baurticeford had shut themselves into their homes and all kinds of travellers had holed up in the taverns and stables, except in those which had flooded. Thankfully the rivers of water ran right past The Oxen tavern and its adjacent stables, apart from some overspill that caused minor flooding where the doors met the street. Their horses were safe for now. The same could not be said for those in some of the stables in the lower part of the town. A couple of steeds had been swept away and crashed into one of the homes by the south entrance. The staunch populace reacted by coming together in hordes to make safe where they could. It was times like this when the borders of estrangement between neighbours were broken down; the outsiders and foreigners who had come from distant places were suddenly treated with equal respect and afforded their fair share of aid from those in a position to tackle the rain. Man and woman alike began to dish out the water from their rain-invaded homes. But the fight had only just begun.

For three more days the rain fell as heavy as it had begun. It was like a waterfall had cut through the sky. There had been around five hundred homes in Baurticeford before the licentious downpour had taken dozens of them away. Only rubble now remained; their inhabitants had been sheltered wherever possible. The room in which Tritan, Sal, Kal and the kid were holed up had become a domicile for refugees and families came and went whilst their fate was decided. The business of the seed had been long forgotten and every one of them, who had set out from Krali fort, played their part to protect the town. They had joined in the efforts to redirect the newly formed river, that now ploughed through the centre of the town, around the perimeters. This had involved spending hours in a hailstorm that had arrived to worsen the situation. The ice had battered against their skin as they hauled the wood supply north of the town and created a diversion that sent the water through the crop fields that rested outside the town walls.

When a large section of the forest had been removed for the work, the river finally diverted from the destructive path it was on. The deputation that the four companions formed had become instrumental in the survival of many of the homes of Baurticeford. It was as if the shame of their ill intentions had been tested. Though fortune smiled down on Kal from the same place from whence the rain had fallen. The entire seed supply had been lifted by the floods and washed away with the shelters that had housed them. He had succeeded in the most malicious part of his plan without having to commit a single ill deed. But

they had all colluded with their minds and Kal wondered if he
had not inculcated the rain the very same way.

They were held up in The Oxen for two whole weeks before
the showers became lighter and eventually the sun broke
through and reclaimed its throne. They were alone again for the
first time since the evening when they had arrived. They shared
in that silent moment a consideration for Baurticeford and its
people, the glances they gave each other were those of equals
who had profited in soul and mind from the vicissitudes of the
town. It was the boy who broke the silence.

'Whenever a man conceives of evil, nature rises up to
remind us she is the one who controls us all.' He recited the
words his father had said to him the last time they had seen
each other, a parting that had lasted far longer than intended.
The kid had memorised the words and finally knew what they
meant. The control one man held over another was an illusion;
they were all prisoners to fate. Kal stood to position himself
above the rest of them; the time for equality was over.

'She has certainly made a bold statement. I for one, think
that I will accept the favour she has reached out to offer us.
We'll recover our things and set out in the morning. Tonight I'll
speak with Roberts and offer our condolences. Those now made
homeless will be welcomed to stay in the fort, and after we
shelter them for a time they'll be begging for what we have to
offer.' Kal looked about the room at the others and nodded. Sal
was remarkably quiet for once and looked away the instant she
met with Kal's proud expression. He turned and left the room.
Tritan rubbed his hands together; they were freezing cold in
spite of the hearth they had set ablaze in the room with whatever wood they could scrabble together. He recognised the cold
trembling he had felt moments after he had taken Wendel's life.
Before he had come to this town the idea of manipulating its
people and ruining their seed supplies had hardly bothered

him. But, resulting from whatever sordid intervention had made their mission simpler, he now felt sick to the pit of his stomach. Knowing the thanks and praise these townsfolk would offer them for their aid and seed, in spite of the ill purposes with which they had set out from Kralii fort, caused a splitting sensation to resonate in Tritan's skull. He wondered why the decision to do wrong to another was easier to bear than the profiting from another's suffering that you had not caused.

TRITAN WAS READYING the horses downstairs; the equipment was all soaked through with boggy mud of the kind that lingers for months after it's cleaned away. The kid was trying his best to scrub the layers of mud from the coats of the horses. It was as tough as running a brush through straw. Eventually they decided enough was enough, the rest could wait until they arrived back at the fort.

'When was the last time you were home?' the lad finally asked Tritan. It was a question he had considered for weeks but there was never a good time to broach the subject. Tritan was taken aback by the sudden interest.

'The place you're referring to, I never considered to be home, and not until I left it did I realise of what value it was to me. But I guess it's been half a season by now. You miss your family, don't you?' Tritan asked.

'They need me, if that's what you mean.'

'I'm sorry, if I knew a way…'

'Forget about it, I know there's nothing you can do. You proved as much back at the landowner's homestead. You're stuck in the mud worse than I am.'

It hurt to hear the truth aloud.

'Nothing is permanent.'

'At least I am close to home, for that I can be thankful,' the kid responded. 'Your village is far to the south?'

'Yes. It's about as far south as you can travel without reaching the coast. I never realised how safe and secluded it was until seeing how ravaged so much of the lands were these past months.'

'But you helped to ravish them! How can you not have known before what you had done?'

Tritan shook his head. 'I can't offer you an explanation that will make sense, because I don't understand it myself. All I know is the world feels different to me now.'

'And yet now you still do nothing. These people's lives have been ruined and yet you still plan to exploit them!'

'It's not my plan.'

'But you're a part of this! You're just a liar!' The boy spat out the last words and stormed off leaving the horses to whicker and Tritan had to try hard to control them. They'd become unusually disturbed as if they had understood what the kid had said and wanted to show their agreement.

Tritan was not given long to consider the conversation, as a man came running up the street towards him with a panic-stricken expression.

'Toby! Thank God you're still here, you must come at once, all of you!'

'Calm down, tell me what has happened.'

'We've had word from a northern settlement; they were encased in ice and snow. I don't know if anyone has survived.'

Tritan's heart sank, he recalled all the rain and endless nights these past weeks, sleeping rough and comforting those whose lives had been upended again, so close to the end of the war. The days had felt like years and as they worked, soaked through to the skin, he'd believed there was some cleansing of his past. He knew the small settlement that the man spoke of and he knew now that Baurticeford had not really suffered so fiercely. Suddenly the washed away homes felt like a small burden, the refugees had some hope, places to stay, people to offer them sympathies. Krali village would have been buried in tons of snow. They had no way to protect themselves the way the fort did. Every house would be beneath a mountain of ice. If anyone had survived the first two nights, they would not have survived a third, let alone two weeks. His soul was crushed as he imagined all the bodies lying beneath the frozen ground; the image of their blue skin and frozen eyes haunted his thoughts. He imagined the children's families' judging stares as they reached out to touch him with their icy fingers. Tritan knew then that love could satisfy hunger more than food; quench thirst more than water and it could destroy your heart with greater ease than the point of a sword. He realised he loved the boy, in all the ways he had never loved Pietrich, his own son. He knew that when he saw the kid, he imagined Pietrich grown older. The boy whose name he didn't even know was like a clue to a future that could have been but now was lost forever. He thought about his son lying on his deathbed, all those years he would never know, all the things he would never do. The spirits of the perished, frozen families called out to him, *come to us, brother*, they said, *come to us and you will see there is another path*. The kid was going home after all.

18

'I can take anything the world throws at me, all the solitude and pain and disappointment. I just wish I didn't love you so much. I can't bear to love someone who feels nothing for me in return. I upended everything to be closer to you not knowing the outcome and after all, when I thought you were mine, I lost you. Now I'm so confused, I don't know where I stand and you seem to love him still, one who has hurt you so much. Abandoned you and your son. I'm still here and no matter how many times you make it clear you feel nothing for me, I go on loving you. I never asked for that. It is not a feeling I nurtured willingly. I am a victim of fate's cruel brush. He has painted for me a life that I would not wish on any other. I may not want for anything... But without a soul intact how can I appreciate any of the gifts that are given to me?'

Marilia stood staring in shock at Thomas. All she had asked him was how his day was going. She had distanced herself from him these past few weeks, knowing that kissing him was a grave mistake. After all, you can't throw wood onto a fire and expect the flames to die. The fire of his love was burning brighter now than any other time she could recall. But in spite of all she felt for him, it meant nothing to her. She knew she should care more, she knew how much he must suffer, for she suffered in the same way for another.

'Thomas, I don't know. I don't know what I should say. Right now, all I can think about is my son, Pietrich needs a strong mother and I can't weaken myself with other distractions.'

'And when he is gone. Who will save you from the torment you will feel?'

'Don't use that against me. Anything else but not that!'

'I would feel ashamed if I had not fallen so low.' He took a deep breath, already regretting the words. 'I am sorry, against my will the demons in my mind wish for me to hurt you. It's not what I intended.'

'We should stay apart for a while.'

Thomas knew the truth of the declaration but he could not hold back his tears. Verity was often more painful than lies.

Thomas gathered himself, trying to bury his torment. 'I'll send the medicine with Eira, she's become very good at tending to Pietrich these past weeks.'

'Yes, Pietrich has seemed almost twice as strong since she began to help out.'

Thomas suddenly looked at Marilia with a curious expression. He knew she was right, he too had noticed some apparent improvement in the boy, but something about it did not sit well with him. This caused Marilia to meet his concern with her own.

'What is it? What is wrong?'

'Sorry, it's nothing. I drifted off. I am going to miss you.'

'It's just temporary.'

'Tonight alone will feel like forever to me.'

'I need time to think.' She took Thomas's hand for a moment. 'Your hands are freezing.'

'I think my heart has stopped beating.'

She kissed his hand for a brief moment and began to cradle his fingers in her own. It was the worst goodbye Thomas had ever known.

THE WHOLE CONVERSATION had taken place in the furthest part of the village but Pietrich had heard it all as though he had sat right beside them. Eira had succeeded in being left alone with him to administer the medications. Which meant disposing of them in the ground on the walk between the healer's workshop and Pietrich's bedroom. She always hid a small vial of enriched herb tea in her pocket that she placed inside the containers that Thomas gave to her. Her mother seemed not to have noticed the diminishing supplies of her store and she prayed her ignorance would continue. Pietrich had certainly suffered more pain as a result of avoiding the prescription but his conversations with Eira had become richer and he had recently been able to speak with the tongue-less man whenever he wished. He was starting to perceive the world that surrounded his grandfather, but he feared greatly for him as all had gone quiet since the visions of heavy snow that fell around the small village where he had hidden away. The temptation to search out his own father was fierce, but he had promised not to try, only once had he gently brushed up against something that felt familiar to him, like his father, but he had shied away as quickly as he had arrived. He still did not understand why it was so dangerous, but his grandfather had tried to explain by beginning to tell him the story of Rose. They had reached the part where mother and child escaped into the mist when the retelling had been interrupted by the heavy snow that had started to fall. Then came the wind and ferocious torrents of hailstones. The tongue-less man had severed their connection that moment and vanished ever since. Pietrich began to wonder if he would ever know the end of the story.

A knocking sound came at the window and he imagined the beautiful face that lingered there, staring in at him while he was lying helpless. Eira often did this to tease him but his revenge was in the hearing of the beating of her heart. Her breath sounded to him like an autumn gust as it danced around a forest, toying with the fallen leaves as it took them in its grip. That sensation was his alone, she would never know the way he sensed the life that flowed inside her.

19

A burning rage of jealousy and admonition surged through his thoughts. Boscelito was tired of the fighting, tired of watching men die and tired of taking their lives but he could not understand why he was being sent away. Surely of all of them he was the one Augustus needed at his side the most? After all, he was the pillar Augustus had rested upon during the worst of the years they had suffered together. Augustus had remained feared by all that knew him, all except Boscelito, for during those moments when all hope was lost and the sadness was too much to bear, he was the one who accepted the tears from the tyrant of men. It was he, Boscelito alone, who had witnessed the weakness in the unbreakable soldier. They had grown up together as if brothers. Boscelito had never known his own birth parents. The Léon household took him as a boy servant and being of almost equal age to Augustus, he was the perfect fencing, riding and scribing partner. Boscelito felt he owed his life to the family. He stayed by Augustus's side when he joined the armies that were assembling to overthrow the councils of Harmion. Borstan, a descendant of one of the founders of the collective council named Harmony to instil the principles they upheld, enlisted many fighting men to help him overthrow the political rule of his ancestors. There were ten legions of soldiers that advocated the peace on behalf of the council but Borstan knew that they would quickly turn to his favour should he show his strength. Borstan had chosen Augustus to lead the 11th Legion, his own private army. Borstan was eager to take power and to re-establish the lost lineage of royalty, to satisfy all his childhood dreams of a crown upon his head. But his ambitions ran short as the resistance that had formed to counter his desires successfully assassinated him and so all of the soldiers loyal to Borstan turned their heads to Augustus for leadership. Although Boscelito disagreed heavily with the new ruler's philosophy, he remained loyal to his old friend.

Boscelito made laborious the task of sorting through his possessions, trying to pack as much as he dare for the mission he had been sent upon. He was sad to leave so many of the books behind that kept him company each night as the rest of the legionnaires drank themselves to sleep. He was a rare man, Augustus had once told him, and the parting words that had been spoken to Boscelito as he was given his orders still resonated as if the world repeated them to him in echoed verses.

To love the current of a river, you have to float downstream.

Boscelito had left without further hesitation, his heart broken, but he knew there would be no change of mind. Augustus had tasked him with searching afar for those who were neutral in the war. He was to turn them to Augustus's cause and strengthen the 11th Legion into an unstoppable force. Little did he or Augustus know at the time that this parting would be the last time they would know of each other as friends.

THE FLICKERING CANDLE roared like a furnace in the small enclosure where Boscelito warmed his hands. He looked down and noticed the wrinkles and varicose veins that showed his age. He thought about that day when Augustus had ordered him to leave the 11th Legion behind and in doing so he had left also their cruel ideology. Yet some part of him still yearned for the friendship that also departed all those years ago.

The memories of his time in the war haunted him. A lifetime left alone in a cell with nothing but one's own thoughts for company, was not grounds for a sane mind. He used to believe that a man must survive with his body intact to salvage any dignity in the time that was stolen from him. But he had been wrong; it is the mind that must survive, for a broken mind is harder to heal. The scars run deeper and once you lose a part of your humanity, that void can never be filled, like a phantom pain from a lost limb. There is no solace in the closing of one's eyes and dreaming, for the dreams become nightmares, attacking the soul and bit by bit they destroy what little humanity remains.

Living like a wild animal had perhaps been one of the only things that kept Boscelito alive all these years. Simple tasks like finding food and firewood to keep warm at night could fill an entire day, leaving little time for the mind to ponder the meaning of existence. He had lost the skill of language the moment he had bitten out his own tongue. A fast irrational decision that he took moments before his capture to ensure he could not be tortured for information. He had learnt many things in his years away and the risk of that information falling into the wrong hands was too great. But his mind still created stanzas. He had memorized many passages from all the books he had studied and the words latched themselves onto him. The histories and geographies and political discourses within those pages had been his only companions.

The past two weeks had been hard. The snow had locked him in his cave and now it was a cage. Boscelito remembered the sensation of missing the light of the sky; he had endured years without natural light in the grey world that Augustus had gifted him. He wept as he remembered that day, when he had watched his son stolen from his mother's arms; the guard had described relentlessly the butchering he had given her once the child was safe. Augustus made clear the boy would be raised to believe she had been killed in childbirth. Boscelito had presumed his son was dead too, until years later when he had heard news that Augustus had supposedly fathered a child, a fierce warrior Tritan, who was used like a mindless weapon. He knew immediately it must be the same boy, the years made sense but more significantly Augustus carried a dark secret with him that no man knew, no man but he. Boscelito had stumbled across the secret unwittingly when they were far younger men. A festival had been in full swing and the two friends were dancing with the village girls. After plenty of ale they were led off to the stables. Boscelito was a handsome and confident man and no stranger to women. But Augustus was a brute and not pleasing to the eye. The girl that had chosen him did so for his station within the Léon family. But in doing so she also exposed his impotence. Boscelito had discovered Augustus with the strangled girl buried in straw the following morning. Augustus was weeping and confessed everything to Boscelito then for the first and only time. The girl's death had been considered a drunken accident and was covered up. Nor was any more discussed of Augustus's condition between the two men.

Jealousy of the things I can do and you cannot, but arrogance for the things I cannot do and you can. Boscelito had used the words as a sort of prayer to remind himself of the man who had so altered the current of his life. He felt that in a way, Augustus was also responsible for the hole he was hiding in now.

Boscelito's supplies had started to run low and the air in the cave was so thin he was barely able to keep a flame alight. He worried for the villagers who lived in the huts just through the clearing where his cave was hidden. He had heard shouts of terror coming from the settlement in the first days of the snow but now it had been quiet for a week, at least he guessed it had been a week by now, for telling time was impossible when you had no way of seeing the light of day. Tiredness became his only clue to distinguishing day from night. He had dedicated a small part of each day to digging through the snow, melting it down for drinking water. He had managed to clear a path towards the cave's entrance about the length of a cart but there was still no sign of the exit. He had hoped that Pietrich would visit him these past days, just to talk if nothing else. But something was wrong; the boy's reach did not seem strong enough to be able to grasp him through the frozen walls.

In a desperate moment, Boscelito took up all the firewood he had remaining, enough for three nights warmth, and rested it all up against the snow wall that restrained him from the outside world. He knew this moment of inspiration was a risk and the danger with inspiration is that it first feels the same whether a good or a terrible idea. But he had no one to confer with and instead he must trust his instincts and be brave.

As he bent down with the candle to set the kindling alight he prayed his bravery would not go unrewarded, for if he failed he would have simply committed an act of stupidity. He would leave the judgement to hindsight and thought no more of it as the fire began to roar. The heat was intense and as each section of snow drifted into the earth, Boscelito wrestled with the heat to move the fire forwards, scorching his hands moments before plunging them into the snow to reduce the damage. The process continued until his hands were a fleshy mess and the supply of wood had all but been depleted.

It was dark now inside the cave. The icy wall still stood but as the final embers faded Boscelito saw a marking on the cave wall. He stood, suddenly filled with hope as he recognised the markings he had used to keep a tally of the age of his meat from hunting. The snow had mostly washed it away but some charcoal signs were still visible and he knew then that he was less than the length of a man from the outside world. He took to digging with his hands, the icy cold making them so numb he barely noticed the pain from the blistering. But this was a slow way to dig and eventually he began to tire.

He didn't stop; to rest would be to fail. If he paused for just a second the fatigue would take hold of him and the pain that he had kept at bay would flood across his body like a storm.

He dug and dug and then he dug some more. Large chunks of the snow above him began to give way and he kicked them aside, paying close attention in case the snow that had built up outside fell inwards. He took to scraping at one far side of the cave and did his best to compact the snow beside it to create a sort of roof. The roof was key to his survival. If a part of it fell now the whole lot would collapse on top of him and the game would be over. Boscelito forgot about all the suffering and all the injustice. He forgot his wife and the soft touch of her skin as he confessed his love for her. He forgot about the brief moment when he had seen Tritan being carried away, freshly born and basked in blood. Now he was alive and the breaking light of the day that reached down to grab him was like an embrace from a long lost mother. It was worth waiting thirty years before he may yet again see his son. It was worth it all. The moment would pass he knew, those fears and horrors would return like the rain, but for now he was untouchable and the voice that greeted him shared in his delectation.

Grandfather, I thought I'd lost you! He's close, so close to you. But he is not alone. They're coming, they're all coming!

20

The storm came suddenly. Dozens of galloping hooves shook the earth and the snow-tipped trees offered their burdens into the sky as the wind carried the white dust through the air like a starling cluster. Each man and woman who rode felt the brushing of icy fingers across their shins for the settled snow was so deep. At the head of the cavalcade was Kal. Beside him rode the full remaining force of the 11th Legion, thirteen men and three women, including Sal who they had sent ahead from Baurticeford to Krali fort in order to gather as much aid as they dared spare for the rescue. Sal had brought them all except the stable hands and cooks. But all that any of the riders saw before them was devastation. Tritan rode in tandem with the kid. They were doing their best to determine where the buried houses rested beneath the white hills that were once Krali village.

They unearthed houses for the entire afternoon, gaining entry through the raised windows where possible but the story of each home was as sad as the last. Families had huddled together for warmth but now were cold and solid like statues, their limbs fused together and interwoven like a plaited bouquet of blue flowers. There was only one house remaining. Tritan knew by the way the boy acted that this last home was his. For the first time the 11th allowed their youngest member to take the lead.

The kid brushed aside the final clumps of snow that blocked his entry to the door. Tritan watched him solemnly as he opened the heavy wooden portal and listened to the crashing icicles as they broke onto the stone floor of the entrance. The sound was chilling. The splintering shards were a prelude to the shattered lives that lay inside. The boy stepped into the tomb as slowly as his body would allow, as if to prolong the fragile hope. The kitchen was empty; he focused his eyes across to the adjacent rooms and saw the continuing emptiness. One room beckoned him. It was where his younger sister had slept and where he had visited her during all the years that she had been afraid of those childish nightmares. It was here that he discovered them all together, atop the bed and under a mountain of sheets and blankets. Their three heads were laid beside one another. They had shared their fate together. The kid knelt down in front of them and brought his hands together to pray. The prayer was a silent supplication. He would never share its sentiment with another living soul. Tritan suspected that the kid had prayed his family had shared their love with each other in their final moments.

'I should have been here.' The words came out like a statement, numb and devoid of feeling. 'I should have been with them, either to save them or to die with them.'

The lad pulled the top sheet over their peaceful faces. It was the last remaining gesture he could make. He closed his eyes and wished he could close his ears too for outside Sy was shouting fiercely. Raging about the wasted effort they had all made by coming here. His voice carried through the thick walls of ice and stone and it stirred a rage in the boy. But he wanted only to think of his family in this moment. He wanted to say goodbye. In that instant his whole life took a different shape and all meaning left him. The past he had lived seemed empty. The future held no purpose. As though the kid's thoughts had been spoken aloud, Tritan rested a calm hand on his shoulder. He should have spurned him. The hate he had carried for the ex-soldier was so strong before but now it subsided for the gift of such a simple comfort. He had blamed the brute for everything that had passed since that day he had first met him. But in the moment of his utter weakness the kid found there was a kind empathy in the resting palm upon his back. It was in this moment that the boy chose to forgive him. Nothing made sense nor did it seem fair. Nothing was fair. But forgiveness was the only light he held on this day, the darkest day he had ever known.

Outside the gathering continued to be unsettled. Sy had sparked an ill feeling in many of those who also believed the journey had been wasted.

'We'll bury the dead but then we should move back to the fort. There's still time to make it back before nightfall.' Kal addressed the tired and weary members of the 11th as he walked amongst them; the cold was stretching its tentacles over them from their feet upwards.

'No, we should leave them as they are, we've wasted enough time as it is and if we want to be certain to return before dark we need all the hours of light we can muster.'

'Sy, do not mistake my orders as open for debate.'

The kid and Tritan emerged from the last house to find the assembly stood awaiting a final decision. The boy addressed them all boldly.

'No one touches my family. None of you here has the right to bury them.' As if to emphasise the point of his demand the lad slammed the wooden door shut and slid across the steel bolt, shutting them all out and turning his back on those he had loved. 'I'll help you with the others but my family stay in their home.'

'I ought to burn their corpses in front of you while I dance with joy.'

The kid stood his ground even as Sy glared at him with an arrogant smirk.

'All of you get to digging at once,' Tritan intervened, gesturing towards them all. They didn't hesitate for long. 'The rest of us will carry the bodies. Anyone who ignores their responsibility or so much as suggests indifference will be run through with my sword and right now I don't care much if I have to kill you all.'

They were either too tired to argue further or too scared. Tritan couldn't tell, but it didn't matter for they all set about the task of burying, silently and with no additional reproaches. It was long and hard work and only Sy moved sluggishly, but he too remained quiet and this Tritan concluded was the best he could expect.

A large communal pit was dug, about four feet deep. The families were laid out side by side together. But ultimately it felt much like the mass graves they had dug during the war to protect themselves from the rotting bodies. Tritan couldn't help but wince at the familiarity. Burying soldiers in such a way had never bothered him but seeing the women and children lying beneath him as soil was flung over their corpses was hard to bear.

The fading light encouraged them all to work faster and it wasn't long before they were packing up and readying to leave. Jaz was giving the horses a quick feed and Sy was already straddling his horse, eager to move at the head of the convoy. Reed, the skinny and quiet man was the last to ready himself for the journey home, but he was taken aback as he searched for his horse that was no longer there. He moved from man to man with a confused expression on his face. Kal noticed his discomfort and trotted over to discover his concern.

'You idiot, you've left her untied again?'

Reed responded with an angry look, but remained quiet.

'Where is the kid?' Kal continued. 'Don't tell me we lost the boy as well!'

They all looked about, including Tritan. It was certain. The kid had vanished.

'Kid… kid!' Tritan bellowed but there was no response. He realised then that he had not seen the boy since he had thrown his last shovel of soil into the pit. A long hour had passed since then. It didn't take long for them to realise the vanishing horse was no coincidence.

'Let's get moving, everyone. At once!'

Kal gave the order but Tritan was long gone, riding north with Diablo. As he rode, he sensed all the wild ideas that must be churning around the kid's mind. To see his family in such a state just moments before could have inspired any number of crazed actions. Tritan feared the worst. All he wanted now was to protect the kid but he knew what that might mean; it could be the end for them both.

Tritan rode hard and long, doing his best to put distance between himself and the 11th as he drew closer to Kralii fort. He thought of all the things he might discover in the derelict fort and wondered how far behind him the ravaging legionnaires would be; hungry for blood at the mere inconvenience. Tritan began to think of the sword hanging at his side. He wondered how sharp it was and realised he hadn't honed it since they had made their way across the razor sharp mountains. He didn't know how many of them he could kill before it became as blunt as a spoon. These weren't simple swordsmen he was plotting against. His attempt to protect the boy would be futile. The bloody future projected into the forefront of his mind, and although he had threatened them all not long ago, it had been a hollow, angry gesture. He knew then that simply fighting his way out would not be an option. He would have to escape with the kid, reliving the hope that Wendel had passed onto him and Tritan felt emboldened with the second chance that now seemed so much sweeter. If it was the last deed he committed, he would at least ensure the safety of the boy, even if it meant the end of his own life.

Diablo galloped down the path with such grace it was as though he could see again. The memory of the passage to the fort helped and even as Tritan's thoughts drifted the horse did not falter. Tritan began to think of Augustus. He hated the life that had been forced upon him and as the kid had once blamed him, he blamed his father. *Father.* The word felt strange to him as he said it over and over in his mind. It was clear to him then that if he survived this charade he would hunt down the man, somehow, wherever he was now. The fear he had carried for thirty years became anger and suddenly he needed his revenge. If he had to kill the entire 11th Legion that remained, Kal, Sy, even Jaz and Sal, to be free to seek out his revenge and discover the man who had dictated his whole life, he would fight with a greater purpose than in all those years of war that had made him what he was. He was a killer, that much was certain and he would awaken again the sleeping animal that lay inside his soul. But now he would kill for himself, not for some orders or a trifling payment like those he had received as a sellsword. He considered the lesson of Castellar that he had memorised from all those years ago. He knew that to take life by his own design had not been the purpose of the lesson, but if it was his own interpretation that now drove him, it was enough.

· · ·

KRALI VILLAGE HAD BEEN LEFT MUCH as the 11th had found it with its inhabitants buried beneath the ice and soil. It sat still amongst the valley as a quiet wisp of a breeze fluttered and dusted the gravesite with the same snow that had trapped the whole village in their homes. The breeze was for no one but the dead and Boscelito stood back into the shadow of the tree that had hidden him as he had watched the burial, to allow the passing wind its purpose. The sight of Tritan had ruptured his heart. For so long he had dreamed of laying his eyes upon his son and there he had stood. Six feet tall and strong, but already old and worn. At first he could not be sure if he recognised the man for he had only seen him as a newborn babe, but the eyes with their steely look were those of his mother. It was then that Boscelito realised fully how much of his life had been lived in his absence. He felt sadness creeping in and readied himself for his own journey north; tracking the riders who had departed with a killing rage that had buried the kindness they had shown to the dead as swiftly as they had buried their bodies. Boscelito became increasingly unsure of his own actions, his own son could see him as a threat. Maybe Tritan would even kill him, uncertain of the menace, as there was no way of telling his son all the truth that was trapped inside him. Somehow though, he would reclaim his son, and as though their lives were finally running in tandem, Boscelito began to dream. He dreamed of revenge against Augustus. The vision was so strong it almost had a taste and smell. He fed on the dream and once again he felt strong. Strong like the day he had left Augustus in the camp to journey to the islands. A strength that had awoken his true humanity.

21

The fire blazed high into the sky and tickled the amber clouds that were painted by the setting sun. A ring of sodden soil had encircled the fort like a moat where the heat had stripped away the thick layers of snow. The smoke and flames were visible for leagues in all directions and at a first glance it seemed impossible to consider a point of entry. The open gate was the only option. The wooden stakes that were tied together with thick cord had been left wide open and the gap between them was the only invitation Tritan received. But the invitation was a sinister one. To accept entry to this place was to enter a treacherous inferno. It was a deathly invitation. The kind of death that no man could help dreading as he imagined the heat peeling back skin and boiling blood, with lungs, blackened and withered.

Tritan left Diablo well clear of the burning fort and waded his way through the boggy earth with a thick rag tied around his mouth to filter the smoke for the few breaths he would be certain to require. He crouched low as he half ran and half crawled, searching for the clearest path to the source of the fire.

The mud clung to him and weighed him down as the intensity of the heat increased, congealing the sludge into a restrictive suit of armour. Realising the protection it earned him from the scorching temperatures he pasted his hands and face. As he trudged through the gauntlet he saw that it was the storehouses that were the source. By now the fire must have been burning for a while and he knew the seed supply inside the storehouses was ruined. The kid had taken from Kal what Kal had intended on taking from the townsfolk of Baurticeford. No one would be controlling the supplies now and after the long storm that had ravished the northern towns, all men and women would be equal in their famine.

Tritan rushed past all the empty barracks, opening his eyes only when he dared, searching out the boy. The smoke blinded him and before long the rag tied around his mouth became as useless as if he was fully embracing the smoke with every breath. Tritan was disoriented and the fort gates were as lost to him as the little sister was to the kid. He remembered the families' cold faces as the fire lent its heat to his burning skin. He took smaller steps, hoping at least that luck would take him back to the gap where he had entered. The small steps were what saved him as he stumbled across a large object in the narrow street between two flaming buildings. Tritan managed to keep his balance and realised he had stepped on the unconscious body of the lad. Kneeling, Tritan fumbled for the boy's throat, locating a faint pulse below his jaw. He threw the kid over his shoulder and dared to open his eyes for a split second; it was all he needed to see that the fort entrance was just thirty strides away to their side. He took each step with bated breath, praying he would not pass out until they were at a safe distance from the spreading conflagration.

The short distance to safety became more elusive. The closer they came to salvation the less likely it seemed they would reclaim their freedom from the raging fortress. Blackness started to cloud Tritan's vision and tumbling stars blurred the surface of his eyes. The world disappeared and all senses left him as he slipped into a kind of dream. The dream was unfocused and his whole life raced through his mind as flashes of angry moments. He was born and died over and over in an endless loop of tranquillity and pain. He laughed and cried and said goodbye to all those he had known before they came to him again. They clung onto him as he fell into an abyss of uncertainty but the further he fell the looser the grasping ghosts of his life held on. A voice called out to him from the darkness. It was familiar yet not one he had heard in his waking life. It was the sweet sound of an encouraging mother, lending her affection to his plight with a soft gentleness that reminded him of his dream of Rose. Ash cleared like parting curtains and he was now wading across a lake towards an island. Or perhaps he was the one being carried. He was lying across the shoulder of his mother looking down at the murky water that churned and splashed as a storm formed waves that swept over his face between struggling breaths. The eyes of the soldiers Elucifice had sent in pursuit of them were staring at their struggling strokes as they neared the island that would trap them. Suddenly a final wave, large and fierce, fell over him just as he took a large gulp of air. He spluttered and coughed and opened his eyes.

'Tritan! Wake up.' The kid was shaking him with intensity. 'Wake up, you great oaf.'

Tritan choked on the muddy water and retched. He was lying on the bank of the newly formed moat and saw the trail that his body had made whilst being dragged out of the bog. The kid had woken just at the moment of his collapse and the saviour had become the saved. Fortune had smiled upon them and Tritan laughed as he spoke.

'I suppose now I can't damn you for your actions, you've redeemed yourself too soon.'

'I didn't expect it would all burn so quickly,' the kid confessed. 'But you have to admit, it was effective.'

'Yes, you've done well to ensure our demise. Maybe it was better to die in the fort because another fire is coming for us and believe me when I tell you that this one will endeavour to burn us as slowly and painfully as they can contrive.'

'There's nothing they can do to me now.' The kid spat the words out stubbornly.

Tritan shook his head, growing more serious as he scraped off layers of solid mud. 'They will find a way to make the suffering worse than you can imagine; they always find a way. I don't expect the people of Baurticeford will thank you either.'

'They'll find a way to survive. Better that they struggle together in unity than bow to the control of your precious legion.'

Regaining his composure, Tritan grabbed the kid, and headed to the place where Diablo had stood calmly, hoping that his master would return unscathed.

'We must leave here at once.'

'Why don't we stay and fight,' the boy boldly suggested. 'At least they'll have to kill us quickly then.'

'No, we need to split them up. Borderland forest is close, they'll have to break into small units to track us there.'

The two companions prepared themselves as best they could in the minutes that followed, before mounting Diablo and riding off towards the forest that bordered Harmion and the mist that separated it from the unknown lands of Orldin. Tritan knew that that was where he would find Augustus. He believed strongly that Augustus would have survived the journey through the mist. It was likely he had been the first since Rose had taken her baby Maldus from the clutches of the old king,

Elucifice, but Tritan knew deep down that he would see his father again. He wondered what trials would await him but he knew that he couldn't take the kid with him; first he would have to ensure his safety somehow. A feeling of anger surged over him and he recognised the adrenaline that had coursed through his veins on the eve of all those battles throughout the war. This time he would fight against those who had once fought beside him. And he would fight alone with a half worn sword and a young lad who was as good as dead if any one of the 11th came within swinging distance of him. He had relied upon brute force for his whole life and in that he had always bested any man. But now he was the hunted prey and tactics would be his most potent weapon. The forest would be the battleground for this private war and the trees his allies, the blunt sword his weapon, and the kid his reason to fight. It was a greater reason than he had had before. But he knew it wasn't only for the boy he would be fighting. A simpler life had evaded him the day he had borne a son. The reason to go on living had grown in him each day and he no longer recognised himself. For the first time in his life, he would be fighting for his family. Tritan dared to hope that he would see them again. It was a fool's hope but it had settled inside him, planting itself unwaveringly inside his heart, claiming its throne; from that moment on it would never let go. He mused over the irony as the seed of hope that he might somehow save his son lay hand in hand with the answers he so deeply craved from his father. Tritan would fight to see his son once more or he would die trying. But first he must confront his past and that past was Augustus.

22

T he sounds were unfamiliar to the kid. The way the branches swayed in the breeze and creaked was more ominous than any of the forests where he had hunted and even the songs of the singing birds held a different tune. It was a series of warnings that he heard, the language was impossible to understand but the sentiment told him to stay away. *This is not your home.* The boy heard the voices in his head and was consumed by the guilt of trespassing as they made their way deeper through the winding paths. The progress they made was very slow for there no longer existed a clear route. To continue deeper towards the mist they had to travel in circles and Diablo shared the burden by breaking through dense brush that scratched away at his thick hide; though the ever brave and gallant steed made no complaint.

They encountered an adequate clearing in which to set up camp but their comfort was little. They dared not light a fire nor sleep in tandem for fear of their pursuers tracking them whilst they rested. Tritan took the first watch on the first night and watched avidly as the kid slept under the light of the moon. His peaceful appearance was a gentle comfort and in return for the pleasure it gave him, Tritan decided not to sleep this night at all and to allow the boy to continue to rest until the sun came up.

The following day proceeded in much the same way. Their silent journey became a pact and their survival was ensured by the patience required to hunt the wilful creatures of Borderlands forest. The slightest sound of a breaking twig could ruin an hour's preparation and they became accustomed to waiting in the same spot like formidable assassins; this new skill could yet prove useful for more than just the provision of their daily meals.

On the third day, around mid-afternoon, the kid decided it was time to make conversation. The pair had never travelled together alone before and he realised how little they knew of each other.

'It's a strange feeling, waiting to die.'

'Kid, we all wait to die, from the moment we are born. But for now we are waiting to live.'

'Do you think it has worked? Several days have passed now and we've not heard a sound.'

'Oh, they'll find us, that is for certain. But by now they'll be scouting in packs of three or four, I am sure of it.' Tritan began to draw in the earth to illustrate his beliefs. 'This is us, and by now, for sure we are days from any recognisable spot and these lines are the formations they will attempt. They will do their best to remain at a close proximity to each other but this forest is huge and untraveled so they must break into at least four caravans.'

The boy gazed intently at the drawing in the dirt. 'It's strange. I expected to be more afraid. I feel kind of… numb.'

Tritan scratched out his depiction of their current situation and kicked soil across it to obscure their tracks before he found his reply.

'Your family must have meant a lot to you. I know it seems a stupid thing to say but, only the loss of something great can kill fear in a man.' Tritan shuffled uncomfortably and stared back into the enquiring gaze of the kid, who seemed to be seeking a reason to care about his own life again. The boy continued to listen, intrigued. 'Fear is a great asset I was always told. I believe it to be true but now that it has come to me for the first time since I was a child, I wish I could sedate it somehow.'

'Why are you afraid, Tritan? All this time since we have travelled together you have seemed to care little for yourself or any of those we have been surrounded by.'

'I guess I never knew what I had, until it was taken away from me. To get it back I must survive somehow and that fact scares me.'

The kid began to sense that he was entering difficult terrain and as his appetite tugged at him he had an excuse to divert their conversation.

'Well, I am getting hungry, I think we ought to start considering the evening meal.'

Tritan chuckled and knew the lad was eager to head out and hunt.

'I'll leave it to you this time. You're a far better hunter than I am. Make the most of it before age adds weight to your bones and deepens the sound of your footing. And be careful not to stray too far. You'll easily get lost so keep me in sight, no unnecessary risks.'

The kid turned to head out with his newly crafted bow, the fruit of his labour these past couple of days. It was a magnificent bow crafted from the strong wood in these parts. At first, he'd struggled to extend the string that was formed of many wound fibres that he had collected under Sal's instruction, but within a couple of days he had learned to extend it to its full potential. Sal had also taught him how to use a bow with greater stealth. Now he would find pleasure in providing a meal for Tritan. It was a first step to caring about anything again. Before he made it far a thought occurred to him and he turned back to address Tritan one last time.

'You know, I considered my escape many times these past months. I didn't think I would be escaping from the legion, just from you. Now we're alone together, I can't recall having wanted to run away at all.'

Tritan felt ashamed when he heard the truth in the words that were offered to him but he knew that there was a trust developing between them. He owed the kid the truth in return.

'I am sorry, you cannot know how sorry I am, but if you decide not to stay I won't stop you. I don't have the right to force you to remain. But I need you to know that I want you to be safe. I owe you a debt I can never repay.'

The kid smiled. It was enough.

'Get a fire going, I won't be long,' the boy reassured him, and then turned and headed into the depths of the densely formed trees and as he tiptoed away from the spot where Tritan stood watching him leave, he made not a sound.

The following hour passed by quickly for them both. The sun moved across the sky casting long shadows against the trees but there was little space to allow the trickling light to reach the ground. It would be dark well before the sun would set in the depths of the forest. Tritan arranged the dried wood that he had accumulated into a pile and lit the fire that they would use to cook the boy's prey. By the time the embers were burning bright he heard the sound of footsteps approaching.

'Your timing could not be better,' he called out. 'Just enough daylight to cook before we have to smother the fire.'

Tritan heard no response. The footsteps ceased and Tritan remained still as a statue. The crackling firewood was the only sound for a time and he looked all about him but saw nothing.

The desire to get up and move was great but he stayed focused. Fear and dread returned to him and shortly after followed the sound of footsteps again. This time there were multiple movements spread apart and he knew he was being surrounded by a half circle of at least four pairs of feet. He began to prod the fire again as if he was unaware of the ensnaring trap that was about to be sprung upon him. Slowly and carefully he rose to his feet and without looking back, walked towards Diablo who was eating a patch of grass under shelter. He saw his sword hanging from the horse's side but walked directly to stroke his old friend's head and comfort him, whispering calm words as if to appear oblivious to any danger.

The four men sprang at him instantly; they were less than a dozen paces each from where Tritan stood but it was enough distance for him to unsheathe his sword and dive over the top of a high bush and take shelter between two large tree trunks. It didn't buy him much time but it was enough to ascertain who he was fighting. The four men were more or less unknown to him; Reed was the only one he had spent any time with and even then they had barely spoken a word. The others were younger men and all new recruits. He had never ridden to battle with any of them and this was a great comfort. Surely they would underestimate him and he would have no regrets at defending himself against this party. Reed hung back with the biggest of the four as the first two charged from each side. The first man carried a heavy steel sword and the second held a short one-handed axe, his free hand he used to push apart the branches that obscured his attack. Tritan, remembering the state of his own weapon, did his best not to make direct contact unless it was a killing blow. He jumped and parried their efforts, allowing the thick foliage of the forest to protect him from the deadliest swings. The first man tripped on the roots of a tree and lost his sword in a berry bush. Tritan left him to his

panicked efforts to regain his sword and leapt towards the man
with the axe who swung the sharp blade through the air. His
technique was like a turbine. Impossible to avoid but this speed
could not be kept up for long so Tritan made no effort to pene-
trate the storming swings until the man stopped for breath. The
pause eventually came and this was his moment. Tritan easily
plunged his blade through the man's guts and watched him
squirm to the floor. As the blade came out it was followed by a
torrent of blood and although a stronger man would have easily
continued the fight, this one conceded instantly. Tritan knew
then that he had been discovered by the weakest of the gangs
that were searching for them. But he couldn't tell where the kid
was, nor whether there was any great danger lurking close
behind these four. He decided not to linger and met the man
who had now reclaimed his sword. But the fall had lessened his
confidence and Tritan easily over powered him with a series of
heavy blows. This man was strong; he held his sword up high
and deflected all of Tritan's best efforts. Each swing had been a
heavy plunge from above, as if furiously cutting wood for a fire.
Tritan feigned the next swing and then plunged a heavy fist into
the man's abdomen. The other's sword fell again and this time
Tritan caught it and swung it down into the man's skull not
waiting to watch the inevitable instant death that the blow
would cause. There were still two more and Tritan knew these
two would be warier of him now. He circled around the thick
trees that had hidden him and kept a low stance lest any
daggers be thrown. The remaining two men came at him
together, both wielding swords. They showed no signs of
relenting and beat at Tritan furiously, entering the three men
into a dance of swordplay that resulted in many surface wounds
to all of them. The battle became long and sweaty and the blood
of all their wounds soaked through their clothes so that it was
hard to tell who was affected worst. Reed moved the quickest

and made use of his companion's afflictions to time his own attacks. It was an unfair move but it proved fruitful as he managed on more than one occasion to cut Tritan deeply. Determined not to continue this suffering Tritan reconsidered his position and began to back away as each swing was aimed towards him. He was tiring already and his attackers showed no signs of relenting in spite of the wounds they now carried. If this had been a practice session each of the men would have needed a week's rest to recover but the only solution for any of them was to kill the other. Reed found a route around to the rear of Tritan whilst the other man made efforts to keep Tritan occupied. Now he was pinched between the two and had to exert more effort to turn and parry to deflect the worst of the blows. He chose carefully when to reel backwards and when to take the weaker attacks in their stride. He was losing too much blood and too much time was passing without causing any true damage to either Reed or the other man. The thought of facing the other members of the 11th after this fight troubled him and he became bewildered at the thought that it would all be over so soon and before even having to face the more skilled and stronger members of the legion. He was back at the fort all those years ago when his death had been presented to him and the same feeling of helplessness ate away at his confidence. His legs were shaking now and the drops of blood began to pour as the wounds opened more fiercely. It was a moment of ecstasy that came next as Diablo joined the fight, ploughing into Reed and sending him crashing into a tree. Several of the legionnaire's bones were broken in the encounter and Tritan took the opportunity to concentrate on the other man; one on one. Alone together they battled and it wasn't long before Tritan had disarmed him and gifted him the point of his sword more than once. But the blade stuck inside the dying man, such was the bluntness of Tritan's sword. Reed attempted to move from his disabling position but felt only the hooves of the great stallion as Diablo kicked out and crushed his skull, knocking the life from him instantly.

The next few moments bore heavily on him. So much energy had been expended and Tritan wondered how he would carry on. As he staggered he saw the inviting floor beneath him and wanted nothing more than to curl up in its embrace but knew if he rested for just a moment it would be the end of him and the end of the kid. Tritan patched himself up by tearing off the dry parts of his shirt and wrapping tight bandages to stem the bleeding as best he could. After the fifth dressing he decided that would suffice and mounted Diablo to venture out and search for the boy.

He rode forth exhausted, driven by the adrenaline of the fight. Tritan mustered what strength he had remaining to call out after the boy.

'Kid... kid! Give me some sign of where you are.'

At the sound of his own voice calling into the woods, it occurred to Tritan for the first time that neither he, nor any other of the 11th had ever bothered to ask the kid his name. He felt ashamed for such an oversight. To be riding now and potentially discover the boy at his end whilst simply calling out *kid* seemed distasteful and offensive. But for now he had no other option than to continue to scream the word. He would make amends and, if he must learn the kid's name in his dying moments, then so be it.

'Kid... kid!'

He called out again, aware that he was giving away his position too easily. But it was all he could do in this moment of uncertainty. It was a foolish move but desperation often called for actions of this kind. Still his cries met no response. He hoped only that the boy was restraining the urge, to avoid discovery by the other parties in their pursuit.

Tritan, atop Diablo, discovered a small stream that opened out of the forest and gave him occasion to ride with speed in a single direction. They followed the stream down until the point where it became a simple trickling rivulet. Once again he began to hear the sounds of his pursuers but now they too were riding their horses. The splashing sounds of hooves in the water were his warning and Tritan diverted back into the thick, dense forest. He dismounted Diablo and began to scale a thick tree that was covered with crooked branches. He rose above the stream and hid behind the trunk, leaning occasionally to scout for the attackers' positions. This time he saw two women of the 11th. There was no sign of Sal. They rode with short daggers that were impractical for anyone who was horse mounted and as Tritan considered his heightened advantage, arrows began to fly from nearby. The first two arrows achieved nothing more than to give away the kid's position but the third and fourth both struck the frontrunner in the chest and the woman fell, instantly dead, into the muddy waters. The second horse reeled up in response and the next arrow caught the horse in the chest, protecting the second woman from its point. She and the horse both fell into the water but though the horse spluttered from a punctured lung, the woman suffered nothing more than a bruised side. She hid behind the horse as two more men came up behind her, eager to identify the source of the flying arrows. Tritan chose this moment to spring from his strategic position above them, manoeuvring his entire weight above the point of his sword as it plunged down into the shoulder of the man at the rear. The fall was great and the force with which the sword penetrated the man caused it to bury so deep that the hilt rested against his collarbone. In turn, as the sword held firm, Tritan plummeted to the ground and only the foot of water beneath him broke his fall. He scrambled along the floor, reeling from the impact of his back crashing against the stony bed of the stream. Now unarmed, he rose to face the two remaining adversaries. The woman was quick, and with a dagger she was deadly. Tritan received two quick slashes to his forearm that he used to protect his body and face. The only thing that saved him then from further injury was the bark he had tied around his arms as an armour plate. It gave way instantly but he came away unscathed from the thrusts of the dagger. But the man who still rode his steed, rammed into Tritan sending him flying. The strength of the horse was such that Tritan was momentarily knocked unconscious and were it not for the kid's precision with another arrow he would have surely been finished there and then. The man fell on top of Tritan, squashing his body into the water as the tip of an arrow stuck out from his left eye; the point of entry at the back of his head had lessened the strength of the arrow and it was fortunate, for Tritan's face was just inches from its merciless edge.

The woman came bounding after him and attacked downwards, aiming around the body of her fallen ally as Tritan shifted and tried to free himself from the weight that bore down upon him. Amidst the confusion, the woman also fell on top of Tritan restricting his ability to breathe. The last remaining efforts he mustered went into his fists as he grappled with her throat. The force was strong enough to cause her to drop her blade and before long her colour was a deep purple and her eyes turned red as she saw her last sight, the fearsome anger and hatred that Tritan held for her. She slipped away and then it was done. Tritan felt no remorse.

It was a while before he managed to rise. The strength required to move the two bodies from his chest was more than he now had but Diablo bit down hard into Tritan's jerkin and pulled him free. They were a sorry clan, Tritan, the kid and Diablo. But now the battle was half done and suddenly there was hope. They could survive this; somehow against the odds they would survive.

Exhausted and in great pain, Tritan had walked off his new afflictions and once again mounted Diablo, the boy was nowhere to be seen. This time Tritan knew better than to call out and trusted that the skilled archer the kid had become would continue to keep his position secret. It was the best way to ensure the element of surprise that was required to see off any remaining members of the 11th Legion. They had yet to be discovered by Kal, Jaz or Sal; the three that would be the hardest to kill. A new respect, perhaps even a tentative bond, had been rekindled between them these past months. He prayed that this same bond would be his saving grace, a single moment's hesitation from any of them could swing the chances of victory in his favour. But worst of all was the thought of facing Sy. Nothing but hatred and death would be offered to either Tritan or the kid by him. It was no accident they had yet to come across Sy. He was waiting, Tritan knew, until they were weakened and the killing would be so much easier. Sy was not the kind of man to take pride in an even match. He would likely sneak up on them from behind to slit their throats and still claim the victory, above all the others, for the part he played.

Tritan was dazed, his mind drifted and his vision became blurred. He was vulnerable now, far from the zenith of his youth. He afforded himself a moment's surcease, as his will drifted from him, he could no longer claim to hold any. The trees that surrounded him came crashing down and they lay beside him levelled. Tritan wondered how it could be possible that the world around him had fallen. After a moment, when the pain shot through his side he conjectured that it was he who had fallen, far from the saddle and onto the earth. He trembled and felt the gelid shivers encasing his whole body. His eyes opened to see the swirling world before him. He knew this sensation. He had felt it before. It was the beauty that the mind offered to the body as the spirit was torn from its cage. He was dying. Somewhere beyond where he lay Diablo whickered, suffering the madness of his impending loss. Such was their bond and such was the way they had lived. Tritan was losing his senses, just a few remaining moments of consciousness as he felt the warmth of his blood seeping from his sides. Towering above him was the fading sight of the rich green colour of the evergreen trees, like emeralds it seemed; he smiled gently. Then the shadows moved in and his tunnel vision became focused solely on the man who came to stand above his wasted body. Tritan felt the urge to take up his sword but his hands would not obey his instruction. An arm reached down to him, but the palm was open as if offering kindness and as Tritan struggled with the blurred sight of the face that he feared would be his end, he saw the gaping hole where a tongue had once been. Then the blackness of the man's mouth became his everything.

23

The air was thick with dread and uncertainty. A silence lingered amongst all the onlookers as the sorrowful atmosphere clung to their hearts and the sight of the comatose child plucked the strings of their concern.

Pietrich had not woken for several days now and it had become almost impossible to administer any form of remedy. He appeared peaceful and his body had not yet succumbed to its ailments. Eira continued to visit her friend and comforted what remained of him. It was hard work and the conversations were now one-sided but embers of hope shine brightest when the darkness of despair spreads its wings. Thomas, under Marilia's instruction, had established a method to keep her son fed and watered. A tube was inserted into his veins each morning and nutrients were injected into the bloodstream. It was a strange and unknown method but it was not yet certain that the boy would never wake again and in this way he retained some strength. Thomas had relished the opportunity to spend time with Marilia again.

Eira remained patient, as the opportunity to be alone with

Pietrich was now scarce, for Marilia dared not leave his side in case she missed the last breaths he would take in this world. But Eira's frustration was sometimes hard to hide. She had learned in private of the last conversation Pietrich had managed to hold with Boscelito. It was an instruction as to the location of Tritan and the legionnaires but the visions had been incomplete and Pietrich was not sure if his advice had helped at all.

Now, Eira, Thomas and Marilia all stood around Pietrich without uttering a word to each other. It was as though each was waiting for the others to leave before attempting to rouse him. Thomas's beliefs became clear the moment he broke the silence.

'We should consider the arrangements for his place of resting. The diversion may soften the ordeal of this daily staring we are indulging in.'

'No!' Marilia spat out at once. 'No such talk will be had in his presence or mine. Not yet.'

'Very well, but I am only concerned now for your wellbeing. He is resting and you must do what can be done to give yourself rest. Sometimes the best form of repose is to busy oneself with other matters.'

'Thomas, I appreciate all you have done, but right now nothing you are saying is helping me, so please remain silent or leave us be.'

Thomas felt the pain of his intrusion at her words and decided to take both courses of action. He quietly turned and left the cottage, leaving Marilia and Eira to their thoughts. There the two stood for what seemed like an age. But knowing that any moment could be Pietrich's last, they endured as long as they could.

Pietrich suffered a constant feverish sweat, which Marilia wiped away with a cool damp cloth. It was an ongoing battle between her determination and his continued weakening.

Despite the methods of keeping him fed, Pietrich had become quite thin and the cute curves of his face had withered away to expose the hard lines of his jaw.

'He still resembles himself, doesn't he?' Marilia asked herself as much as Eira, searching for solace and reassurance. 'I don't wish to see him disappear one day at a time this way.'

'There is still time for him, think how far he has come. It is not days that have made him this way, but months.'

Marilia smiled at Eira and knew she was right. But the smile faded as her own thoughts plagued her mind.

'These past months have gone by so fast. I am struggling to recall his father's face at all. The first time he left I would try to picture Tritan, just to keep the image strong in my mind. He used to smile you know, at the outset, but our beginning was over so fast.' Marilia sighed deeply. 'I haven't given the same attention to those images this time and now they have abandoned me.'

'You shouldn't worry about that now, you've been so busy, how could you expect to remember such things?'

'You're a sweet girl, Eira. You'll make someone very happy one day. Look how beautiful you have become. You're hardly a child anymore.'

Eira moved closer to Pietrich and took his hand. She stroked it calmly and carefully.

'His hands are so cold.' She paused. 'Is real love something that lasts forever? I don't think I can imagine not loving him as I do now.'

'People change and feelings change with them, but whether we love someone or not is never our choice. We can only submit to the heart in that regard. I don't know if anything can last forever though, not even love.'

Eira knew Marilia was not questioning her love of Pietrich with these words, but rather her love of Tritan. Eira wondered how hard it must be to love such a troubled man and to be left no choice in the matter. She considered herself blessed to love such a sweet boy. Sick or otherwise, he had made her very happy in the brief time they had spent together as children. So fiercely she prayed that they would know each other as adults too. Eira closed her eyes and imagined a future that was certain not to occur. She pictured a plot of land and little children of their own running around, she would roll in the mud with them and show them how to work the land with Pietrich and then they would sit down together in the evening to talk about the day and laugh together, looking forward to the next day and the next day and the next. She imagined all those warm nights when they would lay in each other's arms and they would comfort each other during the harsh winters, smiling in spite of the cold, warmed by their love for one another. But it was just a dream and as she opened her eyes Eira saw the weak and frail boy lying in front of her. She knew that he may not even make it to his eleventh birthday.

As if they had sensed the need for comfort in each other, Marilia and Eira hugged and wept. Their tears ran fierce and the moments after were filled with hope again, as if the tears carried away with them the fears of their thoughts.

'Goodnight, Marilia, thank you for being so kind to me.'

'And you to me, I don't know how I'd cope with all the whispering and gossip that is prevalent around the village if it weren't for the strength you have given me. Sleep well.'

Eira left Marilia and headed out into the dark fields as the rest of Knighton slept. Her mother, Kayla, had become used to her late arrivals home and no longer waited up for her. She loved the walk home each evening. The cool southern air was refreshing and the stars shone so brightly. When she arrived at the door of her house she waited with her hand on the handle and considered her entry. But instead she turned about and pulled up a stool and sat, with her back leant against the outside wall. She stared across the fields and watched as the dancing lights of fireflies pranced and sprang about in front of her. She had never paused to watch them before. It was a magical sight and there was no sense in how they glowed so brightly, for they were such little creatures. It was like the stars had fallen to earth to visit her and with each pulsing glow she knew the strength of the life that each of them must carry. It was all she needed to remind herself how much strength Pietrich must yet carry as even the shallow beat of a weakened heart was a sign of life and life clings on. How it dares to taunt death in such a way. How it dares to carry on.

24

The light was terrifying. It pierced the enclosure like a needle as the mist reflected the morning sun's stare. The enclosure was humid and the walls wept. Space was not a luxury in the tiny, stony room and the three small makeshift beds formed from kindling and leaves took up the vast majority of what little there was. The only bed that was currently lain upon was Tritan's. He was in a deep sleep and beside him boiled a small pot of water. Minding the pot was Boscelito.

Three days had passed since the tongue-less man had found his son, just moments from death. The kid had fired upon Boscelito but fortune had it that his arrow would miss, giving Boscelito enough time to prove his well intent. It was hard to convince the boy at first for Boscelito could not speak but after a time it was clear he had meant them no harm and wanted only to aid them. The kid had helped Boscelito lift Tritan onto Diablo's back and then they had walked, carefully and alert, through the forest to the underground chamber where they now hid.

Tritan had slept the entire time since they returned and the kid had hunted as Boscelito minded over his son. Though neither Tritan in his dreaming state nor the boy who was very much awake, realised the connection between them. Only Boscelito knew the truth and he had no way of telling it.

The conversations with Pietrich had ended and Boscelito did not know the reason why, but he believed their time together had come to an end and he knew there was no way to ask his grandson for help anymore. He had bonded with the kid in spite of their silence in each other's company. The nod of approval at the hunted prey and the way he cared for Tritan made the lad Boscelito's instant ally. They left the dwelling only when they must for fear of being discovered by the others of the 11th that would by now have found the bodies of their fellow legionnaires. Hiding Diablo, however, was far more difficult and even Boscelito's attempts to take the horse some safe distance were in vain, for sighted or not, Diablo found his way back to the place where Tritan rested. It was such determination the great animal held not to leave his side that led to the horse standing guard within a few leagues of their enclosure and should any adversaries make their way to them, the horse would no doubt play its part in making some sort of signal. Boscelito prayed it would not come to that but for now his focus was on reviving Tritan to consciousness.

The hours went by slowly, waiting and waiting for Tritan to regain his senses. He made murmuring sounds due to the fever that had set in but it was a relief every time his body kicked out because it took great effort to restrain him through the nightmares and with each passing fit, his power returned. In his semi-conscious state it was possible to give Tritan some food and tea that was laced with healing herbs that his companions discovered in the surrounding area. The forest was thick with nutritious plants in spite of the severe cold. Tritan's wounds had begun to seal and although the flesh was still weak, it no longer broke or bled. Boscelito had closed the worst of them by heating steel and burning them shut but the smaller cuts took care of themselves.

As the evening came and the light of the day diminished, the kid and Boscelito settled down to rest, keeping their ears attuned. It was quiet all around them and any disturbance would be easy to hear, so they slept, awaiting the day that followed, when they would continue their routine.

As morning came, the boy woke first. He rolled out of his spot and began to prepare his bow for the morning hunt. It was some while before he even noticed the empty bed where Tritan had rested. Startled, he looked all about him as his eyes adjusted to the gloomy enclosure, but Tritan was nowhere to be seen. The kid considered waking Boscelito but decided against it and headed out into the forest alone. The air was thick with a cold fog and his vision was limited to just a few paces in each direction. Tiptoeing carefully, he made a circular passage, gradually drawing further and further from their hidden encampment. It wasn't long before he had ventured as far out as where Diablo rested. The horse was still and alone but seemed aware that something was out of the ordinary. The kid reassured the brave steed with a soft embrace before continuing his search. An hour passed by and then another. The boy was truly panic stricken but now the fog that had limited his sight was lifting and he scaled a tree to gain a greater vantage of the area. After he had climbed to the highest point possible and gazed in every direction he decided it was time he headed back to their hidden cave and when he reached it he found Boscelito in an equally distraught state. The tongue-less man was making furious gestures, confused and concerned.

'I've been searching all morning,' said the kid. 'I don't understand why he didn't wake either of us.'

Boscelito continued his gesturing and slid his hands across the air, creating the length of a sword. It was then that the lad realised Tritan's sword was missing along with the man. His heart sank and he considered the foolish action that Tritan had probably taken in their absence.

Boscelito readied his equipment and signalled the kid to search in the direction opposite to where he intended to venture.

The trembling voice of the boy whispered. 'What if he returns? One of us ought to stay here.'

Boscelito shook his head, not wanting to risk waiting. So they both headed back into the depths of the forest, covering as much ground as the two of them could manage.

The afternoon passed by and to no avail. Each of them had spent hours walking in circles and only succeeded in discovering one another back at their hiding place. They inspected the enclosure with scrutiny but there were no signs of Tritan returning. Boscelito and the kid sat in silence together for a time, lost and dejected.

'He'll be back by nightfall, he has to be.' The boy was as unsure of his hopeful statement as was Boscelito. 'We should eat, doing nothing isn't going to help any of us.'

They began to ready a small fire inside the cave, out of sight, cooking a small hare that had been kept fresh, packed in snow. It was good eating but neither enjoyed the meal, as they knew all they could do next was to try and sleep, praying for Tritan to return in the night. Neither of them would sleep they knew, but they had to try. They needed their energy and only rest could provide it. It was the only aid they could give Tritan for, should he return in any state, they would require their strength.

The night was as long as they had feared. They slept no more than an hour apiece and when dawn finally broke and Tritan was still not back, their hearts began to sink. A deep solitude lingered in the air and the time that passed seemed endless. They counted every second and it seemed as though a lifetime passed by. Boscelito couldn't accept that the years he had spent waiting, searching, and hoping that he would one day see his son would be rewarded by just a few days of simple nursing. He cursed himself for having slept when Tritan had woken, not aware of his departure. It felt like a grave failure. The way he had failed him the day Tritan was born.

Boscelito and the kid buried their woes and all hope left them. Yet in the same moment they began to hear familiar slow and uneven footsteps approaching them. They ran out into the open and saw a trail of blood stretching from the depths of the forest, ending at the point where they found Tritan, kneeling in the snow. His head was bowed and he trembled. The kid ran to him to fall beside the man who clutched his reddened sword as though it was his lifeblood. Tritan slowly raised his head to stare at Boscelito and although it was the first time he had truly set eyes on the stranger he felt then a strange union with him. He couldn't understand why but it was as though they had known each other in a past life. The boy checked Tritan over for the source of his lesions but he found nothing. The blood was not his. Tritan took a deep breath, mustering his strength before he spoke.

'Now there are only five.'

AFTER A GOOD DEAL of time eating and taking water, Tritan recounted everything to them. Every step and all the gory detail of how he had taken the three lives this past day that they had been without him. He was still weak but stealth had kept him hidden from the 11th as he stalked the resting foes in the middle of the night and slit their throats. He had sighted Sy in close quarters to Sal, Jaz, Kal and one other and deemed it too dangerous to approach any of them but the other three had been alone and the killing was easy. It had been tiring work but without threat and now their numbers were diminished.

'What is our next move?' the kid asked.

'To be rid of the threat, we must finish this. But it is my task and I can't expect anything of either of you,' Tritan turned to address the tongue-less man. 'I don't know who you are or why, in such a moment of need, you came to us. But you have my deepest thanks. You need not linger here any longer, you should leave this fight and take the boy with you; that is the best both of you can do for me now.'

Boscelito shook his head; he would not leave his side, not after all that had passed. The kid spoke next, as if on behalf of the man who could not form his own words.

'I tried several times to say the same thing while you rested, but he would not accept it. He has intertwined his fate with ours and whether you like it or not, we would do better to remain together.'

'You may be right, but the source of all of this lies in the hands of one man alone. And should I live to go in search of Augustus; that I must do myself.'

'Well, if that is the case, then we have only one choice. We should divert those who remain while you escape into the mist. You need not fight any other of this legion. If I am half right about what lies ahead of you, it is best you avoid another scrape. I have nothing that keeps me living,' he gestured to Boscelito next, assuming his thoughts were in sync. 'This one is old and cannot speak. But he seems determined to see this through. If we can buy you enough time to make your departure, you should allow us to aid you at least that much.'

Boscelito wanted so much to stand side by side with Tritan, to confront Augustus together, but he knew deep down that this diversion was his son's best chance of coming face to face with the man that had plagued them both for all these years. He waved his arms at Tritan and the kid and showed them to a path that was yet untrodden.

After a couple of hours traipsing through the snow they arrived at a windy, stony road and it led to a narrow valley that was cut into an ominous looming rock. It would be a hard path to walk, even for a man and Tritan knew this was the end of the journey for Diablo. He nodded to the tongue-less man and began to ready his things before approaching his old friend and stroking his mane.

'This is where we say goodbye, old friend. Protect these two as you have protected me. We'll see each other again one day, in a better place than either of us has ever known.'

Diablo sensed his departure and whickered; he lowered his head into Tritan's chest and held it there for a moment. It seemed that tears formed in the empty sockets where his eyes had once been. It was painful for them both but the horse was as strong willed as the man he had lived with his entire life. After a time of embracing Diablo, Tritan led the horse to the spot where the kid was standing and handed the reins to the young boy who seemed to have grown older in years these past few days.

'Take it easy with him at first and speak to him often, your voice will comfort him and eventually he'll learn to trust your judgement.'

'We'll pray for you together, I promise.' The boy was sincere and seemed like a man as he spoke the words.

'Pray for yourselves, and do nothing foolish. Run, don't fight. Ride as fast as you can and don't look back.'

'Good luck then.'

'One last thing, kid, in all this time, I never learned your name.'

'Kid is as good a name as any, the boy my parents once named is dead, and you should remember me as I am now.'

Tritan smiled and held out his hand to the boy who had been and the man who now was. The handshake was firm and the kid smiled too as he felt the strength that had returned to Tritan's arm.

Boscelito approached his son next and placed his hand upon his shoulder. Tritan felt great comfort in the gesture and still wrestled with the confusion of the aid this stranger had given him.

'Thank you again for all you have done. I wish I could have known you better.'

The words cut into Boscelito's heart but he restrained himself from taking Tritan in his arms for he knew he would not understand. He hoped deeply that his son would live to see his mission through and that one day he might learn of the true father that now stood before him. He didn't know how but Boscelito held such faith that the truth would find a way of unmasking itself from its deep shadow.

The final moments the band of three spent together were silent, but more was said with the looks they shared than a thousand words could ever convey. Boscelito squinted through his watery eyes and with them told Tritan that he loved him. Somehow he knew that Tritan had understood. Then the ex-soldier of the 11th Legion turned and headed down the path, approaching the furthermost northern parts of Harmion where the land became impossibly treacherous and the freezing mist that clung to the mountains for hundreds of miles, turned into the unknown domain of Orldin.

The kid and Boscelito stood side by side with Diablo and watched as the figure of Tritan faded into the lustrous fog until eventually they saw nothing at all.

There was nothing more to do but prepare their things and

ready their knives and bow. The hunt for the last members of the 11th had begun and the sharpest tool of all had honed the senses of these predators. The tool was the bond between one soldier and another, an unspoken bond that is impossible to put into words and can only be shared by those who know deep down that they would die for one another, without ever having to speak it aloud.

25

Winter was a tame description of the world that fell upon them. The snow was thick and their feet sank deeply into the white icy clouds that embraced their shins like feather pillows. The crooked branches of the trees were tinted with bright grey dust as though they were old men, withering in the cold. The kid readied himself with a determined focus, ready to strip away his final layers of innocence. Atop Diablo's back, he held his bow firm with an arrow slotted into the string. His free hand he used to hold the reins of the horse. He had never really learnt how to ride but somehow it came naturally to him, even with this animal, blind as it was. Diablo had quickly become accustomed to the new rider who led him through the Borderlands forest, their trust fused by the parting encouragement Tritan had given. Boscelito guided them just a few paces ahead, both his daggers drawn and cloaked in frost. A full afternoon had passed since Tritan had ventured north into Orldin. As of yet they had seen no signs of the remaining members of the 11th Legion but this did not sway them from their course. Those who they expected to spring on them at any moment would be focused too and a second's hesitation would cost either party severely.

Their pace had slowed to a crawl on account of the thick snow but with each passing moment they felt relief in the distance gained between themselves and Tritan. After another hour they came by the enclosure where they had settled for the past week and picked up the remaining items of worth. They managed to assemble a reasonable meal before setting out again in the direction that Tritan had returned from. The hope was that the 11th were still caught off guard by the deaths they had suffered during the previous night and if their positions were unmoved it would be possible to follow Tritan's tracks back to where he had found them.

By nightfall Boscelito and the kid had followed the tracks as far as they led but the trail had vanished under the fresh fallen snow. They set up a bivouac between two trees and took turns to stand guard whilst the other rested. There was enough thick growth at the base of the trunks for Diablo to satisfy his hunger before he too rested.

The night was pitch black as the moon was shrouded entirely by grey cloud. The darkness was the best protection they could have hoped for under the circumstances and they decided that there was no need to go further until daylight returned.

At the break of day the journey continued. Once again the pair moved slowly through the forest with their weapons held ready. There was no room for complacency and even a family of starlings flying overhead, gliding on the breeze, could not distract either the boy or Boscelito. The beauty of the birds would remain a secret, like so many others that the forest held claim to.

The snowfall had let up and the hilly bank they now traversed was less of a struggle so they began to move with a more rapid pace. Diablo and the kid led the way, clearing a shallow path for Boscelito to jog through behind them. From the low ridge they were able to see for an hour's ride in every direction. The cloud that had hidden them at night had lifted and now the sun beat a fierce gaze upon the snow, reflecting a blinding shimmer of glistening light into their eyes. Suddenly the boy pulled back on Diablo's reins and they stopped in their tracks. He held up his hand to Boscelito to signal their halt as he spotted rising smoke, far in the distance. The fire that burned before them was a tiny speck but they saw no clear way of heading towards it unnoticed.

'We need to drop to lower ground. We'll be spotted immediately if we continue at this level,' said the kid.

Boscelito nodded his agreement and so they slid down the side of the bank and into the shade at its base where the sun could not see. The smoke was barely visible from here but they kept to a clear route that they guessed would circle around it. After some great effort to move quietly they came to a frozen lake that opened out ahead of them. The kid dismounted Diablo and walked at the front; the lightest of the three, to ensure the ice was thick enough to bear their weight. They trod carefully around the perimeter where the danger was less but still, on more than one occasion, Diablo's hooves broke through to the icy water and he reeled towards the narrow bank at the edge. It was pressing work and their progress was slow and tiring but eventually they reached a narrow point of the ice-covered lake and the end was in sight. The smoke from the fire ahead had diminished and they suspected its signal would not remain for much longer. Time was short but to rush would surely result in one of them falling through the cracking sheets of ice and they dared not risk the treacherous outcome. It took them the best part of the afternoon to navigate the remainder of the lake until finally they came back to solid ground. As suspected the smoke of the fire they'd used to set their path had died away and now they relied purely on their sense of direction. Keen as it was they had no way of telling if the 11th had remained in the position they had set out towards and often Boscelito and the kid looked back to ensure they had not themselves been circled. They approached a corner that had obscured their view and realised that the lake was not so far from the camp after all. Slowly and carefully they edged forward and as the sun dropped low in the sky and their shadows became long-stretched depictions of themselves, they came across a circle of ash where the fire had burnt out. The ravished carcass of a wild boar was stretched out on a beam above the grey stones that formed the base and though they searched for some remnants of meat there was nothing of value to salvage. The boy held firm with Diablo whilst Boscelito tiptoed around the camp to find some signs of the 11th. The legionnaires had clearly moved on and there were several tracks leading away from their position making it impossible to determine which was the correct path to follow.

'They are expecting us. Maybe our only advantage is they may still expect Tritan to be riding with us.' The kid was uncertain of his hope but as each hour passed, Tritan's escape was further secured.

'We could ride further south and light a fire of our own, that may bring them to us?'

Boscelito considered the plan and then dread descended upon him. He ran back to the fire and checked the corpse of the wild boar, studying it with greater scrutiny. He ran his fingers across the greasy bones and smelt the remains. The look he then gave the kid was a sorrowful one and they both knew a trap had been set and they had walked right into it. The boar had been dead for days and the fire was for show. That was clear enough to them now and they stood rooted in their fear waiting for the onslaught that must descend upon them. Silence and dread filled the air as they slowly backed away from the clearing where they were surely easy targets. The multiple tracks that led away surrounded them and they knew they were ensnared. Tritan was not with them and this fact might be the only one currently keeping them alive. The 11th must be waiting wherever they hid for the son of Augustus to show his face and, as Boscelito and the kid tracked backwards, the opportunity afforded by the trap lessened. The kid whispered to Boscelito as quietly as he could.

'They are waiting for us all. There is no other reason for them to hold tight in their positions. The moment they realise we are alone we are done for.'

Boscelito signalled for the boy to mount Diablo and he did so in such a swift movement that within seconds they were retreating towards the frozen lake. It was then that the 11th revealed themselves and an arrow flew towards the fleeing companions, narrowly missing them. But from the direction towards where the kid rode with Diablo, a dagger flew through the air and struck the great horse in the shoulder. The foreleg gave way and the kid rolled out onto the icy lake, the force causing him to crash through it and plunge deep into the waters. His head pounded from the cold and as he tried to resurface he found himself buried deeply beneath a wall of ice. The shadowy figure of Diablo scrambling to his legs was all he saw as the icy waters obscured his vision. Boscelito jumped onto the lake and plunged his daggers deep into the ice, cutting out blocks and searching frantically for the kid but before he could lift the piece that trapped the boy, one of the 11th fell upon the tongue-less man. It was the man whose dagger had earlier struck the horse that now fought with Boscelito atop the frozen lake. Sy, Jaz, Kal and Sal remained hidden. The two men grappled and rolled, falling into the freezing waters beneath the ice. Boscelito saw the kid struggling to push free of the frozen cage, but he was unable to aid him as the legionnaire pulled him down into the depths of the icy water. Boscelito thrust his daggers towards the arm of the man that held firmly to his leg but the water negated his strength and he caused little damage. For a great time they remained submerged and the temptation to breathe in the water was fierce but they all clung on, in spite of the aching pain in their heads and lungs. Diablo, midst his escape, was struck with an arrow and crashed through the waters again and the boy raised his arm to grab onto the strong muscular leg that had broken through and pulled himself free from the ice. The kid looked all about him for a sign of Boscelito but the dark figures of the two men had fallen too deeply into the water. The kid then saw Sy approaching with Kal at his side. Sy held the bow that had sent the fierce arrow flying that had struck Diablo and he drew back another shaft. The boy took a deep breath and dived back into the water, plunging deep as the arrow pierced the surface and surged past his face. He saw then the two men wrestling at the bottom of the lake and swam down to them. He went straight to Boscelito and imparted some of his breath into the tongue-less man, reviving his strength slightly for a moment. Boscelito thrust his dagger into the legionnaire who was gulping in the icy water and took the life from him as the man took his last breaths and his lungs filled with the glacial water, freezing them as he died.

The kid helped Boscelito wriggle free from the sinking corpse that clung onto him and they emerged above the lake's surface and crawled to the bank where Diablo was retreating towards the forest. The horse had been struck by another arrow in the hind and was struggling to walk. The kid spotted Sy and Kal closing in as another arrow was loosed towards them. Instinctively Boscelito pushed the boy in front of the horse to protect him from the sight of the shaft. The horse was struck again in the back and reeled up in pain and then the three companions fell down onto the icy bank. It was over. Sy aimed another arrow and sent it flying into the steed that lay helpless, protecting the kid and Boscelito. Diablo was panting deep breaths of painful sadness, too many arrows had struck him and they all knew that the time remaining to them was little. Then came the taunts.

'What a pathetic show. I had hoped for more after all these days of searching.' It was Sy that shouted the words that so enraged the kid and Boscelito. But they were stuck and remained lying hidden by the great body of Diablo whose life was drifting away with each passing moment.

Just a stone's throw away now, Sy and Kal with swords raised high approached the defeated adversaries. But it was Sal and Jaz who joined the fight next and it was this moment the pair had chosen to show their true allegiance. From up above, Jaz, the great hulk of a man, threw a large boulder into the ice just in front of Sy and Kal. The ice broke instantly and the two men plummeted into the lake.

'Run you clowns! Run!' Jaz screamed to the boy and Boscelito. The kid looked up and saw Jaz standing up high on the bank and beside him was Sal, her bow aimed at Sy and Kal. The kid and Boscelito didn't wait around to understand the treacherous manoeuvre and fled from the scene towards the forest. But the boy looked back at Diablo who could no longer stand and felt a great distress at leaving the animal to its dying fate.

'We can't just leave him like that, it's not right!' he screamed.

Boscelito shook his head, there was nothing either of them could do. He pulled on the kid's shirt and dragged him away into the wooded area that hid them from the fight.

Kal and Sy resurfaced and glared up towards Sal and Jaz with hatred.

'Traitorous bastards!' shouted Kal. 'I'll gut you for this!'

The response came swiftly as Sal's arrow flew straight to his heart. Kal died instantly, no final words or last stand would honour his years of soldiering. In a moment as swift as the flapping of a starling's wing it was all over for him. Sy diverted from his path instantly and ran towards the corpse of Diablo to shelter himself from any further shots. Jaz dropped down the bank and headed towards the youngest and meanest of the 11th. He pulled out his hand axe and circled around the horse to where the man lay.

Jaz lunged down with the axe. But as the forceful strike came, Sy rolled aside and deflected its cutting blow and, with the hidden hand that clutched the tip of an arrow he shoved the point into Jaz's throat, cutting through the windpipe. Jaz fell back as the breath left him. He dared not remove the arrow for it would speed up the inevitable end he had been fated to suffer. Instead he moved towards Diablo and cradled him as their breathing slowed and their lives passed in tandem from this world into the next. If Jaz had still the breath for words he would have said it was a good death.

Sy fled the scene towards the forest in pursuit of the kid and Boscelito, closely followed by Sal, who had remained atop the bank that ran parallel to the edge of the lake. From her position she was far enough behind those who had entered the forest that she may miss the crucial moments that followed.

Boscelito had lost his daggers to the cruel waters of the lake and the kid, armed only with his bow had dropped the quiver that held his supply of arrows. Only two that he had held onto with his string pulling hand remained. Exhausted from running the pair stopped in a small clearing and assessed their situation. With no blades between them, even though they outnumbered Sy, they would be no match for him.

'We have to try, no more running away,' the kid spoke boldly.

Boscelito answered him by moving to the nearest tree and with all his strength he ripped free a branch about the length of an arm. It was a crude weapon at best but the boy was right. The time for running was done and if this was to be their final stand, they would stand together. The sound of approaching footsteps drew their attention and then, through the clearing, came the scar-faced man with his sword drawn ready to spill blood. Sy looked fierce at the best of times but smothered in Jaz's blood and with the scar that Tritan had inflicted on him he looked truly terrifying. He mocked them once more. 'It hardly seems fair, an old man and a boy, unarmed. I'll make you a deal, tell me where Tritan is and I'll kill you both swiftly.'

'Sy, you'll never find him. He is beyond your reach and I have a feeling this place is the last you'll ever see,' said the kid, his voice quivering.

Sy began to laugh and the laugh became a cackle of insanity that reverberated around the forest. The boy pulled back the string of his bow and directed the arrow at the legionnaire. The laughing ended as Sy held his sword in position. They were just steps apart from each other but the kid caused no fear in Sy who slowly pushed towards him. Boscelito circled around the man until they were in the shape of a triangle. The boy loosed his shaft and Sy cut it down the next moment. He charged towards the kid but Boscelito was on him, moving swiftly, like a much younger man. The branch came down and crunched against Sy's arm causing him to spin, leaving just enough time for the kid to reload his bow. Sy turned his attention to Boscelito and swung the sword down, breaking the branch in two and with it he cut deeply the tongue-less man's forearm. Boscelito dropped his branch and reeled over, prostrate. Sy went to swing his sword again but the kid fired his final arrow into his back and then held the bow like a club, charging at him. Sy spun around, furious but unaffected by the arrow that stuck out from his lower back. Adrenaline drove him and as the lad swung the wooden bow towards him he met it with his sword and split the bow in two. Boscelito regained his footing and grabbed the arrow that protruded from Sy's back with his uninjured arm and twisted it in the wound. Sy screamed out and turned, striking the sword deep into Boscelito's body. The old man fell to the floor and as the blade was pulled clear, he vomited bile across the forest floor.

The kid was stunned, knowing he must act quickly but instead remaining frozen and useless. Once again he was destined to stand by and watch a man who had cared for him be murdered. The strike that came next was quick and clean as the blade held in Sy's hand thrust through Boscelito's chest and he fell to the floor. As Sy pulled out the sword he heard no sound as the old man leant his head against the trunk of a nearby tree and closed his eyes tranquilly as though he had preordained the moment, and in that final second he seemed to be at peace.

Sy turned back to the boy who was now whimpering. Alone again he was once more a child, helpless and afraid.

'Don't worry, kid, you'll not be dying quite so fast as that, I promise.' Sy licked his lips as he said the words and slowly pursued his final victim. But the boy turned and ran towards the nearest tree and began to climb it as though he was a feral animal.

Sy bellowed at him mockingly. 'You can't hide up there forever!'

Just as Sy spoke the words a tip of steel pierced the back of his skull and exited through his mouth. Sal stood behind him and readied another shaft but she did not need it. Sy was dead before he hit the ground.

'Kid, come down, it's safe,' Sal shouted up to the boy who

was clinging onto a high branch but as he went to make his descent he slipped and fell for what seemed like an age, eventually crashing into the ground by the base of the tree and cracking his skull on the roots. Sal ran to him, panic stricken.

'Kid... kid!' she screamed.

Leaning over his body she saw his eyes were closed and she shook him fiercely. He began to blink and looked up at her. 'I'm buggered if I'll let a slippery branch be the end of me.'

Sal smiled at him and helped him to his feet. They looked around at the carnage and the kid wondered what cruel twist of fate had kept him alive. He had seen the end of the 11th Legion, save for Augustus, and he suddenly felt bewildered. He had actually believed he would die alongside the tongue-less man, fighting the remaining soldiers. Now he stood without purpose but full of life and the entire world rested to the south of him. He was thankful to share the moment with Sal.

The boy walked to the tree where Boscelito had breathed his last and as he squinted through his watery eyes he saw a bloody patch of snow at the base of a trunk. But Boscelito was nowhere to be seen. Sal had followed him and scrutinised the location.

'We must be looking in the wrong place,' she said.

The kid shook his head.

'No, we're not.'

hards of rock glistened like silver. The land was rich and though the cold was unrelenting the dryness of the air allowed the greenery that clung to the sides of the smooth stone to glow like tendrils of emeralds. The ground was slippery and icy as the deluge clung to the smooth surface making the traverse slow and treacherous. Tritan had by now travelled alone for nearly three days and he guessed he had barely scratched the surface of his journey through the passage that was hidden beneath the thick looming mist. It was a strange mist; unlike any he had known. Each breath was felt in the lungs as though there were whispers of dry water trickling through the body, fine as sawdust. His thoughts remained with the kid and he missed their recent conversations. There was so much he had not learnt about the boy and he regretted the fact he knew nothing at all of the tongue-less man who had aided them in their final moments together. But his focus now was reaching Augustus. He could sense the presence of the old warlord with every step he took and knew somehow that years before, Augustus had walked the same path that he was now treading.

Visibility came and went through the long days and the nights lasted for an ever shorter time the further Tritan travelled from the lands he knew well. He had abandoned most of his belongings save for the clothes that protected him from the adverse weather. His sword and a ration of dried meat that was all but exhausted were his only other possessions. Thus far the route he walked was unchanging and if he ever worried that his direction was false, he could do nothing to divert from the set path. The valley that was cut into the rock was narrow and often obstructed by fallen boulders that were nearly impossible to climb. The walls to the side of the path were high and smooth and there was no way of ascending them. His only choice was to continue further and further into the unknown. The familiar sounds of singing birds and wildlife had all but ended and he wondered if anything other than himself was alive for leagues in any direction. The thought of running out of food worried him but at least water was readily available wherever he turned. He had taken to soaking up the dew from the stones with a rag and drank small sips constantly. Tritan had to rely on the mysterious surroundings for his provisions and had to believe that when he would need it most, food would present itself to him in one form or another. He had to allow himself that much hope at least.

Sleeping was a challenge for he had no shelter and the light of day that returned almost as quickly as it diminished forced him into a state of near insomnia. The previous evening he had slept only two hours and he knew that he would sleep increasingly less as each day passed. His thoughts became confused and his mind wandered often, darting between his past and present. All the years he had lived seemed to have led to this moment as though fate was forcing him to go in search of his father.

Tritan was not yet past his years of physical strength and he had recovered well from his recent afflictions. He recounted the story of Rose to himself over and over, imagining the mother travelling through this strange land with her infant child. It gave him strength to imagine the tale was true for he knew that her journey would have been far more arduous than his own and it aided his efforts to subdue the darkness that descended upon his mind. Every time the task seemed hopeless he remembered that a mother's love had been strength enough for her brave escape through this mist. But unlike her he was not escaping, he was the pursuer of a higher purpose and he thought of all those he loved and knew it was for them as much as himself that he was undertaking this foolish task. He thought of Marilia, his loving wife, whom he had never treated fairly nor told of his love for her. Worse yet, he thought of his son who may already have fallen prey to his illness. But he had to hope that the child that was his own still clung to life the way that Tritan clung to his purpose.

After several more days, exhausted and heavy-eyed, Tritan had become thin. He had finally run out of what little food he carried two days past and his clothes now hung from his body as a sheet hangs from a washing line. He feared he would soon begin to lose the weakened muscle that still held to his bones and then his strength would certainly lessen and the constant hiking would be harder to bear. He knew that, by now, lesser men would have fallen victim to the early stages of starvation and there was no way of telling how far he had come or how much longer he would have to endure this suffering. He was delirious and the cold sank deeply into his bones. Resting for just a few minutes caused him to experience a shivering numbing pain. His only choice was to keep moving.

The sun clung to the horizon and barely rose or sank anymore. It made it impossible to determine the time of day and he had given up guessing. He no longer needed to stagger his meals, there were none to be had. He came to a wall at the end of the path that was steeper than any of the boulders he had previously scaled and readied himself for the climb. The rock was smooth but there were a few craggy pits that allowed him to grasp at a hold to lift his weight. His body felt as light as a feather now and it was fortunate that his once muscular arms had not yet fully withered, making the ascent almost manageable. After an hour of pulling himself up the vertical cliff he saw a rim that might offer some sort of vantage point. The first he would have seen from since he began the journey. His forearms burned with a fierce pain and it felt as though taut rope had replaced his tendons. His fingers had become so numb he could hardly tell if there was strength left in them, but he relied on them just the same and hooked his heel onto the ledge above, forcing his weight upwards and thrusting his free hand above to grasp a sole crack in the rock. He strained and screamed as he eventually rose to the rim and rolled onto it. Finally there was relief from the climb and he lay on his back, staring up into the mist that drifted over him. He took a moment for himself as the blood returned to his limbs. The throbbing sensation that came next was unbearable and spasms engulfed his body.

Forcing himself to his knees, Tritan saw the end of the cliff that he had scaled and keeping himself low beneath the strong wind that could easily knock him from the summit, he peered into the distance. An infinite space of white was what he saw, the valley had come to its finale and it was as though he peered at the end of the world. In every direction there was a drop that seemed so deep it might never end. The mist parted for just a moment; long enough for Tritan to see that his only choice was to climb down into the abyss that stared menacingly up at him, hoping there would be a flat plain beneath the fog. The cold had begun to take hold of him again and his muscles were seizing. Useless and aching as they were, he would have to move fast or he would be stuck on this peak without hope of recovery. All around him was stone and there was no sign of life; somewhere in the distance was the faint outline of a forest. The trees were so far beneath him that they did not appear to be real. It was as though he was viewing the world from a plateau belonging to the gods and he felt the deep insignificance of his own life. He was as a pawn in a game that invisible deities played to amuse themselves. Such were the feeble souls of all men; pieces on a game board not knowing they were moving to the will of masters.

Tritan began his descent and tried his best to steer from the temptation of glancing down. One foothold at a time he dropped further and further, knowing that this was the point of no return for he would never be able to scale back up this infinite mountainside once he had lowered himself onto the plains below. His only encouragement was the tips of the trees that grew in size as he dropped further and further.

In a sudden moment a strong breeze came and whipped across him. He hung firm to his position but above him several rocks were loosened and fell towards him. All he could do was to bury his head and pray for them to miss him. For the best part they did, but one sharp stone caught his left hand on the knuckles and his grip was broken. Unable to hold his weight with his other hand he fell instantly. The fall was like a hallucination as he spun uncontrollably upside down and he began to see vivid visions of his life. He became aware instantly of memories he had buried deep in his mind and they flooded to him all at once. It seemed like a spiteful joke to have lived through so much to now be plummeting to his certain death.

A crunching sound, loud and disturbing, came at the

moment that Tritan landed sideways on a ledge that protruded from the mountain wall. His breath was stolen from him and were it not for the cold he would have certainly felt the severity of the clashing of his bones against the stone. He felt sick, but stretched out his hand to quickly grab at his sword that had slipped free of its sheath and clattered beneath him to the edge of the ledge where he had nearly lost it. Outdone and feeble and too afraid to move, he simply cast his eyes to the sun that lingered on the horizon, ready to set for the brief interlude of darkness that was night in this place. He stayed there, watching the fiery orange ball tickling the edges of the world, before once again it began to climb. Higher and higher back up into the sky, its strength returning. The brightness blinded Tritan and he shut his eyes, passing into a subconscious nightmare of pain and cold.

HOURS LATER TRITAN AWOKE, unsure if he was alive or dead. Had he dreamed this journey and died previously only to suffer this Elysium alone, to endure an eternity with nothing but his own mind for companionship? He dreaded the thought. Better to be the child soldier again. Better to have never existed at all. With a slow and awkward movement he raised his fingers across his eyes to shelter them from the glaring sun. The mist had cleared and he knew he had come to the beginning of a new world that he had never before seen. As the vista opened up in front of him he realised his journey had only just begun.

After an excruciating hour, traversing and lowering himself from the ledge he finally touched the ground. As his feet felt the flat surface of the plain he saw for the first time a colour other than the shades of grey and white that had surrounded him for days. It was the vermillion stain he was no stranger to. Blood seeped down his leg and covered the floor. He hadn't noticed the wound previously but as he pulled back his leggings he realised that he had landed awkwardly on his sword and caused a severe gash across his leg. He did his best to dress the wound but it ran deep and the bleeding barely slowed. Defeat and anger took hold of him, and he knelt down to the ground and began to bash his fists on the solid dirt, bruising his hands. Moments later he regretted the outburst and the wasted energy that it had consumed. But now was not the time to stop and ponder his stupidity. He must continue on as far as he could before the faintness took hold of him.

Tritan became dizzy and began to see double as he approached the forest before him. Familiar sounds of the wild returned and before long he realised that the howling sound he had believed to be the wind was something far more perilous. It was a wolf howling and with each cry the sound drew closer and closer. It had smelled his blood before he had even known he was injured. He drew his sword, though he was barely able to bear its weight anymore and he prayed fiercely that the wolf would simply pass him by. Tritan prayed. To whom or to what he did not know but his silent pleading went unanswered as the growling beast came closer and circled its prey. It was barely visible against the snowy surface and stood out only when it moved between the dark brown of the oak trees that was its domain. A moment later the wolf was gone again and the growling ceased. That only unsettled Tritan further who spun in circles looking for the beast. But the wind was all that came to him, a howling treacherous sound that was almost deafening. Then all of a sudden the great grey creature sprang at him silently and from out of nowhere. It knocked Tritan to the ground, sending his sword flying away into the distance. Tritan quickly grabbed his dagger from beneath his jerkin and turned his head from his debilitating position but he was alone again. The wolf was sizing him up and playing a cruel game. Tritan held firm to his position and concentrated fully on his hearing. No sounds came save for the continued gale that whistled in his ears. He turned and searched the ground for the wolf tracks but the wind had blown away the paw prints that had been created in the dust.

The ground seemed to move in front of him and he realised his head was spinning. He took a deep breath and tried to settle his mind but sickness took hold of him and the world around him began to drift as he staggered sideways. Then the earth itself rose up to meet him and before he realised what it was the wolf pounced onto his chest and drove him into the ground. He wrestled with the wild animal, desperately trying to keep its gnashing jaws at a distance. Tritan raised his leg and pushed his knee into the wolf's chest while attempting to strike it with his knife. He came close to drawing blood from the wild animal but the wolf was quicker and rolled away for a brief moment before resuming its attack. Tritan used his free hand to hold the wolf away from his face but moments before he was able to strike again with the dagger, the wolf sank its jagged teeth into his calf. Tritan screamed out in pain and thrashed about with his knife slitting open the wolf's front paw but this only angered the beast further. Tritan rolled away and caught sight of his sword again and kicked out with a fortunate strike that sent the wolf reeling backwards for a moment, long enough for Tritan to grab the weapon. He took up the hilt and swirled to face the foe but the distance between them was already so short that the length of the blade was useless to him. He acted instinctively, swinging down the hilt of the sword instead, hammering it into the wolf's skull and knocking it unconscious instantly. Tritan didn't hesitate. He slit the animal's throat and then like a wild man of the old days, he began to hack away at the raw meat, cutting chunks of flesh into smaller pieces that he then ravaged. Tritan became a base creature, acting the way any other would when driven to the point of survival. For survival was all that was left to him in this barren land. He ate well, ignoring the blood that seeped down his chin as he continued to feed. Tritan felt alive, so alive. It was like he had drunk a magic elixir and the thrill lasted for a great time.

When sense returned to him and conscious thoughts of his human mind were once again possible he began to cultivate the meat for his onward journey. He packed the pieces into a cloth and dressed the two new wounds formed of deep holes created by the wolf's fangs. It was a severe wound, worse even than the gash created by his sword. For these marks were jagged and deeper still. He could not worry about that now, his energy had been replenished and he knew he must continue so he set off into the forest, wrapping cuts of meat that he slid into his jerkin. Tritan made it just a few steps before he heard yet another wild sound. But this one was far higher pitched and he realised the yelping sound he heard was coming from a tiny hole at the base of a tree. It was there that he found the small wolf pup and realised that he had trespassed onto the grounds of a wolf's den. The wolf he had killed was merely protecting its young the way any parent would. Tritan hated himself in that moment when he realised what he had done. At the time it had been merely self-defence and after all he needed the meat. But now all he felt was guilt. He had been the intruder and now he had left this poor pup all alone and afraid. It was young. Much too young to fend for itself and before he knew why, Tritan took the quivering creature into his hands, bundled it in a warm cloth and tucked it into a deep pocket.

DAYS CAME and went and darkness never returned. The nights were as bright as day and even in the thickest parts of the strange looming forest it was impossible to rest. The trees grew in strange shapes as if the branches themselves recoiled from the sky and hunched back towards the earth, searching for solace from the overbearing light. In spite of the flatness of the ground the roots of the great trees broke free of the earth making it swell with their sinister shapes. There were parts where it was impossible to see the ground and to tread through the depths of this wild place was unsteady work. No creatures lingered here; the only signs of life were the trees themselves and the rich moss that clung to the base of their trunks. It was a labyrinth. No way to see forward and no way to see back. Tritan attempted more than once to scale the highest branches but they became too thin to hold his weight in spite of the thin excuse of a man he had become. At one point he managed to climb dangerously high but above him in every direction were the thin fingers of wispy branches and their leaves were so thick it restricted the view to his close surroundings.

The scraps of meat he had scrounged did not last long, especially as he now cared for the wolf pup and despite his better judgement, he knew he must feed it something. Tritan tried to ignore that the meat was its parent and the pup, itself unaware, had ravished the food as quickly as Tritan had. Now they had taken to sucking the moss that grew plentiful for it was their only choice. The transition from fully-fledged carnivores to this diet of vegetation had not been easy and at first the pup had refused to consider the greenery as food at all. Only terrible hunger had changed its mind after two days chewing on Tritan's clothes as if the leather would bring nourishment. It didn't.

Another couple of days passed by and the only change to the gruelling routine was in the dampness of the air. Now the deluge of a terrible storm met them. The rain bore down on them and it was as if there was no space between the drops. It was a match even for the floods in Baurticeford. Tritan became soaked through to the bone and the wolf pup with him.

Searching for some semblance of shelter meant merely to tuck beneath the overhanging trunk of an obscure tree as it leant to its side. The ground remained thick with the rain but at least it diverted the falling waters from hitting them from above. Tritan stayed hidden in this miserable place for hours, his mind once again attacking him with its uncontrollable thoughts. He recognised the sensation; depression. It was a horrible way to be and Tritan, though he still retained his logic, could not help but calculate all the ways in which he now suffered and how he deserved it. He was no stranger to the ways in which the mind can weaken a man and his purpose, and now he was completely at the mercy of his subconscious. He could no longer believe his journey was justified. Instead he began to consider he was finally being truly punished for the things he had done in his life. He thought of the innocents that had fallen victim to the swing of his sword, and the loved ones he had mistreated and taken for granted as if they lived only to serve his selfish desires. He thought about his foolish hope as if there was some redemption in traipsing after the man who had raised him. Tritan had fooled himself into believing that it was the fault only of Augustus that he had done the things he had done. But that too was Tritan's selfishness. How had he never taken responsibility for his own actions? How foolish to think that he could ever be forgiven for what he had done. Such dark thoughts grew inside him and rose up like a wild fire, burning his failing body from the inside out, eating away his hope.

As his mind weakened, Tritan became increasingly aware of the wounds on his legs. He peeled back the sodden cloth and saw the inflamed teeth marks and although the gash from his sword had sealed cleanly, the deep holes from the bites had become infected and the flesh surrounding the marks were bright red and full of pus. He was falling apart, body and soul. Maybe this tree that hovered above him would be his final resting place. After all it was like a tomb and Tritan allowed himself to crawl into a foetal position as though he was returning to the womb, giving his life back to the world that had spat him out more than thirty years ago. He considered the irony of having been at the base of another tree the last time he thought he would die.

It was some hours later when Tritan woke. He knew not for how long he had slept but he knew it must have been a good stretch for his body ached and his mouth was parched. *Finally,* he thought. But the rest had done little to put his mind at ease. The rain had at least stopped and he was thankful for that. He decided that this patch where he lay would not be the last place he would know, but he no longer believed he would find his father, only that he had to move in some direction. Any direction, as if it was possible to run away from the plague-filled thoughts that battered him relentlessly.

Tritan stood and checked on the wolf pup that had also managed to sleep and it squinted as it tried to prise open its eyes to see the hulking man that looked down at it. The pup was a soft and cute looking creature and the sight of it caused Tritan to well up, he had never been there when Pietrich was so young and helpless. He had missed all those years where his baby would have suckled in the comfort of its mothers embrace. He had missed the first spoken words that Pietrich would have uttered and he had missed his first steps. His son was ten years old now and Tritan had never even thought to teach him how to ride a horse for the brief time he had been there. He felt nothing but a cavern of shame in his chest that restricted his breathing. He realised for the first time, that in all the years Pietrich had lived, he had been present for less than one. Maybe not even a half of one. He was angry. Tritan's shame became rage and he hated himself. How could he have left his son's side in his dying state? Because he was outcast? No. Because of his own stubborn pride and hatred for the healer that had rescued him from death. The village had forced him to leave but he had not tried to overcome their sentence. In truth, at the time it had come as a gift to him. It was like being punished with freedom, freedom to live or freedom to die he did not know. But now he realised that it was merely an invitation to pursue a prison of his own making, the one that he'd now locked himself inside. The prison of his own dark mind.

Tritan's footsteps had become slow staggers; he could barely hold his weight on the wounded leg as he hobbled through the mysterious forest. As he walked his mind drifted to thoughts of his wife. He wondered what it must be like to love a man who was never there. To fear for the safety of someone who sought out danger like an addiction and then he thought of all those wives who would not have seen their husbands again. The ones who he had sent to the grave; there were so many of those. Far too many dead fathers, sons and husbands. He had never considered that each of the lives he had taken had left loved ones behind in their wake. As if to answer his thoughts he suddenly saw in front of him the figure of a strange individual. He had to blink to satisfy himself that it was no illusion. But clear as day, at the base of a tree, there knelt a woman, dressed in a white wedding gown. She was laying bright blue mourning flowers as if she sat beside a grave. But there was no grave to be seen. The woman was young, in her early twenties and Tritan called out to her, but she did not respond. He walked closer to her and noticed the colour of her skin was unnaturally pale. She is a ghost, Tritan thought. He had heard stories of how guilt could cause the mind to send visions of those that suffered by one's own hand, but he had believed it to be nothing more than the crazed sentiments of weaker minds, drifting into insanity.

Tritan walked up beside the woman and watched as she mourned an invisible being. He leant down closer to touch her

shoulder but his hand passed right through her. She was not
real but he saw her as clear as day and the ice cold sensation
that passed across his hand as he swooped through her transparent figure was unmistakable. He felt fear prick up the hairs
on the back of his neck and he slowly stepped back from the
woman. But as he stood just a few feet from her back, her head
turned a full half turn and black eyes shot a glance up at him.
The pain he felt from those eyes was immense. It was as though
he felt all her life's suffering condensed to a mere instant. Tritan
turned and began to run but as he did so he saw all around him
dozens and dozens of other women. They had all turned to look
upon him and he was afraid, so very afraid. There was nowhere
to turn and Tritan could do nothing but avert his gaze to protect
himself from the dreadful feelings they were projecting upon
him. The whiteness of their garb and skin was an even match,
contrasted only by their eyes and the colour of their hair. Tritan
moved towards a tree which he climbed but as he reached a fair
height he saw above him, standing on an impossibly thin
branch, another one of these ghostly women. He caught a
glimpse of her stare and felt a stabbing sensation in his heart.
His hands lost their grip and he fell to the ground, thudding
against a jutting root as he landed. The woman was now over
him and he held his hands to his face to protect his eyes from
her glare. He felt the cold sensation once again as she leant
down and touched his arm. It was as if she touched the very
inside of his body with death. Tritan grabbed his dagger and
thrust it upwards into the abdomen of the woman and this time
he felt something solid. He had struck something real.

When he opened his eyes he saw the body of the woman
lying on the ground, there was no blood coming from the
wound but she was still. Tritan crawled to see the damage he
had done and worried fiercely that he had killed her. How he
wondered, for she was already dead? Then horror struck him as

he looked upon her bloodless face. He saw unmistakably the features of Marilia. He lurched back and stared upon the body of his murdered wife. It could not be true. It was not possible that this was real. Tritan took a breath and fled. He ran so hard and for so long that in spite of losing his breath his body continued onwards, his heart pounding in his chest, trying desperately to circulate enough blood to keep him conscious.

When Tritan eventually stopped he dared to double back to assess the situation and found no signs of any of the women, nor Marilia. He was by himself once more, but now the index finger on his left hand felt strange. He looked upon it and saw the tip of his finger had turned to a deep black. He squeezed it as hard as he could but there was no sensation at all. It was as though that part of him had died. How he wanted to distance himself from this place; no matter what else he might find, he could not linger here another moment. Tritan began to walk, ignoring the ache he felt in his leg as his pace quickened. Eventually he came across a strange clearing; he thought that night had finally returned until he realised that what he saw was the blackened corpses of the forest. The trees had all become skeletons of charcoal and a strange ash floated in the air around him. He became aware of cadavers scattered about the dead forest. There were so many dead animals, buried deep beneath the grey dust. He held his arm to his mouth to avoid breathing this treacherous air. None of it made sense. A tear trickled down his face, smearing the grey ash across his cheek.

Snap. A branch above him cracked and before Tritan knew what had happened he was flung into the air. A rope had tightened around his ankle and pulled him upwards. He saw the world hanging upside down around him. He tried to swing free but it was hopeless. He dangled for a time and all his efforts to wriggle free were to no avail. Somewhere in the clearing a hooded figure approached him. This figure was no ghost, but a skinny man, fully cloaked and peppered in strange markings. His face was obscured by the shadows created by the hood that loosely shrouded his head but Tritan could tell he was old. He carried a long staff in his hand that was beautifully carved but before Tritan could look more upon it he saw a dozen other figures following closely behind the old tribal man. The first of the group to approach him was a young girl. She sniffed Tritan and circled him with curiosity while the others stood in a full circle around him. The rest of the tribe all held spears, but the spears were antiquated carved branches with sharpened stones. Not the kind he was familiar with. They began to speak to one another in a strange language that Tritan had never heard before. Not one word resembled any dialect that he had ever encountered.

The tribe leader, whose face remained hidden, finally approached Tritan to make his own assessment. The shadowy figure came close to his face; close enough to smell the putrid odour of his breath. Tritan's blood rushed to his head and his skull pounded. The old man turned to address his tribe and held out his staff, shouting what seemed like a series of strict orders. Before Tritan could try to determine what fate was being decided for him, the old man spun and cracked him across the head with the bulky edge of the staff, sending him into an unconscious state. The world around him vanished, quickly and fiercely as though he were a faltering candle flame snuffed out in a storm.

27

A n old belief stretching back across the ages is that our dreams come to us when we need them most. The first type of dream warns us of danger or awakens us to our true desires, thoughts buried so deep that we do not realise they are there. They help us to combat our worst fears and encourage strength to overcome our anxieties. The second form of dream we call nightmares and should we not rise above the fear they instil inside our hearts, they truly consume us.

Tritan's dream was constant and each time it reached its conclusion no consciousness came. He only returned to the beginning of the story to relive the day again and again. Surprisingly, it was the first dream about dying Tritan had ever had. Many details were false, like the fact that in the dream he had a sister. He could never understand why this was the case for he had always believed that he was an only child. It was all he knew so he had never questioned the fact. Perhaps it was the lack of a female presence in his early life? But why then had he dreamt separately of his mother on many occasions. These were the riddles presented in the subconscious and Tritan felt the questions circling the walls of his mind as he slept. It was a strange half sleep for he held awareness of the dream. He knew he slept and yet he could not wake. It was in the old barn that the dream took place. The walls were thick and little light crept in through the small windows but the roof had half fallen in, scattering broken slate across the floor and that was where the sun beamed down fiercely. It was a dusty space and the old furniture was covered with sheets as if forgotten by those who had possessed them.

Tritan's sister lay by his side. He had once again returned to the beginning of the dream. Soon she would be screaming and running for her life. She did. Tritan chased after her, calling out, trying to warn her of the impending danger ahead but she would not listen. She never listened. They ran and ran through a barley field that had grown as high as their shoulders. It was a thick maze of warm beige tentacles and he almost lost her but eventually they reached the far side of the field where it became flat and they turned to face the dozen horseback riders that pursued them. The dream sister screamed and fell where she stood but Tritan, as always, lifted her to her feet and directed her towards an old fortress, one of the ancient royal castles that had once guarded the land. This one stood proud as though transporting them back to a time thousands of years past before the many storms and wars razed so many magnificent structures to the ground.

The large wooden doors that led to the outer courtyard were ajar and Tritan and the dream sister fled through them. The riders were just seconds behind them. They fled into an old chamber, filled with armour and paintings and lavish silks that hung from ceilings as high as giants. Nothing this ornate existed in the Harmion that Tritan had been born into. But the dream had passed a memory to him. Perhaps the memory of those whose bloodline he belonged to. Whoever they may be.

They stood surrounded by the riders, swords closing in. Tritan pushed his sister towards a small spiral stairwell that headed upwards towards the bell tower. The bell began to toll and the sound was so loud it drowned out the clatter of her footsteps as she made her way through a doorway. As Tritan rushed behind her a sharp pain shot through his spine and he fell, crashing to the floor. As he rolled to his side he felt the sword that protruded from his back. The next sword came down upon him and his vision was lost. But his other senses remained. He could smell the sweat and the blood. He could hear the screams above the ringing of the bell, bouncing off the solid stone stairs and as the dizziness came to him the sound of his sister's screams echoed piteously down the stairwell. He waited. Waited for the moment when the next sword would strike him and he would once again awaken in the old barn, lying beneath the straw wondering how he could alter the events in the nightmare for it happened the same way each time.

Tritan heard the yelling pain of his sister as he slipped away from her but this time the waiting continued for an eternity. The blackness remained and echoes of her screaming faded until all that was audible were the dull sounds of dripping water hitting the stony ground around him. But there had been no water in the dream. The smell of sweat had become the smell of death and old decay, and suddenly Tritan realised he was no longer asleep. He had woken into another nightmare. This time the nightmare was real.

Tritan rolled his eyes about the place, trying to find some faint outline of a shape to determine where he lay. But there was no light at all. He moved his arm slowly and carefully around the floor and felt the damp straw beneath his back. He brushed his palm across the side of his head and felt a bump the shape and size of an egg. It ached but did not feel fresh and he wondered for how long he had been left unconscious in this position. He suddenly remembered the wolf pup and went to feel his pocket but it was empty and all sign of the pup had gone. All his other possessions had been sequestered from his person, his sword and even his thick winter layers. He supposed those had been taken to prevent him finding comfort in this dark place, whatever it was. Thankfully the chill of the outside world was lost to the space he was now in and he felt warmth unlike any he had known in weeks. As he moved to stand he realised he could not. His leg had lost all strength and to worsen his situation he had a vine tether secured around his ankle. It was coated in a strange sap that strengthened it and without his sword there was no chance of removing the bind.

A small flickering light approached from the distance. Under the circumstances it was almost blinding, but Tritan could now make out that he was behind bars in a small cell. The bars were made of a strange wood that was smooth and almost perfectly straight but it seemed strong as iron. He had never seen anything of the kind and were he not in so much pain he might have taken a moment to admire it. This cell had clearly been the result of a recently ordered renovation for its shape was strange, like a fox's den. The walls were all rocky and the floor too was of a natural form. But the wooden bars and the cleanliness of the cell were unnaturally fresh, as though he were its first occupant. Incongruously there was a putrid smell coming from the far corner of the cell. The corner was obscured in darkness but as the holder of the flickering torch took each step closer to the cell the shadow moved across the wall and slowly but surely the figure of a man was revealed. Tritan stared at the body and moved as close as he dared before gagging. The corpse belonged to an old man, covered head to toe in tattoos. His skin had been preserved by some strange method for though no expert, Tritan knew this man had been dead for some years. The long white beard remained clinging to the skull and Tritan remembered the old tribal leader who had stood cloaked before him, moments before he had struck him unconscious with his cane. Despite the decayed form of the leathery flesh of the corpse the two tribesmen were the spitting image of each other. Though he had not seen the features of the hooded man's face, the length and texture of the beard had been almost identical. The tattoos on the right shoulder were the exact same, three small lines that had been formed by the use of a burning hot tool. These were the only things Tritan could recall about the tribal leader. He had not been conscious long enough to take on board more detail and he was no longer the soldier he had been previously. That man would have taken a mental note of every aspect of his lead captor before the blow would have come. But no more, that man was gone. Now he was just a man. No. A boy, searching for his father with no army at his side and no sword on his belt.

Tritan turned towards the flickering light but saw only a skinny shadow before him, someone staring down at him through the bars. After a moment's contemplation the figure turned and fled down the tunnel from where they had come and the light fled with them. Tritan was again plunged into darkness and he knew that soon someone of importance would be made aware of his awakening. He dreaded the moments that would follow and wished he had remained lying face down, pretending to sleep. But it was too late. He had been seen awake and soon someone else would come for him. He didn't know why he was still alive but he feared he would soon find out the purpose of his capture. He had once again escaped death and knew that his current fate would be something worse. He waited and waited to meet his impending doom, longing for his Elysium.

Tritan felt a throbbing sensation in his injured leg. In the darkness, he pulled back the cloth that had stuck to the open wound. He felt carefully around the edges of the wound and realised that the skin was raw, swollen and sensitive. The infection had worsened and he feared for the resulting outcome of this affliction. He gritted his teeth and tried as hard as he dared to move onto his feet. It was slow and painful but he managed it. At the very least he may still be able to hobble in the darkness.

He continued to wait for someone to return for him but they did not come. So Tritan determined himself to rest instead. He assumed at some point they must either come for him or he would be left to starve. The second outcome seemed unlikely for it must have taken some effort to move him underground and into this cell. To leave him to simply perish seemed a great waste and a foolish choice for this tribe, no matter how primitive they were; surely they must hold a greater purpose for him.

Tritan rolled onto his side to allow his injured leg to remain free and closed his eyes and tried to sleep again. The next time he woke there was a candle burning by the entrance to the cell and a small wooden bowl of soup had been provided for him. He grabbed the broth and consumed it almost in one gulp. It was cold and must have been left some time ago. He considered calling out to his incarcerators but he could form no sounds. Perhaps it was better to wait as long as they saw fit before doing with him as they wished.

As Tritan placed the wooden bowl back to the floor the noise echoed around the enclosure. A few moments later he heard another sound coming from the movement of some heavy instruments in the distance. The banging came at him from several directions and he guessed that he was in a cave network of some description. Then the footsteps came. As if on a gust of wind, fate came to claim him and dragged him slowly from where he lay. Two pairs of strong arms pulled him from the chamber and as Tritan could barely stagger, they hauled his ragged body across the rocky floor of the cave, through the darkness towards the clanging sounds that grew louder as they approached.

Tritan was flung into an open chamber; it was a large hall, dimly lit by the burning torches that rested in hooks attached to the natural walls. He was dumped unceremoniously at the centre of the room and stayed perched on his knees with no energy remaining to him.

A horde of men, women and children had gathered to see the spectacle. At least thirty people of all ages, dressed in thin, modest cloth, circled him, speaking in a tongue that was a mystery to their captive. Somewhere in the distance and amidst the fray of confusion lurked the tribe leader. He paced slowly and unnoticed by all but Tritan. His face remained obscured by the hood and the darkness of the shadows stared into Tritan's gaze. Their look continued for some time and Tritan was resolute to discover his purpose from this man and from him alone. But for now he would not be afforded that pleasure. The young girl who had assessed him as he had hung upside down, ensnared in their trap in the decaying forest above, came to face him. She smelled Tritan's lank hair that had grown into a mess of straw-like tangles. She ran her gentle fingers across his jaw, brushing against the weathered and greying beard that showed the signs of his approaching middle age. Tritan looked into her eyes and for a moment he could swear he saw kindness.

The tribe girl snapped her fingers and instantly two men came to lift Tritan onto his feet. They spread his limbs, exposing him in a position that shot fear through his heart. Another man and woman came from the distance, dragging a wooden frame along the dirty, dusty floor. They raised it behind Tritan and placed the bottom of the pike into a deep hole to keep it upright. Tritan was tied to the frame and strong binds, made of the same vine as had been used in his cell, were secured around his wrists so that he could not fall. They let him go and his body slumped but remained dangling there like a scarecrow; he was their puppet and the show had barely begun its opening act.

The moment of benevolence that followed confused Tritan greatly. The girl approached with a bowl of thick green paste that one of the elder women of the tribe had prepared. She smothered the paste on Tritan's wounded leg and wrapped a string of leaves around it to hold the paste in place. It was a cool and calming sensation and he welcomed it. He almost smiled at the girl but her actions were so methodical and emotionless that he decided the act was not selfless.

Tritan gazed all around the chamber at this strange collection of primitive beings. He saw families huddled together, respected elders resting their wearied bones and young children running and playing around the pillars that joined the floor of the cave to its ceiling. This community was lost to the rest of the world and maybe even lost to time itself. It seemed as though they had existed in the simplest way for an eternity and thousands of years more could pass and their culture would remain intact and unspoiled. Tritan realised he envied them and their beauty. Did they even know what life held in store for the rest of humanity? Their secret was a gift and Tritan recognised the feeling he felt towards them. Jealousy. It was a fierce jealousy. How he longed to be with them, to remove himself of his past and the knowledge of a greedier world of men who fought for power. How serene it would be to occupy this world and live within its embrace. The cave was like nature's cradle and these tribal beings were the infants she had deemed to be special, hers to protect and preserve, above all others.

Sprawled out on the floor in front of Tritan were two women. They scratched in the dirt and shouted their mysterious words. The symbols in the earth were a strange collection of circles. Without any true meaning he could discern but clearly the tribe was enraptured by what they saw. The women gestured to the walls of the cave and ran their flaming torches across the murals and Tritan saw for the first time the artwork that was magnificent and harrowing. Blackened charcoal had been used across the ages to draw depictions of battles and tribal triumphs of the hunt. Men with spears were shown fighting ferocious wild beasts three times their size. This tribe followed the most ancient way of life and had never needed to grow beyond its means.

The tribe leader proceeded towards a point on the wall and held his flaming torch towards the rocky surface, lighting it up and the flames flickered like dancing flies. The shadows kissed the walls and the light that was cast beside them revealed the roots of a great tree. The roots were jutting out of the walls and climbed towards the ceiling where they vanished into the rock. Each root had a channel burrowed into the rock and branches were drawn on the ceiling above. Then the hooded man turned to face Tritan again and this time he approached him. As he walked it was as though Tritan was caught in a trance and the figure floated forwards as though he were weightless. His steps were slow and methodical, as though they were withholding the pleasure of a great discovery so profound that he dared not rush the moment of ecstasy.

The shadowy face continued towards Tritan who was now shaking and sweating from fever and nearly on the verge of passing out. The position where they had fixed him had caused all the blood to run down towards his legs and he was barely capable of keeping his eyes open. *Just long enough*, he prayed. Long enough to see this man for whom he really was and, as if the tribe leader had heard his wishes, he pulled back the hood that obscured his face and moments before the darkness consumed him, Tritan saw his father. It was Augustus who spoke.

'Yes, of course. Of course.'

28

D arkness causes fear in the sturdiest of men. It reaches out to grasp them and wraps its cloak of terror around them and when they stare into the darkness they see the darkness in themselves. The young begin by fearing the shadows for they cannot see nor know the dangers hiding in the obscure corners. They seek immediately their mother's protection and desire the warmth and comfort of the light of day. But if one such child should spend too many years in the darkness alone it will consume them and it will be the light they fear most. For the light reveals all hope and love and beauty. To an isolated man these are the most dangerous things in the world for they break down the barriers of steel that darkness forges around the heart, leaving its fragility exposed like a newborn chick in an unguarded nest.

Tritan awoke curled like an infant. Plunged once more into the arms of the pitch black that filled the network of caves. He sensed that he had been moved into another space for the air smelled fresher but this space was small. He could touch the walls all around him without moving from where he lay, as though he had been thrown into some sort of pit. His eyes now adjusted to the darkness, there was at least a trickle of ambient light from the evening fire that illuminated his surroundings above. It was hazy and hard to focus but he saw a wooden slatted roof made of the same material as the bars in the cell from where he had been moved. The slatted structure seemed merely a man's height above him and in spite of the pain shooting through his leg, Tritan stood and grasped the bars that were secured by ties of the sap soaked vine. He yelled out furiously with all his strength and the echoes of his roar flew throughout the caves and returned to him and he knew that the tribe would have heard his scream. He roared again and again until his voice was hoarse and then he fell back to the ground and wept. To distract himself from his sadness he observed the condition of his leg. The leaves were still attached though the paste appeared to have dissolved and a white pus had formed, seeping out from the edges of the dressing. His body was pushing out the infection and he prayed it was not working itself deeper into the flesh.

Tritan reached out to feel the walls around him again. The space he was in was so small that it was impossible to lie down without curling into an awkward shape. As his hands moved across the rocks he saw the faint outline of a handprint that had been forged by blood. He rested his palm across the print and was taken aback, as his own hand fitted its shape perfectly. He wondered what fate had befallen the previous captive and how long ago this print was made. It seemed worn by time and could have been years past since it was made or even centuries.

Footsteps approached above and the hands of two tribesmen untied the vine that secured the beams of wood before removing them and dropping a rope ladder. One of the men shouted down to Tritan and gestured for him to climb. Tritan waited silently until the man called out to him again but remained where he sat. The man jumped down into the pit to join Tritan who barely had the strength to stand let alone fight him. He conceded to their demands and, with assistance, pulled himself up and ascended the rope ladder before the two men helped carry him along the rocky corridor. This time they took greater care with him and helped him to walk and before long Tritan was back inside the large chamber, surrounded by the entire tribe and once again they secured him to the wooden structure.

Augustus was in the distance, painting a fresh depiction of a battle. It showed a horse with a young man riding atop his steed that had an arrow jutting from its left eye socket and Tritan knew the horse was his dear Diablo and the young man was he. He recalled the battle where his horse had lost his sight but had remained strong and continued bravely with the arrow protruding from its head. Tritan had fought like a savage on that day, raining down terror on his enemies and protecting his old friend. Many days after the battle the horse had suffered an infection in the other eye and Tritan had been forced to cut out the one that remained, leaving the two empty sockets exposed. The warnings he had been given by the 11th to put the horse down had offended him and instead Tritan had taken to training Diablo to ride blindly, trusting Tritan and Tritan alone. He was just seventeen at the time.

Tritan missed his friend and wondered what fate had befallen the horse and the kid and the strange tongue-less man who had fled as a distraction, allowing Tritan to journey to this place where he was now captive. He had succeeded in discovering his father but this was not what he had planned or expected. To be tied up by a tribe that had clearly fallen to Augustus's leadership. He thought about the body of the tribe leader that had been left in the cell and wondered how Augustus had managed to overpower him and take his position.

In some way he knew that it was a task only Augustus could accomplish but he could not figure out the reason why. What could this tribe have offered him after all these years? Had Augustus found what he was looking for as he retraced the steps of the old legend of Rose? Tritan was not sure if the truth would ever be revealed to him but as each moment passed, little by little, he would unravel the mystery.

Augustus turned to face the tribe and gesticulated wildly, shouting out to them in their tongue. The sermon sounded poetic and Tritan was enraptured by the sounds that he did not understand. It was only in the moment when Augustus turned to point at him that he was struck again by fear, clearly he was the subject of the sentences that were being spoken.

Now the tribe returned Augustus's ranting with their own shouts and cries. There were excited cries of pleasure and several members began to bang on deep-toned drums formed from old solid trunks and the tightened skin of hunted animals. The drumming was incessant but intoxicating, like a ceremony or ritual. The young tribe girl approached Augustus and he whispered to her. In her hands she clutched a small clay bowl and a sharp bone knife. She nodded at his instruction and proceeded towards Tritan and tore the jerkin from his chest. She ran her hand across his trembling body and traced the outline of a scar with her finger. The next sensation was of a warm trickling as the razor sharp bone cut deep across his scar. The blood trickled down his abdomen and the tribe girl collected the red drops into a small bowl. The cut was not too deep but enough that he bled sufficiently to fill the bowl and once she had filled it she returned the bowl to Augustus who carried its contents to the roots of the tree that jutted out from the rocks.

Augustus wailed in time with the banging of the drums, beautiful sounds that carried throughout the chamber and the pain in Tritan's chest was almost abated by the heady dreamlike song, as if music could cure the pain of the body by easing the mind.

Augustus began to paint the blood onto the cave wall, creating small branches and leaves that connected to the roots. The image was a wonder but the roots were large and spread across almost half the chamber wall. The level of blood in the bowl ran low quickly and again the tribe girl proceeded to fill it from Tritan's wound. She passed the bowl to Augustus who continued his ritual and when the bowl was once again empty he gestured to the tribe girl to fill it a third time. This time she answered in response to his instruction and pointed to Tritan who was now dizzy from the loss of blood. Augustus shouted at her and objected to her refusal but she insisted they could not continue. Augustus took the bowl from her hand and went to stand by Tritan, staring deeply into his eyes. He saw a man on the brink of slipping away and waved his hand to the tribe who stopped their drumming. Augustus walked away from the chamber and the tribe girl rushed to Tritan and cried out to the healers who approached with the strange paste that had been used to seal his wounded leg. One of the elder women from the tribe covered Tritan's midriff with the paste and plastered the wound with the cool leaves that held it in place and the bleeding slowed instantly. The tribe girl took a pail of water and lifted it to Tritan's mouth. With his remaining strength he sipped the pail dry before his head slumped into a half comatose state.

When he opened his eyes once more, Tritan was back inside his pit with the slatted beams secured above. He was once again lying in a foetal position and shivering from the cold as his body fought against his wounds. His old scar had sealed cleanly but the bite wound on his leg continued to produce pus and the dressing had been forced clear of the affliction. He heard the sound of the gate being loosed above but did not avert his eyes from the ground where he lay. It was too soon. Far too soon to continue their incessant rituals of bleeding for he could not survive another turn in the chamber above; surely they must know that.

The calm and quiet footsteps circled around Tritan and the gelid shiver of fear shot through him, but the hands that came down to touch him were gentle. It was the tribe girl and she began to work on his wounded leg, removing the old dressing and securing a new covering of paste and leaves. Once she had finished she climbed the rope ladder and left him to rest. He dared not acknowledge her in case his movement was mistaken for strength. He slept.

THE CAVE WAS quiet and still and neither light nor sound existed in the clutches of the rocky labyrinth. Tritan mumbled to himself as he imagined the words of Augustus singing to the tribe that had fallen prey to his every demand. But now the words became those that he knew. He began to understand the strange language and only moments later did he realise that Augustus stood in the shadows above his pit with a flaming torch in hand.

'We hoard from birth, taking ownership over everything we see. Now at the end of life, all that I have obtained is in here,' Augustus said, tapping his skull. 'For sixty years I have fought for my ideals but time has changed the world and they are no longer relevant. What is it for then that we do the things we do? We spend our lives trying to be bigger in the world that is so vast. But I find greater meaning in the smaller things now, a simple walk amongst the trees to listen to the sound of a morning bird sing. To watch a caterpillar crawl across a leaf as the morning mist disperses in the valley. Why then should we not make ourselves smaller? So those little moments can resound with greater reverberation. At one time I led over eight thousand men. I would walk past the barracks of a night and see their faces. They meant nothing to me, nor did I mean anything to them. But when I rode with just a hundred men, I knew them all, cared for them all. Empathy is a hard tool to grasp for any man. To apply it to a mass of strangers is impossible.' Augustus paused for a moment, as if something disturbed him. Then he continued. 'I recall the burning of the edifices of worship. A masterstroke in the early stages of the war, before you were born, that shattered the lives of tens of thousands and all in a single evening. We rounded up all those who were stuck in the old ways, locked them in their halls with their deities and set them all aflame. I watched as the building before me burned and the screams collapsed into the roar of the inferno. I felt for those hundred innocents then. But what of the other tens of thousands who perished that same evening? For them I shed not one single tear. It is for this we men can cause so much pain, and justify the destruction we cause as we pass through life. I know now that the soul of a man who takes a single life, with his own hands, suffers greater than the king who sits protected behind his walls, while others kill thousands at his behest.'

Tritan looked up through the grate above the pit where he was restrained. The flickering shadowy outline of Augustus was all he saw, the outline of his overgrown beard cut jagged shapes onto the cave walls behind him. Tritan loosened his dry throat and struggled with all his concentration to form words. 'I remember another man who spoke words like those, you had me kill him while I was still a child.'

Augustus considered the words but proceeded as if he had not heard them. 'I fear I have none of my own decisions remaining, only the will to plough onward. I have been falling for so long, I fear I may never touch the ground again. That is why, in spite of whatever guilt I possess, I can still do what must be done. I have given you all your pain and stripped you of all potential but that which I would forge for my own purpose. Even after I thought you dead I affected the things over which I had no control, for my influence festered in you. To bring you here now it must have been so. A poisoned seed that grew long after it had been sown. Now I must ask you once more to be my tool. Though as you well know, I make no request. I only offer the sorrow of a would-be father, as I feel now that you have come to me again as though you truly were my son.'

Tritan didn't understand the meaning of the last sentence. Had Augustus plunged into such madness that he had severed all his ties as though this tribe were his only family now? 'You have trapped me in your shadow my entire life. That is the true prison you have locked me in. It is a bolted cage, unlike the one you hold me in now, for which no key exists.'

'Oh, but there is a key, Tritan. It lies in the heart of the oldest story of them all.'

29

The mist clung to her as strongly as she clung to her baby. The rocky passage was almost impassable but Rose, with the babe secured to her back, reached up to the craggy rocks and pulled herself higher and higher. Atop the ridge that overlooked the white salt flats, the mist was so thick it was as if you could leap into its embrace and fall softly to the ground unharmed.

Rose looked back over the precipice she had spent the day climbing and, of the hundred king's men sent to pursue her, only a dozen now remained. She carried herself across the flat-lands with her son and made her way through the labyrinth forest until eventually she came to a clearing. The sight was beautiful. Hundreds of animals ran in packs around the perimeter of a clear water lake that stretched from one side of the clearing to the other. Mountains hung at its back where the sun tickled the ridges as it began to set.

She heard the footsteps of her pursuers and turned back to face the lake. There was nowhere to run, but in the middle of the lake was a small island and without giving it further thought, Rose leapt into the water, her baby still strapped to her back, swimming furiously towards the island. She reached the shore and turned to see eight men watching her from across the water. She knew they would have to dive in to reach her and so she waited. Eventually the men spread out along the banks of the lake and then slowly waded into the waters from each side. She was surrounded. It was then she resolved to do something she'd never believed herself capable of. *Better to die her way and by her means.* She took out her pocketknife and slit the arteries of her wrists on both sides. She fell, instantly, dizzy and weak. Her hands immediately lost their use but she somehow managed to clutch the knife between her two wrists and moments before she passed out, she plunged the knife into the chest of her baby boy. They would die together. She had taken from the king the pride of killing his prey and sacrificed herself and her baby rather than be captured by this horde of soldiers. The men returned from whence they came, dejected though their task was complete. But they did not make it far for a mysterious gathering of men and women robed in animal skins and armed with spears attacked them. None of the king's men survived.

It was the next day that the tribe returned to the lake to find a silver barked tree with bright red leaves flowing from its branches at the centre of the island. Miraculously the tree was fully grown though the day before it had not existed. At the base of its trunk was baby Maldus. His wound had healed completely and he cried fiercely, full of life as he lay by his dead mother's side. It was in this moment that the prophesy of his bloodline was born.

TIED ONCE MORE to his wooden frame, Tritan heard the story from Augustus the way the tribe had told it to him. It was hard to take in and even harder to believe. In a matter of moments,

Tritan had learnt that Augustus was not his real father. Worse, the tongue-less man who had protected him was the old friend of Augustus and had truly loved Tritan's mother. *He* was his true father. Tritan was on the verge of tears and rage and what else, he knew not for there were no words to describe how he felt; but the story had not ended. Augustus went on to explain what Boscelito had found, determining his decision to turn his cloak. The boy Maldus had been raised by the tribe but when he was grown he realised he was not one of them and became resolute that he would return to the lands where he was born. The tribe locked him away, fearing for the ill omen of allowing this prophesied child to leave. But Maldus was so committed to discovering his homeland that he fought his way out of the caves and journeyed south, travelling back down the very path his mother had brought him all those years before.

Tritan dropped his gaze from Augustus, barely able to meet his eyes as the old man spoke. 'They have waited a long time, thousands of years for you to return, Tritan. A descendent of the miracle child, your own mother was one of a rare settlement of islanders whose lineage traces back to Maldus after he returned from Orldin. Maldus settled on the islands and lived out a quiet and peaceful life. The truth of his history is told in the folk tales of this tribe and those who dwell in the outer islands of Harmion. None of it is written. So you see now, the importance of who you are. Now you have come back to me, my adopted child, ready to do your duty one more time, before it is too late and the heart of the world stops beating.'

Tritan went to speak but no words came to him. He had lost the father he thought he'd had and only recently he had travelled with the man who had truly fathered him, though he had not known it. Was life so cruel that it would deal him blackened cards for every hand? His whole life had been a lie and he knew not how to determine for which actions he was now responsible. Had he played the part of a puppet for so long that he was nothing more than a weighted instrument to be cast into the fires and forged like a steel blade, ripe for killing. Although a sword makes no choice in the manner in which it is used, still, it is the steel of the blade that cuts the flesh.

Finally, Tritan moved his mouth and produced a guttural sound like an infant learning to speak for the first time. 'You have ruined me. I am ruined.'

'Yes, you are a ruined man, but ruins are imperishable. A monastery that stands proud at the top of the hill is weak for it is valuable. The rubble at the side of a dirt road means nothing to anyone and has no value. And yet if you know how, you can build with the rubble and make the world anew.' Augustus paused and ran his hand across Tritan's head, feeling the scraggy hair of the man he had raised. Tritan found the touch offensive but in his captive state he could not protest. 'All things are connected in this world. The tree brought new life to Harmion and as the tree dies, the land dies with it. You have seen the things I have seen. You can take solace in the knowledge that only you and the blood that flows within your veins can make things right.'

Tritan hung his head. He cared not for his supposed value, for he did not believe it nor did he want it to be true. He felt sick to the pit of his stomach and cursed himself for his decision to pursue Augustus. Once again he felt as though he had failed and that fate had been taken out of his hands, even at the point when he believed he was finally taking control of his own destiny. *What a fool.* Tritan looked about the chamber and saw the part-painted tree, glimmering red and reflecting in the firelight, the red of his blood.

The ceremonies continued in much the same way. For days Tritan was used as a means to produce blood for the depiction of the tree on the wall. His blood seeped through the cracks in the dirt and tickled the roots of the tree that protruded from the roof of the cave. By the time Tritan could no longer hold his eyes open the tree had been half painted and once again he was cast into the dark pit where the tribe girl visited him and dressed his wounds. The scar on his chest was barely visible anymore for so many cuts obscured it.

A white light flickered in his eyes as a blurry vision of red came into focus. Tritan was lifted from the ground by the two strong hands of a young soldier. Lying on the floor was the bloodied sight of his mother. He was so tiny and filled the palms of Augustus's hands as he was lifted to the skies and presented to the surviving members of the 11th Legion. Tritan wailed and screamed and heard the sounds of his own making, the howls of a newborn babe. A banging sound resounded all around him as he floated aimlessly into the sky. It was as though he was flying. The banging became stronger and stronger until he woke and returned to the large cave chamber, surrounded by the tribe who had continued their ceremony. He looked down to see the form of a grown man once more and the blood that poured from his chest was caught in the same wooden bowl as before. He wasn't even in pain anymore and could no longer tell for how long he had been bled. How many days had he been forced to repeat this endless ritual? His beard had grown out more and when his eyes eventually managed to flicker a glance at the wall he saw the mural of the tree was almost complete.

That night the tribe didn't even bother to return Tritan to his pit. They simply left him dangling from the wooden frame where he was tied. Clearly they believed his use to them was coming to an end. In spite of the exhaustion that was destroying him, Tritan stayed awake and looked about at the tribe as they slept. The young girl seemed innocent and appeared younger than when she was cutting him with her bone knife. He wondered if she was also being used against her will. The tribe followed Augustus because he had overpowered their old leader. It seemed as though they were quick to follow any signs presented to them that a higher power was at work and for a moment Tritan felt as though he knew the answer to his salvation. But Augustus still scared him in spite of the fact he finally knew the truth; it was still hard to believe. He had spent his whole life in the man's shadow, believing that he owed him a debt he could never repay, but it was Augustus who owed him a debt, the life of not only a mother, but also a father. But to rise above Augustus now seemed like a dream or a story from a song. But this was his life and it was real and such triumph only existed in folk tales.

It had been some time since Tritan had felt bothered by his leg and only the draught that ran through the caves made him realise it was still exposed. He could see the flesh flickering in the fading light of the torches that were burning out and the wound seemed to be forming into a scar. The pus and infection had passed. The crude methods of healing had worked. He wondered if the completion of the painted tree would be the moment the tribe would kill him.

As the chamber plunged into darkness, Tritan finally slept. He dreamt once more of his mother's corpse, lying bloodied on the ground, and Augustus presenting him to his army. The only family he had ever known.

When he woke again he realised that the tribe had already cut him once more whilst he had slept, so accustomed to the blade he hadn't even stirred. Augustus was busy painting the tree and the tribe was celebrating. It was done. The mural was complete and now was the hour that he would truly know his fate. A warrior from the tribe approached Augustus; he was carrying provisions for a day's journey and had a cloth wrapped around his head. He lifted the cloth to cover his mouth and

Augustus kissed the man on the forehead before he set out into the wilderness. Augustus turned to face Tritan before he spoke.

'Now we see together, after years of waiting.' He stroked the jutting roots as if searching for a sign of life. The tribe gazed in wonder. Tritan felt only pity for them, for somehow, deep down he knew they had failed.

30

Light-footed patters ran around in the darkness, sniffing and searching. The creature could smell the sweat of the tribe and it caused pangs of hunger to run through its stomach. For weeks it had survived off the scraps left lying about and managed always to remain unseen. The pup had been at an age where the absence of a parent should have left it waning in misery, waiting for its death to come and capture it. But something had kept it alive, some hope or some sense that perhaps it was not alone.

The wolf pup had grown in size during the time of Tritan's capture and had managed to stay hidden from the tribe. When the fading firelight dwindled, it would emerge from its hole and in the pitch black, use its sense of smell to navigate the cave. Only once had it been spotted by one of the children at the opening of the cave network but when the child's mother had called out for them to return from the forest where the persistent grey ash was scattered through the air, the wolf had managed to retreat instantly and the sighting was never mentioned by the fearful child.

The wolf's eyes had changed from the blue colour of a pup into the golden yellow of a predator and it was nearing the age when it would be more able to fend for itself. Soon it would begin to hunt and in the shadowy corners of the cave network that had become its home it would easily prey upon its victims without them ever knowing it was there.

It was late and quiet all around and the wolf navigated the open chamber freely and undisturbed. It wandered towards Tritan who was sleeping, limply hanging from the wooden frame. It nuzzled under his feet and sniffed the wound that its parent had made. At first it seemed as though the wolf would clasp its teeth around the wounded leg and feed but then it began to lick Tritan's skin, cleaning the filth from the healing flesh.

Tritan began to shift in his sleep but he did not wake. By the time he opened his eyes the wolf had gone and he was never aware that it had ever been there. The only evidence was the paw marks on the dusty, stony floor but it was too dark to make them out and unless someone was studying and searching for tracks, they would remain unnoticed.

A chilly, eerie gust swept through the cave and with it came the warrior from the tribe. He ran into the chamber hurriedly, calling out for all to wake. Everyone roused at once and the first to rise was Augustus. He greeted the warrior but saw instantly the look of terror and anguish on his face. Augustus took from him the blackened branches of the dying forest and studied them with a bellicose intensity. Anger flickered across his face as the warrior, covered head to toe in grey ash, spoke to him with rapid persistence. Augustus threw down the branches and turned where he stood, pointing accusingly to Tritan. The tribe all turned and followed his glare and were it not for the recusancy that Tritan felt, he would have shuddered at the eyes of the primitive confraternity.

Augustus ran across the chamber and thrust his face into Tritan's, so close they could smell each other's breath. 'Why do you continue to fail me?' He raised his hands to clasp Tritan's jaw with his palms and he squeezed so hard it made the younger man's face contort. 'If I sense a smirk upon your face I'll cut you one that will last the remainder of the short time you have left.'

Tritan held the stare and made no sound. He was ready to die. In fact, he had become ready in all the weeks he had been a captive in the dreary cave and now was a good a time as any. He had come so close so many times before that all fear had gone. He had lost count of all the times he had escaped death's clasp but now he saw before him the man who had eluded him all these years. Augustus took the bone knife that the tribe girl had used and cut the binds that held Tritan to the frame. He instantly slumped forward and fell into Augustus, no strength remaining in his body.

'So weak, so pathetic.' Augustus bent down to spit in Tritan's face but a moment before he did, he spotted the black-ened finger on Tritan's hand. The dead flesh had spread from the tip and now covered half his finger and Augustus stood back in horror, a look of recognition on his face. 'Tell me, in what way did they come to you before they touched you?'

Tritan rolled from his position to frown at Augustus and looked down at his finger, also noticing for the first time how the black flesh had spread further. He wondered what interest Augustus could still have in any affliction on his body but with-held his urge to query him.

Augustus, calming slowly, stood to hover above Tritan. 'Young boys, their eyes as black as night, chased me through the forest, hundreds of them. They gave me this some years ago.' Augustus pulled away the jerkin at his midriff and revealed a black stain that covered a large part of his body. It stretched from his stomach to his ribs, front and back. 'It began as no larger than a speck. Soon it will consume me and then it will all be over. You were my only chance. Now we will both suffer the same fate.' Augustus's moment of rage subsided and he looked at Tritan almost with sympathy. 'Fitting I suppose that it must end the same way for you and I.'

Augustus stood and addressed the tribe, once more before walking off into the shadows, and leaving Tritan on the floor for the tribe to gather up and return to the pit.

It was a cold night and shivers ran up Tritan's spine. There was something reassuring about the rituals that had taken place, for Tritan believed when they were over he would be discarded, set free even. Now he had no hope on which to lean. To be left in this pit to rot away was as likely an outcome as any and it did not seem a pleasant way to go. Tritan rolled about trying to find a comfortable position and as he did so a piece of parchment fell from an inside pocket. It was tattered from months of sweat and had specks of blood scattered across it but the drawing was unmistakable. It was the picture Pietrich had drawn for him, a picture of home. Tritan hadn't even realised he had carried it with him all this time and wondered at the phenomenon that he had never lost it during all he had been through.

NIGHTS TURNED into days and days into nights. Hours felt like weeks and the only thing that broke the monotony was the daily serving of dried bread, water and a small ration of meat. Tritan had lost track of the weeks and wondered what season it was. Thomas had predicted his son would not last the winter but by now they must be approaching spring. If he could only somehow make his way out of this prison he would travel straight back to the village and suffer whatever fate would await

him there. It seemed ridiculous to have travelled so far for nothing. Had he really believed he would find some magic or immortality in this place? To now be so far from the one thing he
desired most in his last days, to see his family one last time and
tell them how he loved them. So much he had taken for granted
and so stupid he had been. He imagined conversing with his
former self all those months ago. He would tell himself to wake
up and realise what he had around him was beautiful. So many
men could not hope to expect a half of what he had been gifted
and he had thrown it all away like an old blanket.

After many nights, the tribe girl came to him again. Tritan
wondered what for because he no longer held any value to the
tribe. Their hope had been quashed. Tritan wondered if they
thought Augustus a liar, for making them believe that the
descendent of Maldus had returned. But the tribe girl lowered
herself into the pit and checked over his wounds. She seemed
satisfied at the progress and before she left she handed him his
meal. It was a better serving than usual and he guessed she was
responsible for that fact. Augustus had not been to see him
since the day he had discovered the dying black flesh on his
finger and it seemed like a dream that he had ever found the
man in this place at all. He had come all this way only to learn
the truth of his parentage, but it changed nothing. He was still
the slave of the leader of the 11th Legion, even if he and
Augustus were all that now remained of them. He wondered
what fate had befallen Kal and the rest of those he had left
behind. He prayed that the kid and his true father, Boscelito,
had managed to escape without ever coming across them.

Late one night, as the pit was plunged into the darkness
with which Tritan was now so familiar, a pair of eyes gleamed
down at him through the wooden slats above. The eyes were
not human, though at first he could not tell to what creature
they belonged. The yellow slits reflected down at him and he

realised it was the wolf pup grown. Tritan suspected it was only fitting to be gifted death by this savage animal, having taken its parent away. He waited, almost eagerly, his heart beginning to race as the wolf gnawed through the vine.

Tritan was tired and unarmed and although the wolf was still young, it could easily best him. Moments after severing the vine, the wolf began to nuzzle its head through the gap it had made. But instead of jumping down into the pit, the wolf stood back and continued to bite away chunks of the vine until the hole was large enough for a small child. Tritan stood in amazement and began to sense an ally in the wolf. He was right to, as after a little time, the hole had become big enough for even Tritan to climb through. He could not tell what the wolf would do if he scrambled free but he had to try. This chance would not fall into his lap more than once. Tritan jumped, trying desperately to grasp the edge of the pit, but it was just out of his reach and he had little energy to stretch higher. After a few efforts he conceded that he just wasn't capable and, as if the wolf had read his thoughts, part of the vine was nudged just a foot down into the pit. It was a short strand that still clung to the wooden slats but it was all he required. Tritan ran at the wall and kicked himself up reaching out for the vine and clutched it with his good hand before tugging with all his might to raise himself free.

When he rolled out onto the cave floor he felt a rush of relief, even though he had barely begun to earn his freedom and he did not know these caves at all. He had always been led through them and each time in a half dreaming state. It was so dark he could barely see his hands in front of his face but he began to feel his way along the corridor as the heat of his skin rose and burned fiercely like the open fires of winter. The wolf ran off and disappeared and Tritan suspected that he was on his own once more.

He made his way through a series of turns and circled back to the entrance to the pit. He quietly cursed himself under his breath but used all his focus to remember each time he had turned and in which direction. When he made it back to a three way split where he had earlier taken the right corridor he decided to go straight ahead but soon questioned if it was the right choice as, after a few minutes navigating the path, he ended up in the large chamber where he had been tied to the wooden frame, and discovered the entire tribe asleep.

The wolf was in the distance, prowling and sniffing at the sleeping children and Tritan wondered how hungry it was. He had to act quickly before the tribe was disturbed by the roaming animal and so he tiptoed quietly towards the far side of the chamber. He remembered the first time he had been brought from this direction after he had spent some time locked in the prison cell and he closed his eyes to recall the moment when he had been dragged from there. He assumed that those cells must be nearer to the outside for at his initial capture they surely would not have carried him far.

Eventually he made it to the cells where he had originally been held. He remembered all those dark nights; left alone to ponder his fate, with the body of the old tribe leader that Augustus had betrayed, staring at him from the shadowy corner. Retracing his steps made it all feel less real somehow, like a distant memory of being born.

As Tritan approached the cell doors he came across a single burning torch hanging from the walls. It was burning strong so Tritan took it in his hand to help guide his way to freedom. Each step was made with care and he sharpened his senses to the tunnels that split off from where he trod. He longed to hold his sword once more. With it he felt almost invincible but he doubted in this state that he would even be able to hold it above his head. Better to remain unseen and pray that he did not come face to face with any of the tribe. Suddenly he was filled with the urge to creep through the shadows like an assassin in the night and find the place where Augustus slept. It would be easy to send him into an eternal slumber. But he would surely be caught and now all he should think of was the slight chance of seeing daylight once more. It was too much to begin to believe he would ever see home again; for now he would focus only on his path through this cavernous labyrinth.

After passing through a long corridor he began to sense the path before him rising upwards. It steepened as it curved and the muscles of his legs burned and trembled. As he rounded a corner he saw a slight trickle of light painting the craggy rocks of the walls. He forced himself not to rush forwards but slowly made his way towards the daylight. It was blinding and his eyes could not adjust to the glare. Indeed he was so unable to look forwards that he never noticed the tribe girl standing directly before him. She shuffled forwards and he heard her footsteps before he saw her. But as he forced his eyes to stare towards the exit of the cave he saw the silhouetted figure of the girl and in her hands she clutched a great sword. It was Tritan's sword and she trembled as she held it out towards him. *Was she enemy or ally?* Tritan raised his hands slowly to put her at ease but she held her stance, lifting the sword higher to prove she knew how to wield it in spite of its size and weight.

Tritan made slow and precise movements, closer and closer but the tribe girl remained as still as a statue. As he raised his hand to his mouth and held his finger across his lips he prayed to her with his eyes that she would let him go. She betrayed his hope in the next moment by shrieking as loud as she could and expelling all her breath. Behind her from a hidden passage instantly emerged two others from the tribe and Tritan had no choice but to turn and run, back into the depths of the cave from which he'd been so close to escaping. Tritan threw the flaming torch to the side as, in spite of its aid, he knew it was better to remain hidden in the shadows. He ran and ran and when his lungs nearly collapsed in protest he forced his body to run without air. He was dizzy and could feel his eyes almost failing but in this darkness it made no difference. He used his hands to guide his way through the passages and when the moment came that he was satisfied with the ground he had covered he collapsed against a wall and began to suck air into his lungs. He took slow quiet gulps in spite of the desperation of his body but he knew he must remain quiet, he had only one chance to escape. Somehow he must outfox those who dwelled in these caves. He must remember his training as a soldier. Not the soldier who had fought in battles but the one who'd carried out quiet missions in the night, the one who had still been just a boy, the quiet assassin who was forced to infiltrate the enemy camps and silently take the lives of the sleeping enemy. But he would not take any lives in this place. He could not justify that, not now. Not anymore.

Tritan heard footsteps approaching from one of the tunnels and the flickering light of fire came with the sounds. He moved again. This time he chose a slow pace and made his way towards the large chamber just past the prison cells. He remembered the chamber gave access to an open cavern that was pitch black and if luck was on his side he could slip into it unnoticed while the rest of the tribes-folk scattered themselves deeper into the tunnels. To have come so close to the outside was torture. He had breathed salvation in those few seconds and then they were instantly snatched from him. But he would make his way back to that passage; he must make his way back.

Tritan's wish was granted and he saw from the darkness the shadowy figures of his pursuers passing from one end of the chamber to the other. The last of them was the tribe girl, she still carried his sword. He let it go, maybe he would never have need of a sword again. Maybe his past was running away from him as fast as the tribe ran into the depths of the cave.

He composed himself and made for the exit once more, this time he remembered the way. The adrenaline pumping through his veins kept his mind alert and gave his body new energy. He soon came to the winding spiral that led upwards and this time the light was less offensive. He quietly crept towards it, not wanting to betray his position again. Last time he had been careless with the torch, now he dared not do anything to make himself known. The daylight flooded forwards, wrapping itself around him in a gentle embrace. He felt like a child, plunging himself into a lake for the first time, feeling the cool water trickling across his skin and the sensation was pure and beautiful, like returning to a homely place that held such comfort.

He felt himself smile as he stepped into the forest and a second later the smile left him as a sharp hot sensation came to him. He looked down and there he saw it. A spear had struck him through the chest and droplets of blood ran along the wooden pole and fell from the pointy stone to the ground, painting the blackened ashy floor a deep shade of red. Tritan staggered forward, completely disbelieving what fate had befallen him; he turned to see his killer and there stood Augustus framed against the exit of the cave. For how long he had followed him, Tritan could not tell. Augustus made his next move moments later, taking the bone knife in one hand and the tribe leader's staff in the other. He walked slowly towards Tritan who had fallen to his knees. The knife came across his throat; he felt the familiar blade that had been blunted by the ceremonies that had passed. This was going to hurt and Tritan knew it.

Silent steps approached the two men and they were so quick that neither had time to react as the wolf jumped onto the back of Augustus and sank its teeth into his neck. Tritan reacted instantly by grabbing the bone knife and made a move to slash at Augustus but in his weakened state he was too slow and Augustus grabbed Tritan's arm with his spare hand, the one that was not wrestling with the wolf, who continued to tear at the man's neck. Augustus lunged a strong elbow down onto the wolf's head sending it reeling and then began to overpower his false son.

A scream came next. It was the tribe girl. Standing above the two men. They both stared at her in disbelief. No one could tell what thoughts were swimming through her mind. She answered their questioning faces by plunging Tritan's sword deep into Augustus's abdomen. He fell to the floor and she withdrew the sword and like a trained executioner, thrust the sword upwards under his rib cage and straight into his heart.

The moments that followed rushed over him as the waterfall of memories flooded his mind. Tritan had lost the man who had raised him, and how many times had he dreamed he might be the one to decide Augustus's fate. That privilege was now taken from him forever. His whole life seemed to change in that instant, all he had endured and all the suffering he had caused seemed like a joke to him now. He would have justified it all were he to have confronted Augustus but he had been too weak and too afraid.

Tritan wondered if he would be the next victim but instead the tribe girl helped him to his feet and handed him the staff to use for support. He had not even noticed the rest of the tribe emerging from many hidden outlets and they now surrounded him. Thirty men, women and children stared down at the man with a spear through his chest. They watched him stagger upon the staff and each of them took a slow bow, lowering themselves to their knees before him. Tritan could not understand the gesture but he knew he did not deserve it, nor did he want it. He handed the staff to the tribe girl and stepped away. Hoping and praying that she would take their attention away from him. She did. They all turned to face her at once like a choral ensemble that had rehearsed for a performance and it was as if it had been written in her destiny. She carved a notch in the staff below the dozen others and raised it above her head.

Maybe now Tritan would be permitted to die in peace. He would take one moment of quiet for himself before shutting his eyes and lying down in the ash to embrace the ancient forest and to die with it.

31

Time stopped and the world stopped with it; no one else would die and no one would be born until time returned to the world. But how could time exist in the mind of one who had died? This must be the afterlife that so many had glimpsed, but Tritan couldn't stop wondering how he still managed to contemplate anything at all. It was like being submerged in a deep black ocean, without light but without the need for air. Just floating with nothing but an eternal moment of emptiness for company. He no longer had a body but was instead a spirit being carried along by the wind. His vision was gone but instead he saw the world in a different way. It was hard to discern at first. It was as though he could see through the eyes of not only every living creature but through every other entity in the world; every stone, every tree and every breath of air. *Everything is connected,* Castellar had once said. The words had made Tritan consider what it really meant to have a family before he had had one of his own. Now he had lost all his family: his son, his wife, the father he had barely known and the false father who had raised him as a killer. But that was the old

Tritan, the one who had died. Now he was connected to every-thing, his family and the whole world.

He fixed his consciousness on the place where he had last laid down when he still had a physical form. But he could not see his body. He rushed through the ashy forest at a speed that he had never conceived to be possible and there he saw some-thing that even in this state he could not believe. His body seemed to still be moving without his mind to carry it, guided by the wolf and crawling along in the dirt. The two strange crea-tures that were deep below him had covered much ground and he could see through the earth beneath them and into the cave network. He saw the roots of the tree that had been painted with his body's blood and they ran towards a large lake beneath the place where water had once filled the blackened basin.

After several moments, that he assumed could have been hours in the world he had left behind, the wolf plunged deep into the lake basin, tugging Tritan's body in its jaws. The wolf was still too young and weak to carry him but he watched his body clawing across the floor and there he saw for the first time a magnificent tree. It was modest in size but the shape of its branches was unique, though painted entirely the colour of charcoal and certainly there was no life in it. The only sign of life was a single leaf hanging from the largest branch and coloured deep shades of red, orange and purple, still clinging on the way Tritan's body was also holding on to something. Even in death its defiance was remarkable.

The tree amidst the lake was surrounded by the ancient forest, completely submerged in its grasp and beyond the forest the surrounding mountains wrapped themselves around them all. Tritan sensed something moving inside the tree, a tremor or a breath, almost human. As he reached out to ascertain what life still remained in the tree he felt the very being of the world flowing into him and for a moment he wondered if the faint heartbeat he sensed was his son's, as though he had brushed against Pietrich for just an instant, an instant long enough to know there were still the embers of life glowing deep beneath his silent, resting form.

Tritan's body reached the bank of the island in the centre of the lake and the wolf encouraged it to roll on its side beneath the tree and there they lay still together as Tritan looked from above, waiting for his body to finally give way so he could be taken by the light into the next world. He saw his blood seeping from the wounds into the earth; there was so much blood.

Suddenly everything darkened and all the visions that had come to him disappeared. He tried once again to fly freely above the island but it was too late, that moment had passed. A familiar feeling came back to him as he felt his fingers twitching. The pain in his chest flooded back into his mind and he opened his eyes. Tritan was lying face down on a grassy patch of the island where everything was freshly green where before it had been rotten. He gazed around and above him and where the sun flickered through the branches he saw a full living tree, restored from its state as a charred corpse to a vision of glorious life.

Tritan stood, surprised at the ease with which he moved. He checked his wounds but there were none, his scars remained and his blackened finger still felt lifeless. But the hole in his chest had gone and his legs felt strong. All around him he saw the murky waters changing to a clear crystal blue colour and as they touched the banks on the side of the lake, the ground began to transform back into a rich, life-filled colour.

All at once the thoughts of home came to him like a bombardment of joy and pain. Suddenly Tritan cursed himself as he thought of his wife, Marilia. So often he had pined over the idea of seeing his son again but now he realised he had hardly considered Pietrich's mother more than once in these past months. He knew it would not be an easy audience and though he craved for her forgiveness he was sure he did not deserve it, *After all you can't un-brew a tea.* All the wrong that he had done to her was like a series of stains. Perhaps they would fade in time but they would never truly be washed away.

Tritan heard footsteps circling the great tree and followed the sounds to where the wolf was prowling. It was assessing him cautiously as though it had witnessed something far beyond the grasp of its nature. The wolf backed away from Tritan but seemed wary of the water that had risen from the earth. Tritan remembered all those days of ceremonies, watching his blood being painted on the roots of the tree. Could his blood have truly been the trigger to bring the tree and so the forest from the brink of death? He did not believe it. But without doubt the tree had somehow saved him and if there was just a glimmer of hope that his son still drew breath, maybe it could also save Pietrich.

Tritan tore a piece of leather from his jerkin and wrapped it into a mini double-skinned pouch. He then filled the pouch with a few of the brightly sprung leaves and filled the container with water from the lake before sealing it with a cord from his shirt.

It was time to go home. But he would not leave the wolf alone in this place. He owed it his companionship, should it wish to take it. He slowly walked towards the curious, frightened animal and opened his arms. Considering him for a moment, the wolf trod carefully forwards before allowing Tritan to take him in his arms and place him on his shoulders and together they swam across the lake towards the bank and began to follow the trail that had brought them to this place.

They walked together for the whole day, man and wolf. Two unlikely companions drifting through the forest and past the cave dwelling that they barely gave a second thought. As they journeyed south past the clearing where Tritan had lost his life for a time, they found the shimmering sword lying in the dirt and the corpse of Augustus lying beside it.

Tritan had lost the chance to take his own form of vengeance but now he knew he had the chance for a greater redemption. It was forgiveness. He would forgive Augustus in death where he could not best him in life. Tritan began to dig a hole in the soil and the light of day slipped away. When he was satisfied with his work, he buried his false father. There would be no tombstone to mark his resting place but with no further need for the sword or the past life it had bound Tritan to, he stuck the weapon firmly in the ground and took a moment, with his hands clutched around the hilt, to consider all that he had been through. He turned his back on the steel blade and the life he had led and the two companions readied themselves for a long night of hiking.

Tritan felt elated, his mind cleansed and his body healed. Time was the only factor against him now as he set out on foot with the wolf, not knowing what he would discover should he ever make it home. The joy he felt posed a great risk as he wondered what sadness might yet be waiting for him in the village where he had abandoned his family.

'At last it is time to go home,' he said out loud. The wolf yelped a cry as if praising a pack leader for determining a great hunt. The darkness of the forest came but Tritan knew the sun would rise again in any moment and he dared not sleep. He would not sleep again until he lay by Pietrich's side. He made the promise and then the night swallowed him and the wolf as they disappeared into its cloak.

32

B illowing smoke rose from the chimneys of the stone houses and the workers filled the fields to sow seeds and trim the fruit trees. Spring had arrived in Knighton. The village had survived the harsh winter with their minimal supplies and preparations for the next year had begun. An ominous set of clouds lingered overhead as the day passed by.

'A storm's coming,' said Kayla to the other villagers. 'Could be the first spring storm. Eira, love, run and lock down the stables, I'll follow shortly.'

Eira nodded at her mother's request and as she ran she passed the tree in the centre of the village square. She still visited it every day to check that her leaf remained in place. There it held on, the weak and fragile leaf. In spite of the buds of a new blossom forming, she still ensured it would remain as though she dared not allow winter to end, though it had truly ended weeks ago. She reminded herself of the words that Thomas had spoken the day Pietrich fell ill; that he would not live to see the end of autumn or the winter's snow settle. Now those snows had melted away. As she ran off she caught a smile from Marilia who nodded to her with approval. The girl was committed and Marilia loved her for that.

Marilia had preparations of her own to make; she insisted on keeping Tritan's old barn preserved, though she was considered mad for doing so and, though it pained Thomas, it was the one vice he allowed her.

By evening the preparations for the storm had been made. The windows had all been locked down in expectation of heavy rain. It would be a long night stuck inside by candlelight, but there was some pleasure to be had with huddling together with loved ones during such times. It was these nights that Marilia missed Tritan the most. Though she could not recall him ever having been there to accompany her; instead, on those stormy nights, he had kept to the barn to reassure his horse Diablo, resting in his drunken state. One night she had trudged out in the rain to the barn and lay down beside her sleeping husband, wrapping his large arm across her soaking body. It was that night she missed the most.

It wasn't the same with Thomas. Though she had eventually given in to his persistence she had never learnt to truly love him. That was the secret she held for herself and she wondered if her son would approve of the match were he able to wake and hear of such news. Never mind, it was her decision to make, be it for the best or be it a mistake. No one was there to question her choice and even Jonah had conceded that she was better off with the healer's company than none at all.

As Marilia finished preparing the old cottage she headed down to light a candle by Pietrich's resting side. From the shadows Thomas approached and rested a reassuring hand on her shoulder. Marilia spoke first.

'It is as if he is waiting for something, waiting to say goodbye maybe?'

'He has already said goodbye to you in his own way,' he responded affirmably.

'I don't think it's me he is waiting to say goodbye to.'

Thomas shifted uncomfortably at that and did his best to divert the conversation. 'It's remarkable the strength he has shown us. I never would have predicted it.'

Marilia turned to face him. 'It must be the medication you prepared for him. Eira is a committed assistant. Together you keep him alive.'

Thomas nodded but quickly pulled Marilia into his arms as if he wanted to hide his reluctant expression from her. Something was amiss but he could not figure out what.

'Let's sleep,' she said. 'I feel like an early night might suit us.'

'Yes, you're right, I am sure the storm will wake us many a time in the night. Better to rest now while we can.'

They left a candle burning by Pietrich's side and headed out of the old cottage to cross towards Thomas's home. Marilia had decided to leave Pietrich in their home, as she believed the familiarity was a comfort to him, even as he slept endlessly.

She blessed the skies that she lived in such a safe village, where everyone was a family together. It almost made up for the hole in her heart.

The heavy rain came as predicted and all the villagers kept safe in their houses. The only open window was the one belonging to Kayla. She loved to watch the downpour during the storms. It was a comfort to her to see the rain lashing down whilst she remained dry and warm inside her home. It was from this window where she sat that she saw a strange shadow lingering outside in the distance. The unmistakable shadow of a man leading a horse and following shortly behind them seemed to be a smaller creature. Kayla swore she could see a wolf but it did not seem to be pursuing the man furtively. It was as though it was part of the mysterious party.

As the figures passed across the village, the dark silhouette stopped only to fasten the white steed to a post that was mostly sheltered from the rain. The wolf also remained under the shelter as the man carried on towards Marilia's old family home. He slowly lifted the wooden slat that barred the front door of the cottage and entered inside. Kayla darted to her feet at once. She could not believe that it would be Tritan but deep down she knew of no other man that it could be. She must warn Thomas at once; how dare the soldier return, on this night and in secret.

Inside the old home, the hooded man wandered through the kitchen and pulled the sodden hood from over his face. Tritan found the kitchen was strangely bare as if the home was now unlived in but he found an old cloth and wiped his face dry. He searched the cottage for signs of Marilia but she was nowhere to be seen. He did not let that hold him back. First he must head to Pietrich's quarters and there he found his sleeping son, resting in the moody orange light of the single burning candle.

Pietrich looked so pale and thin compared to when he had last seen him. At first Tritan was certain he was dead but he knew it would not make sense for him to have been left here unattended if he were not merely asleep. Tritan held his fingers to the boy's throat and felt the tiniest flicker of a pulse. But it was a pulse and he fell to his knees with a great relief. He immediately took out the leather pouch that he had kept safe beneath his cloak and twisted the leather into a spout and poured a trickle of the water he had carried all these past weeks into Pietrich's mouth. The boy did not drink at first but Tritan tilted up his head to encourage the liquid down his throat. In spite of his eagerness he administered the liquid slowly and carefully. He knew that Pietrich's state was dire and he dared not risk choking him.

Moments passed with no sign of change. Pietrich remained still and did not seem to breathe. Tritan reached out again to check the faint pulse and it seemed to have stopped. A heavy frown crossed Tritan's face. He didn't understand why the drink had done nothing for the boy. Had his body simply held out so long just to feel the presence of his father one last time before passing on from his life? Maybe he had imagined the tree had restored him to life and the water was as useless to the boy as a smile was to a wall. Tritan wasn't given a chance to wonder what had happened as he heard a disturbance outside.

'Tritan! Come out here at once. If it's you in there, come out to meet us this instant! Don't dare to avoid me.'

Tritan knew the voice; it was Thomas. The sound was ferocious, an anger that he had not known the man to possess. Could his return after all this time be so offensive? Tritan hesitated for fear of leaving Pietrich, but then headed out of the cottage and back into the rain. As he came through the door he saw that the larger part of the village had gathered to witness his return. Thomas stood side by side with his brothers and Tritan could see they were armed. It was they who were surprised when Tritan walked to meet them, empty handed.

'I came back for him, to see him again, if only for one last time. I have no more quarrel with you and I mean no harm to any of you.' Tritan addressed the whole village but his words were aimed towards Thomas. Meekly standing behind the healer was Marilia, her eyes focused on the floor and she did not meet Tritan's gaze.

'It's too late to turn your back on that fight, Tritan. You must take responsibility for all you have done!'

'Then I am yours to do with as you wish; I hold no sword

nor will I strike back. Take my life if you wish. If that will settle old feuds I will accept that fate. After all I owe you my life.'

Tritan slowly walked closer and closer into the circle of villagers that now surrounded him. It seemed as though everyone had forgotten the rain as it pounded down upon them. Tritan saw the girl, Eira, standing with her mother Kayla. Jonah and the rest of the villagers all looked on eagerly. No one had expected his return nor did they expect him to give up his life so freely. Thomas had promised himself this outcome must be pursued should he ever see Tritan again but now he was fearful. How could he a kill a man who welcomed his end whilst the woman he loved stood behind him. Could they instead resolve their differences with words? Should they? No. Tritan had caused him so much pain; he would not forget nor forgive him. Thomas drew a sharp knife as Tritan held his arms open, then exposed his body to the man. Raindrops trickled down his body and ran across his scars, new and old. Thomas knew Tritan's body as well as anyone, almost as well as Marilia and he stared, bewildered at the new lines that marked his flesh.

'Do not linger, Thomas, the longer you wait the harder it becomes.'

Thomas stepped forward to meet him, the knife readied in his firm grasp. But before he had time to take any action a loud scream pierced the night and cut through the thunderous claps of the storm. It was Eira. She had run to the tree besides the gathering and found her leaf, lying on the muddy ground; broken and soaked. The storm had finally overwhelmed it and she feared the significance of what it meant. But a moment later, a miracle unravelled before them all. The cottage door of Marilia's home burst open and the blind boy, Pietrich, ran out into the rain.

'Father, Father! Where are you? I cannot see.'

Tritan spun around to see Pietrich staggering through the rain in no particular direction.

'Pietrich! Son, I'm here.'

Pietrich heard the sound of his father's voice and he ran towards him and wrapped his little arms around Tritan's waist. The boy was blocking Thomas's path who could not believe what he saw. None of those present could believe it.

'Don't hurt him, don't hurt my father, please!'

The villagers were spellbound. How was it that Pietrich was now so full of life and energy. His voice had not been heard by any for such a time. He had not moved a limb in months, though now here he stood, protecting his father. The boy shouted to them all as if he could hear the disbelief and hatred in their breath. 'I need him. Maybe none of you others do, but I need him. Let him be.'

Marilia had stood mouth agape this entire time. She composed herself and regained her calm before rushing out to meet her son. She dropped to her knees and ran her fingers through his hair as if she did not believe it was actually him, but instead some other boy possessed by a dream.

'My love, what has happened. Are you okay?'

'Mother, I'm fine, only I cannot see, please tell them to stop, tell them to leave him be.'

Marilia looked to Thomas as if to echo her son's words but Thomas had already backed away, the knife slipped back into his cuff. The expression on his face was disgrace. He held a secret that no one else knew and it shamed him in that moment. Marilia looked at the father of her child and for the first time she could recall, she swore she could see his tears. But they were mixed heavily with the rain pouring down his face and she wondered if it were not some trick of her mind.

It was Jonah who stepped forward next. 'Let's get the boy

back inside, this rain is no place to hold a reunion. There's a lot to discuss but it can wait until morning.'

The villagers began to nod in agreement as the moment of shock passed and they all remembered that they were fully exposed to the storm. Everyone drifted off to their homes in silence as Tritan led Pietrich back into his old cottage and now Marilia followed them. Thomas didn't even try to object; he simply walked away with his head down, dejected and alone.

Inside the old, stark home, Marilia led Pietrich back to his bed but he stood in defiance. 'Mother, please. I am not tired.'

She shook her head. 'My sweet boy, please. You must try to rest. Let me speak to your father alone.'

Pietrich nearly objected again but decided against it. He knew he would hear everything they would have to say and thought better than to refuse her. He lay back in the bed where he had spent so many months. He was no longer ill and forced to lie still by the affliction that had sedated him. Now a strange new energy flowed through his limbs, but for his mother's sake he would obey her instruction.

Marilia and Tritan moved back into the kitchen and stood there for a time, considering each other's presence. Tritan sat at the large wooden table and waited for Marilia to compose herself to sit beside him.

'I need something strong,' she said to him as much as herself and she rummaged for a bottle beneath a cabinet. She pulled out a bottle of brandy and two small glasses, which she filled generously and then sat beside her husband. Tritan did not object to her offering but as she sipped the brandy he simply watched, leaving his own untouched. It was the first time she noticed the change in him, but now was not the time to question his newfound resilience for the drink.

The conversation never started. Instead they took it in turns to gaze at one another and pondered all the things that had been left unsaid. They breathed heavily and sighed. It was enough for now. Neither Marilia nor Tritan could tell for how long they sat together. Only the passing of the storm and the light of morning breaking through the cracks in the cottage door revealed the dawn.

As the crowing of a rooster somewhere outside broke the silence, there was a knock at the door. Jonah entered without waiting for an invitation and Eira followed closely behind him.

'Morning, I doubted you had slept, I could not either.' The estranged couple nodded to him graciously as he sat down to join them. Eira remained upright, standing meekly in the corner of the room. 'I had hoped to bring Thomas with me this morning, I believed he ought to examine the boy closely, but he has left the village and his horse is gone too.'

'Gone? But where?' Marilia questioned.

'No one knows a thing. Not even his brothers. They are concerned for him, but no matter for that now. Eira has told me something gravely concerning. Please, girl, tell them exactly as you told me.'

Eira shifted uncomfortably and looked towards Marilia. She dared not meet the fierce gaze from Tritan's eyes.

'Well, I...'

'Go on, child, you are among friends,' Jonah said reassuringly.

'I'm sorry!' she said, as if readying herself for an important confession. 'But when everyone began speaking of Pietrich, they told me that the healer's medicine had finally brought him back to us.' A cold silence filled the room before she continued. 'But the truth is, I haven't been giving him the tonics since before winter began. In fact Pietrich seemed to improve for a while after that. I know it was not my choice to make, but Pietrich begged me. He so desperately wanted his mind to be sound and for a time it was, but then he fell into that coma. I could not betray his wish so I continued to pour away the medicine after every visit. I hadn't intended on telling you for I knew you would hate me for it, even now after all that has happened. But when I heard that Thomas had fled this morning I knew I had to tell someone and Jonah thought you deserved to know.'

The silence returned. It was suddenly chilly and Marilia felt the icy cold of the spring morning traversing her spine. Jonah took Eira's hand reassuring her, as if he would remain her ally in this revelation, no matter what.

'I don't understand.' Marilia shook her head. 'But how could Pietrich have held on so long without it?'

'Think carefully for a moment, can there be any reason why Thomas—'

'No!' Marilia broke into Jonah's train of questioning. 'Do not finish that sentence.'

'Very well, but now you know everything there is to know.' He turned to face Tritan next who had simply stared into his untouched glass of brandy. 'Tritan, I'm sorry to bring this news to you having only just returned from wherever you have been, but it is not something that could wait.'

Tritan slowly looked up at Marilia who was in tears, her face hidden behind her hands. He took a moment to choose his words carefully before directing them to Jonah. 'Jonah, you always cared for this family and for me more than I deserved. Just answer me one question. Who else knows about this? Kayla? Thomas's brothers?'

'No, only us here in this room.'

'Then that is how it will remain. Too much speculation over something we all understand truly little. The village is to believe that Thomas had made a better medicine than he himself could have predicted. And Eira, the blessed, loving girl, carried out the administrations on his behalf. My return and Pietrich's sudden recovery are no more than coincidence. He could have simply heard my voice and his body finally decided it was time to rise.'

'But I cannot believe that the two things are merely coincidence. Medication or no, Pietrich was surely suffering his last days. Something must have happened?'

'I'm sorry, but that is the way of it.'

Jonah took a deep breath and looked searchingly into Tritan's eyes, hoping for some sign of a hidden truth that may yet be revealed. But the ex-soldier hid his emotions, as well as one possible truth, behind the steely mask he had worn all these years.

'Very well, I suppose then we can all agree that the only reason for Thomas's sudden departure is the heartache caused to him by your return. But know that if you make a martyr out of him, you will never be truly forgiven in this place. By a few, yes perhaps, but not by all.'

'Then it is as it should be, for I do not deserve the forgiveness of all, nor in fact the few. But I will do my best to earn it.' Tritan redirected his look to Marilia at this and their eyes met. There was a deep understanding between them but there was also sadness. The kind of sadness that could spell only the end of something that perhaps, in another life, could still have been.

33

Forgiveness is a difficult concept to grasp. It can offer us so much peace and yet we are always reluctant to forgive those who have dishonoured us. Always we assume we are the only ones who suffer in this life as though those responsible for us do not have their own flaws and struggles. Generations do not merely separate us by age but by mind. As we look to those who raise us we search for hope and understanding. But we must accept that understanding is as an elusive beast to them as it is to us. We are marked by the days we live, scars of the mind are stronger than the ones we carry on our bodies. When we close our eyes and enter the blackness of our souls we no longer see the hurts our bodies have carried, but we cannot escape the thoughts that make us who we are.

TRITAN CLOSED the scroll that was glowing a warm orange colour by the candlelight. His quill became dry and he headed out onto the farm to begin his day. It was an important day, Pietrich would turn eleven this afternoon and he must help prepare the celebration. His son had not regained his sight in the time that had passed since Tritan's return though it was hard to believe it was almost a year already.

Tritan had more or less settled back into his old life though now he worked hard at being the father he had never been in the years before. He was still mostly estranged from the villagers but they admired the change they had seen in the ex-soldier. His attention to the boy was his strength and he had seen to it that Pietrich would learn to ride and understand the words of literature even if he could not read or hold a quill himself. The wolf had thankfully been permitted to remain in the village after Tritan had trained it to act as a guard of the village boundaries and it had also become a guide for Pietrich, keeping him company most days around the village. The companionship between animal and child had been the ultimate reason that Tritan and Jonah had managed to convince the others to allow it to stay and it was more or less treated as though it were a tame village dog. Only once the wolf killed a stray chicken that had escaped from its enclosure. Pietrich was distraught at the thought of losing the wolf and, as though the animal had sensed his hurt somehow, it never acted in such a way again.

Tritan walked out into the fields and began to prepare the white steed that he had claimed on his journey home. It was a marvellous horse that he had stolen in the middle of the night from a stable outside Baurticeford. Tritan had promised himself he would return it to the owner one day but the horse responded so well to Pietrich that Tritan decided he would carry the guilt instead. One day he would travel to the town and pay for it, he decided. It seemed to sense, as did the wolf, that the boy's vision was impaired and there was something strange about the way Pietrich bonded with these creatures. He seemed to understand them in ways that no one else could. He also seemed to have acquired an acute talent for hearing in exchange for the eyesight he had lost. It was common that when someone lost one of their senses another would grow stronger, but Pietrich seemed more gifted in his hearing than Tritan could understand. He spoke often about village gossip and important matters that he had not been included in and Tritan had to warn the boy to be careful to whom he repeated the things he had heard. Once, some months previously, Pietrich had tried to tell Tritan that he had heard from a man claiming to be his grandfather and that they had conversed in his dreams. But Tritan had told the boy he had been very sick and his imagination had been wrought with fever. Pietrich had tried to insist but eventually gave up attempting to convince his father that the conversations had been real.

On the night before Pietrich's birthday, Tritan had visited Marilia to ask what Pietrich wanted to do to celebrate and she allowed the boy to decide. Pietrich had instantly chosen that, with his father's aid, he would begin the day by having yet another lesson atop the horse. Tritan admired the passion and commitment his son had shown for such practice. He was a diligent student.

As Tritan tied the stirrups of the white steed in the field he saw Marilia emerge from her cottage with their son. She directed him towards the gated fence and then allowed him to make his own way through the fields towards Tritan. At first, when the lessons had begun, Tritan had waited outside the cottage entrance and led Pietrich by hand through the village and out to the fields, but now he simply watched as his son became more familiar with his surroundings. It was important to allow the child to make his own way. After all, he would not always have a parent there to guide him. But it seemed the boy would learn to become more capable than either Marilia or Tritan could have hoped. The simple sound of a hoof tapping against the soil was enough for Pietrich to make his way towards the horse.

Tritan embraced his son before raising him above his head and lifting him onto the horse. He passed him the reins and slipped his boots into the straps before patting the horse's back and sending them off around the fields.

'Happy birthday, lad,' he said under his breath.

Tritan smiled back to Marilia who waved at him in return. It was a moment of peace between them both. Tritan wondered if she would ever accept him back into her life. He would not force the issue for it was her decision to make. It was enough for now that she allowed him to spend so much time with their son. They had become close friends at least and spoke of many things together, mostly about Pietrich's future, but some secrets still remained. Like the time she had spent with Thomas during Tritan's absence and the fact the healer had disappeared without notice the night Tritan had returned. As Jonah had promised, Thomas had become a victim in the eyes of the villagers. The man who had saved the boy and then fled with his heart broken. But as time passed by he was forgotten and now no one spoke of him.

Later that day the village congregated in the main square where there was a wide selection of food and drink, dancing and music. The winter festival had been moved to coincide with Pietrich's birthday, as there was not enough produce to celebrate both occasions. It was a marvellous spectacle and everyone danced; even Tritan was convinced to take a turn on the stage with Marilia alongside Pietrich and Eira. He surprised everyone at how sure footed he was as the musicians gleefully played a folk jig. He could not explain it himself but wondered whether his childhood lessons in swordplay had anything to do with his rhythm. How strange, he thought, that there could be such similarity between the peaceful and joyful things in life and those that cause harm. He put the dark thoughts aside and allowed himself to be swept away by the sound of the fiddle and drumming. It was a truly wonderful afternoon.

Jonah had taken his seat as usual to tell stories to the children of the village and they all crowded around, keenly listening to the history of Knighton and their heritage.

Kayla secured the position of organising the hog roast and boasted at having hunted the beast herself with help from a few of the other villagers. Tritan had been there that day but had purposefully drifted into the background when it came time to skewer the hog.

The party was in full swing and the sound carried from one end of the village to the other. Almost no one noticed as a half dozen horseback riders entered the village. They were cloaked in heavy garb and armed. The music stopped suddenly and everyone turned to face them. The most startling thing about them was not the aggression with which they rode, but the silver plates attached to each of their breasts, marking them as members of some sort of order. Tritan studied the emblem but did not recall having ever seen it. Jonah had risen to confront the captain of the riders but Tritan soon stepped forward to put himself between the riders and the rest of the villagers.

'Good evening,' said the group's captain. 'We apologise for disturbing your celebration. But our business is simple and it will not take long.

'Get to it then, man,' Tritan responded without fear.

'We are here to inform you that this land has been claimed by the true heir to the region. His anointment as ruler was secured one month past and it is our duty to inform all the villages, towns and settlements throughout the lands of Harmion of his positioning.'

There were murmurs of disbelief scattered throughout the village. No one had lived through the rule of a single leader throughout the lands for nearly sixty years. Even during the times of the harsh war, the villages had been left to continue their self-sustained way of life.

'There is no recognition here for any such rulers, least of all ones who remain nameless,' Jonah retorted.

'His name will be revealed in good time. We are not here today to impress upon you any difference to your way of life. Only to pass notice that change is coming. In the next spring you will be informed of the changes that are to be implemented and the elders of the village will be summoned on behalf of the community to sit in council. For now we simply come to look for the son of Augustus. He lives here in this village, I have been informed. We only wish for him to return with us.'

The village was silent. Tritan froze. How had they known of him, let alone that this was his home? Perhaps Thomas had betrayed him after he had fled. But Tritan knew deep down that there were a hundred possibilities and it would not do to dwell on them. But he was afraid, would the villagers give him up? It would be better for them all if he were to step forward or be pointed out and get this business done. Whatever it was that these strange men could want with him, it was not worth risking the lives of the others. Kayla passed through the crowds and stood beside Tritan giving him a look that shot fear through his heart.

'It's true what you say; he was a man of this village. But he left us one year ago. We presume he is now dead or lost, wandering in one of the towns to the north. He abandoned his family and caused such unrest that were he to return, it is unlikely he would be welcomed graciously.'

Tritan was pained to hear of himself spoken in such a way, the lies Kayla told to protect him were laced with so much truth that he felt ashamed of himself. But it was a kindness Kayla had offered Tritan in that moment, the woman whom he would have before expected to betray him first.

'That's a convenient tale with no basis for evidence,' said the captain.

Kayla protested her argument. 'I have no care for the well-being of that man. In fact if he were here and I could give him up to you I would. Better for the rest of us to be left alone from whatever business you want with him.'

'Well, should he come back here, you will not decide his fate but instead welcome him and house him so as to be able to inform us upon our return in the spring. For now we leave you to your celebrations. May the winter months be kind to you all.'

And with that final statement the captain turned and rode with his guard back out of the village. The air was left still and the evening's music did not return. The party was over; it was time to go home.

The next day was long and Tritan did his best to forget the men that had ridden into the village, but he could not help wondering what business they had wanted with him. *Would one of the villagers eventually give him up?* So many questions spinning around his mind made it hard to concentrate on Pietrich's lesson. The boy sensed his father's anguish and rode the horse back to the spot where Tritan sat, gazing out towards the river beneath the backdrop of the southern mountains.

'Father, I think that's enough riding for today,' said the boy.

'Of course.' Tritan stood and helped Pietrich step down from the saddle. The boy could hardly help notice that Tritan always relied heavily on one hand when lifting him. 'Sit with me a while, son.' The two of them planted themselves beneath a tree and sat for a time in each other's company, listening to the rustling of the leaves and the rushing sound of the waters flowing downstream.

'Will you go with those men next spring?' Pietrich finally asked.

'No, I'm going to stay here with you. Are you worried I will leave again?'

'Yes, Mother thinks you will have to go. She is worried that someone will point you out to those men when they return.'

'She is right to be worried, but we mustn't lose faith in the kindness of our neighbours.'

'What do they want?'

'I do not know, I wish I did, but I did not know any of them. It is a question that keeps playing on my mind but I believe the answer is not one I wish to know.'

Pietrich leant his head on Tritan's shoulder and they enjoyed their moment together. Tritan wondered what it must be like for the boy, to spend his days without his sight. He wished he could trade places with his son and offer him his eyes but some things are not ours to give so freely.

Tritan prayed to himself that he would always be there to protect the boy; he would never leave him again. But even as he made the promise to himself he caught a glimpse of the black skin that reached from beneath his glove. The whole hand had now been ruined by the affliction and he could barely use it to grip a glass of water. It would not be long before the others started to notice. He did not know how he would explain it to Marilia or to Pietrich. But that was a trial to be overcome another day. For now he would think only of the gift that time had granted him and he thought of all of those in his life that he cared for and finally for the first time he allowed himself to accept their love. The love of his son, the sweet boy who had been his protector, and of his own mother who he had never known, but in those brief moments between his birth and her death that love was magnified in meaning. His father's love was so strong that he, Boscelito, had endured a lifetime of pain, waiting, only to know Tritan for such a short time. He hoped one day to find him again.

But most of all, he knew that Marilia had loved him fiercely and he knew her love would never soften, no matter what kept them apart.

With the passing breeze that brushed his skin, spirit and soul, the truth settled in his thoughts, like a resting calm sea that had longed for stillness. The final warm breath of autumn drifted over him and he was left in such bliss that he knew that all the goodness in the world was worth all the suffering. He looked into those beautiful blue eyes that belonged to Pietrich and saw reflected back at him his own heart. It was the greatest moment of peace he would ever know.

EPILOGUE

A low morning mist clung to the base of the trees that flourished with an ethereal grace. There was so much life, so many vivid shades of green, like olives and emeralds melded together to create a pallet of natural beauty that bore no resemblance to the ashy death that had before lingered in this otherworldly region.

Hurried and energetic footsteps plundered the forest as the tribe girl rushed through the winding pathways that were covered in vines and roots and where flocks of creatures ran with the winds that rustled the branches. She clung onto the staff and now she bore scar tattoos from head to toe. For the tribe, she was a new leader for a new time; a time when life thrived and the tribe dared to venture outside daily to relish in the landscape.

She ran with the creatures of the forest, the deer and the horses whose strides created a rhythmic beat as if an eternal song graced the lingering days. There was no more need for hiding. Like the barren fields to the south that now flourished with rich soil, the tribe had had their lands returned to them in their former glory. The girl ran through the clearing that emptied out into the basin where the lake stood proudly amidst the mountains. She trailed her fingers through the water and smiled up at the tree that was so alive and breathed its strength into the world beneath it. She had never lived in a time where the world seemed so complete. It was a gift from the man that they had captured, though she would never know it was truly given by him, nor did he know he had given it.

The girl washed her face with the water and looked to the horizon with no more doubts. It was her time, a time of peace, undisturbed. A time unwritten where the future, though uncertain, was shrouded in harmony.

FIN

A WORD FROM RICHARD

Thank you for reading HARMION. The story will continue soon with part two: THE VERMILLION ISLES.

I would love to know your thoughts, so please consider leaving a review on Amazon or Goodreads. This also helps spread the word about HARMION and will make this writer very happy indeed!

Building a relationship with readers is one of the very best things about writing. I occasionally send newsletters with details on new releases, special offers and other bits of news relating to the Harmion and The Time Thief series.

And if you sign up for the newsletter I'll send you a FREE Harmion prequel novella - THE KILL LIST. The Novella will charter one of Tritan's most challenging missions during the Forty Year War.

You can sign up for my newsletter at: www.richardaswingle.com

facebook.com/raswingleauthor
twitter.com/raswingle
instagram.com/raswingle

ABOUT THE AUTHOR

Richard A. Swingle is a British fantasy novelist from Brighton, in the UK. This is his first publication, part one of *The Harmion series*. He comes from a background of working in the Film and Television industry and has been actively writing since the age of 14 when he discovered his passion for storytelling through making short films.

Since then he has developed his storytelling interests as both a musician and novelist and continues to work as a director of photography in the film industry.

Visit: www.richardaswingle.com to find out more.

Other Publications:

HARMION SERIES

The Kill List (Prequel Novella)
Harmion
The Vermillion Isles

THE TIME THIEF SERIES

The Heart Thief
The Spirit Thief *coming soon!*

ACKNOWLEDGMENTS

A special thank-you to my father, Anthony, for working tirelessly to help me edit and polish this book.

To my mother, Janet and sister, Anna for all their support over the years.

To Adam, a long term collaborator whose invaluable contributions made this book possible.

To Jamie for his support and interest in the Harmion world, whose illustrations helped inspire ideas.

To Jo, Chris, Dill, Giulia and Jess for spending the time to read an early version to give crucial feedback.

To Elissa for putting up with me badgering her over the years for all things book related.

To Melanie for her eagle eye and sweeping editorial skills.

A big thanks to all of those involved in the many iterations of *Harmion* over the years, you know who you are.

And a final thank-you to Mhairi for encouraging me never to stop and for inspiring me to be the best version of myself.

KICKSTARTER BACKERS

A huge thank you to the following people who backed Harmion on Kickstarter.

Frederi Alderweireldt, Marta Pierazzuoli, James Khan, Dan Wy, Sandy Tonks, Mhairi Underwood, Anna Dunn, Emma Mitchell, James McAleer, Merle Blue, Luke Andrews, Paul Grove, Adam Hoskins, C.L. Blanton, Olivia Murray, James Gillingham, Angelia Pitman, Scott Williams, Julian Pletts, Dan Turner, Chris Clayton, Owain Hopkins, Jo Johnson, Janet Swingle, Leanne Kean, William Charles, Topher McGrillis, Jess Moriarty, Nils Sorensen, Nanaya Shiki, Will Dunn, Leanne Johnson, Hayley Rouse, Madeline Fogelman, Neil Oseman, Pauline Lomax, Paul Horton, Platypus Underground, Phil Cooper, Christopher James O'Shea, Kevin Johnson, Alasdair McWilliams, Ian Sandford, Peter Riley, Jamie Gibbs, Smitty, Chris Wright, Brian LaShomb, Rod Meek, Thomas Somerled Tijssen, Gary Champagne, Kainoe, Jesse Knepper